To: Kate
Best Wishes!

[signature]

THE RIVER RAT

MURDERS

FRANK L. GERTCHER

Wind Grass Hill Books

Terre Haute, IN

The River Rat Murders is a novel set primarily on the Wabash River during Prohibition. Although fiction, it rings true to the fascinating history and colorful characters who lived, loved and died in the bawdy towns along the river during the 1920s. However, any similarity of the storyline characters in this novel to persons living or dead is purely coincidental and not intended by the author.

The River Rat Murders © 2019 Frank L. Gertcher
Hard cover EAN-ISBN-13:978-0-9835754-4-3
E-book EAN-ISBN-13: 978-0-9835754-5-0
Paperback EAN-ISBN-13: 978-1-930546-27-1

Cover design by Phil Velikan

Cover photos: gangster: ©Ysbrand Cosijn/Shutterstock.com; car: ©Dimitris Leonidas/Shutterstock.com; woods: ©Sasa Prudkov/Shutterstock.com

Packaged by Wish Publishing

Printed in the United States of America
10 9 8 7 6 5 4 3 2 1

I dedicate this book to my father, Frank Gertcher Senior (1910-1998).

A man of many talents, he lived the part of a Wabash "river rat" during Prohibition.
He told me stories about those times, people and places.

ALSO FROM FRANK L. GERTCHER

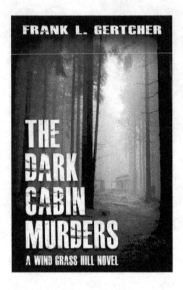

The Dark Cabin Murders begins in the spring of 1841. John Edwin and Maude Worthington and their 11-year old son Thomas arrive in Maryville Indiana. Shortly after their arrival, the elder Worthingtons con pious old Adam Gibson out of the title to a dark cabin near the Devil's Dell. Emboldened by their success, the elder Worthingtons try to swindle the newly arrived and obviously wealthy John Murrow out of his money. Unknown to the Worthingtons, Black John is a slave trader, thief and murderer, and he is on the run from the law. The Worthingtons lure Murrow to the cabin. He never returns. Reverend Jeremiah Harmon and his young son James note the disappearance of Murrow. Over the next few years, they observe the rise to affluence of the Worthingtons. They suspect foul play but have no proof. As the years pass, James and Thomas grow into men, husbands, fathers and, as the Civil War breaks out, soldiers. Yet a dark secret seems to follow Thomas throughout his life. Near the end of the war, John Edwin and Maude are murdered in their mansion near the dark cabin. Does it have anything to do with the disappearance of Murrow? And what will become of Thomas?

Readers of murder mysteries will relish the many facets of The Dark Cabin Murders, *which is anything but singular, involving readers in probes of inner being as well as mysteries and events that ultimately examine wider issues of the impact of life choices.*
— **Midwest Book Review**

In a series of well-told episodes, the author delivers a realistic version of time and place... [including] a searing account of the brutal, bloody, hand-to-hand combat of the Civil War. — **Blue Ink Review**

...An imaginative morality tale about free will, crime, punishment, and the possibility of redemption. — **Kirkus Reviews**

THE RIVER RAT MURDERS

PROLOGUE

I am Caroline Case, and you have found my diary. I left it with my private papers, so I know that a friend would find it.

You must already know my reputation; most local folks do. I grew up on the wrong side of the railroad tracks just north of the stinky refuse dump in a coal mining town on the Wabash River. The name of the town doesn't matter, the river towns were all the same in those days: bawdy, sinful, exciting.

In the beginning, there were four of us: Father, Mother, my little sister Lenny and me. My father was a heavy drinker. He was not abusive in any way; he was just drunk most of the time. He worked as a laborer and occasionally as a miner, but he couldn't hold a job. My mother was a saint, deeply involved in the local church. She took in laundry and worked as a seamstress. Unfortunately, drunks and saints don't make much money, and our small family lived on the edge.

I was only 13 years old when my father died from a fall. He was drunk, of course. My mother died two years later. Officially, her death was from dropsy [congestive heart failure], but I know it was mostly due to a broken heart. Despite his faults, she loved my father.

After my mother's death, my sister and I stayed with the neighbor Moultrie family for about a year. They were a good family, but they were also poor. Lenny stayed with them and continued in school, but I left when I was 16. I knew that I was a burden.

Thus, my adventures began. My way up was through dim dance halls, road houses, tavern back rooms and later, a rather elaborate houseboat on the Wabash. I learned my "profession." I became wise in the ways and vulnerabilities of men.

My "on the job" education was obtained through experience, trial and error. For example, I learned to observe and analyze people, situations and my surroundings in minute detail. With perfect recall, I memorized even the smallest details. During critical moments, I learned to let fear pass over and through me. I remained calm and analytical in stressful and even dangerous situations. These abilities were honed to a high level early on; they were necessary for survival in my often harsh and unforgiving environment. As time passed, I gained confidence.

I also quickly learned the value of money. Initially, money provided the means for a meager, hand-to-mouth existence. I counted every penny. Over time, I rose above poverty. The accumulation of money became an obsession. I learned to critically rank-order opportunities and invest based on expected risks and returns. My teen-age years passed, and I began to accumulate wealth. I vowed never to be poor again.

I was a Madame by the age of twenty-four. I bought the houseboat from its original owner. Later, I became an entrepreneur, with interest in a speakeasy and ownership of a grand Victorian house of "sinful pleasure." I have no regrets. From these entrepreneurial beginnings, I moved on, which proved to be the start of many new adventures.

It was the spring of 1921 when I started keeping notes for my diary. I think I am a good writer; I did study in school, even though I quit when I passed my 16th birthday. Afterwards, I became an avid reader of everything from newspapers to dime novels. By analyzing the structure of written works as well as content, I learned to "turn a phrase," so to speak.

My diary began after the murder of old Alec. He fell, hit his head on a rock, and rolled into the Wabash, or so the county medical examiner said. I knew it was quite different, but no one would listen. I began collecting evidence and keeping notes. These evolved into a diary of sorts. I consistently added pages to this volume until September 1928, shortly after the fifth murder.

This diary is my legacy. This first volume includes an intricate, sometimes dark, often thought-provoking tale of bootleg whiskey, gangsters, corrupt politicians and five related murders. Who were the bad guys, really? I chose to weave this tale into the fabric of my life on the Wabash River.

Hannibal Jones is my closest friend. He is different than most men, and we have a very special relationship. Together, we solved the mysteries surrounding the murders. We know the guilty, not so guilty and much more. However, while we lived in the Wabash Valley, we chose to keep our knowledge to ourselves, at least until my diary was discovered by you, my friend.

You may well ask: "Why didn't you tell the authorities about Alec and the other murders?" The reasons will become apparent as you read the following pages.

Initially, I kept hand-written notes for my diary in a small box. I wrote the notes after extraordinary events happened; occasionally I wrote each day for several days in a row, most often weekly and sometimes after skipping a month or so.

Beginning in 1928, I began to organize my notes into a bound notebook, page by page. Since then, I have refined my work.

Years have passed. My diary will be of interest to the authorities, since I know where the bodies lie. I also have evidence to show how they got there.

The following pages of volume one, refined and edited over the years, tells my story from 1921 until 1928. The authorities may find parts of my narrative titillating, sometimes fun, occasionally sad, rarely sordid, yet always, at least to me, adventurous. You, the reader, will draw your own conclusions.

1

THE DEATH OF ALEC

I am known along the Wabash River as Madame Caroline. My base of operations is a large houseboat. It has a very nice apartment for me and four smaller rooms for my "girls." The boat has a covered porch at the stern, with several chairs, great for sitting in the cool mornings with hot coffee. It also has a kitchen with a table for six, a coal stove for cooking and heating and a sink. We keep drinking water in a five-gallon milk can. Kerosene lamps provide light. A small rudimentary "bathroom" provides the necessaries. All in all, our little home is very comfortable, thank you.

Friends occasionally tow and push my houseboat from town to town, depending on business and the inevitable notoriety with local enforcers of public morality. We travel up and down the Wabash, mostly between Vincennes and Montezuma, with stops along the way at West Terre Haute and Clinton. Business is good.

Why am I writing this? I started because my old friend Alec Feleovich, who lived in Clinton, was murdered last week, on Friday, July 1, 1921. The events surrounding his murder are seared in my memory.

Sheriff Big Bill Johansson and medical examiner Dr. Eben Speakwright say it was an accident, but I know better. I have decided to investigate, and this set of notes will be a record of my findings. I fear that others will follow old Alec, for there is a dark secret in this town.

Before 1920, old Alec, like many others on the river, made a meager living by commercial net fishing, trapping fur-bearing critters in winter and dragging the river bottom for fresh-water clams, more commonly known as mussels. Fish, mostly catfish, were sold in several local fish markets. Fur pelts, stretched and dried, were sold to fur buyers who traveled the towns in winter, buying up local catches of mink, raccoons, muskrats, foxes and so on. Mussels were cleaned of their meat, which was used for fish bait in the nets. The shells were sold by the ton to the "button factory." In turn, the shells were cut into "mother of pearl" buttons and sold to clothing manufacturers. It was hard work, but the Wabash was bountiful, and old Alec, except for occasional wild Saturday nights in local taverns, was pretty much a law-abiding citizen.

Collectively, river-folk like Alec, along with those of us in the riverside red-light business, are called "river rats." In general, we have adopted the name as a sort of badge of honor amongst ourselves. However, we usually bristle when outsiders use the term in a derogatory way.

Before he was murdered, Alec was my friend and neighbor when my houseboat was in town. Alec's shack is set back in the trees, above the usual river flood line, just east of South Main Street, in Clinton. It's still there. His boats are tied up very near my houseboat. Someone will take them soon, I suppose. My girls called him Uncle Alec, and he would always smile and wave as he passed by. I miss him.

Prohibition has changed river life. Before 1920, booze was pretty much legal, even though towns along the Wabash had many restrictions. Beginning last year, prohibition became a national ban on the production, importation, transportation and sale of alcoholic beverages, or so the newspapers say.

There is also much folderol by church groups. However, especially along the river, production of illegal booze has become a very lucrative business. Last year, old Alec and several other local river rats became bootleggers.

Many in the Valley, especially rowdy coal miners and not a few prominent members of local society, participate with gay abandon.

"Bathtub gin," "white lightning" and "speakeasy" have become common terms. What fun!

How did we get to this point? As I was growing up, and later from my vantage point in the back rooms of saloons, roadhouses and other establishments consistent with my chosen vocation, I observed the war against booze with amusement, sometimes trepidation and always avid interest.

The local papers, pious church sermons and high-falutin' gossip by tea-party ladies kept the ball rolling. In their defense, I suppose, it began with good intentions. Drunkenness, family violence and political corruption from saloon associations prompted many church groups to lobby for the end of the booze trade. For a while, I had some sympathy with this point of view because of my father's drunkenness and eventual death as a result. Oh, well.

Over several decades prior to 1918, the local newspapers provided details on the political and legal fronts. Many communities along the Wabash introduced alcohol prohibition ordinances, with enforcement by local police and sheriffs. It was a hotly debated issue, especially in my rather special environment along the river. Of course, there were always laws against my profession, widely ignored, by the bye. My clients included local policemen, a mayor or two and more than a couple of sheriffs.

Prohibition supporters, who we river rats derisively called the "drys," presented prohibition as a much-needed reform for public morals and health. Dry crusaders gained a national base through the Women's Christian Temperance Union, and after 1900, the Anti-Saloon League, or so the newspapers said.

In often profane language, my many customers vented their displeasure. Carousing with my girls went hand in hand, so to speak, with consuming copious amounts of booze. One arm around a buxom girl and the free hand holding a drink: what else could a man want?

With understandable self-interest, the beer brewing and distillery barons led the opposition. They mobilized "wet" supporters, including many local German immigrant folk.

Wass zur Hölle? The Germans saw no reason for pious church groups to dictate whether or not they could drink as much beer and other alcoholic beverages as they wanted. After all, drinking was part of their culture inherited from the old country.

Groups of wets got funding for lobbying from big brewers and distillers, and the fight was on. I read their ads in local newspapers, and saloon gossip filled in the details. Terre Haute's two breweries, the Terre Haute Brewing Company and the People's Brewing Company, both vigorously lobbied with the state for continued production of beer.

However, the German community was on the outs with local society during and immediately after the World War. German immigrant families, of which there were many, were often ostracized by more established and politically powerful groups. German immigrant political influence waned, in spite of their large numbers.

In 1917-18, the Indiana beer brewing industry was shut down by the Indiana legislature. Terre Haute's two big breweries were forced to lay off many employees while limiting production to non-alcoholic products. The final nail in the coffin of legal "old man booze" occurred in 1920; the shutdown became nationwide under the 18th Amendment to the U.S. Constitution.

Pious newspaper articles praised the virtues of the 18th Amendment and its enabling legislation, known as the Volstead Act. This act set down the rules for enforcing the federal ban and defined the types of alcoholic beverages that were prohibited. For example, religious use of wine was allowed. Surprise! Private ownership and consumption of alcohol were not made illegal under the federal law, but our local laws were stricter. Many communities along the Wabash banned possession outright.

The stage was set for bootlegging, which involved making beverages from just about anything that would ferment, often corn or rye, and form "drinkable" alcohol. This "white lightening" was aged at least a week. Sometimes it was given a brown color by adding tea and who knows what else. "Rotgut" was an appropriate description.

One evening last summer, old Alec told me that he had set up a still in a secluded small cabin up river from town. He said that his income had tripled, he worked fewer hours, and he even had time (and money) to patronize my girls with more than a smile and a wave of the hand. He did so, the very next evening after our conversation, with great enthusiasm. I laughed as I took his money, and he laughed with me.

For a while, business boomed for old Alec. I became one of his customers, and my clients loved his product. I often watched from my houseboat porch as Alec returned from upriver on Fridays, late in the evening. He would row his boat up to his usual spot on the bank. Several large gallon tins, filled with some "unknown" liquid, usually rested in the bottom of his open boat. Alec would unload his cargo and hide the tins in a trash pile high up on the river bank near his shack. The next morning, a modified Model T "pick-up truck" would clatter up to Alec's shack, money would be paid, and the tins were carried off by the pick-up driver. Empty tins were returned later and stashed in the trash pile for Alec.

Late last year, things changed. From my porch, I observed several arguments between Alec and the pick-up driver. From overheard words at a distance, I could tell the arguments were over money.

Then one day, the pick-up driver was accompanied by a man in an expensive looking suit. I observed from my porch that this man had slicked down black hair under a broad-brimmed hat. He also had what we called a "go to hell" moustache. I could also see a bulge under his suit jacket, and he would occasionally slip his right hand under the bulge. The pick-up driver did the talking; his companion just glared. I could see Alec as his face changed from self-assurance to uncertainty, and then to fear. Finally, he took the offered money and went back into his shack. The driver and his companion got in the Model T and drove off with the tins.

A week or so after the above encounter, again on a Friday, Alec rowed up in his boat as usual. I waved from my porch. Alec's face carried a grim smile as he unloaded his tins.

"Hello Alec, is everything OK?" I called out.

"Yes, Miss Caroline," he responded. "Dose buyers wanted to cheat me out of the money for my stuff," he continued as he picked up one of the tins from the bottom of his boat. He shook the tin gently. "What was 100-proof is now 50 proof, he concluded with a grin. "Half-price, half proof!"

"Be careful, Alec," I said. "The man with the pick-up driver looked scary to me."

Alec saw my expression of concern. "Now don't you worry Miss Caroline," he replied. "Besides, Big Bill looks after me."

"You mean the sheriff?" This was news. Alec nodded, and his grin got bigger. Big Bill visited my houseboat on occasion. His favorite was Susie, my oldest and most experienced girl. Bill's dalliances were done in spite of the fact that he had a wife Amy, a prominent church goer, and two teen-aged boys.

I knew Big Bill's marital situation, of course. Although it was left unsaid between us, Bill knew that word could get back to Amy about his extracurricular activities. This fact gave me an edge; Bill never interfered with my business. It was a reasonable working relationship.

However, Alec's comment concerning Big Bill implied something else. Was Bill involved somehow with bootlegging?

Alec watched as I fidgeted a little. "I'll be fine, Miss Caroline, jus' fine." With that, he started up the river bank on the path toward his trash pile. He carried two tins. I watched as he made two more trips, whistling as he worked.

"OK," I thought to myself, "if he isn't concerned, maybe I shouldn't be either."

The following week, I watched Alec make another run. Again, he whistled as he stashed his tins. I didn't witness the pick-ups and payoffs, but from my limited observations, Alec seemed happy enough. "Oh well," I thought to myself, "I have a business to run." I put Alec out of my daily thoughts.

A third week passed. Early on Saturday morning, July 2nd, the river was very quiet. The water gurgled gently as it flowed past the sides of my houseboat. I got up early, got dressed except for my shoes and fixed myself a pot of coffee on the stove. After pouring a cup, I stepped out on the back porch. My girls were still asleep. Friday night had been busy, and they were exhausted. "Quiet is good," I thought to myself as I leaned on the railing and sipped my coffee. I looked at the scene downriver.

Alec's boat was in its usual spot. However, something didn't seem right. I leaned forward and looked closer.

With horror, I finally recognized what was wrong. "Oh, my heaven!" I exclaimed out loud. I dropped my coffee cup, and it splashed in the water over the stern of the boat.

"What's wrong, Miss Caroline?" A sleepy voice came from the kitchen. Susie stepped out on the porch, wearing a gaudy silk robe and pink slippers.

I pointed toward Alec's boat. "See?" I said.

Susie rubbed the sleep from her eyes and looked. After a moment, her hands flew up to her face. "Oh, my heaven!"

We both stared at something protruding from under the boat. Feet and legs stretched from the water's edge up onto the bank.

"Susie, get your clothes on!" I sat in a chair and pulled on and laced my shoes. Susie slipped out of her robe as she dashed back to her room.

She soon emerged, wearing a pull-over shift dress. There was nothing underneath, and it showed. She hopped about on one foot as she pulled on her last shoe. The laces remained untied. The scene would have been comical if circumstances had been different.

We scrambled to the narrow board that served as a gangplank, made our way off the boat, and then along the riverbank toward Alec's boat, about fifty feet away.

As we arrived, I saw Alec's oars as they lay on the bank next to his boat. I picked one up and gingerly pushed the boat away. Alec was on his back, and his face rose slowly from the water.

"Oh, oh," muttered Susie softly. She backed up and fell on her behind. She stared at Alec. "Oh, oh," she said again, as she chewed on the knuckles of her right hand.

I stared intently. Blood seeped from Alec's nose and mouth. There was blood in the water. His eyes were open, staring up at the sky.

"Help me!" I exclaimed, as I reached down and grabbed Alec's left foot. Susie just sat there. "Oh, oh," she said for the third time.

"Susie!" I yelled, and looked back at her over my shoulder. Her eyes turned from Alec to me. Reason returned. She slid on her behind down the bank a few feet and gingerly got a grip on Alec's right foot.

We both pulled. Alec's body and water-soaked clothing were very heavy, but after much pulling, slipping and falling, we got him up on the bank, out of the water.

We both saw that the left side of his head had been crushed. More blood and gore seeped out on the muddy bank.

I looked around. Alec's boat was tied to a nearby cottonwood tree with a half-inch rope. I looked back to the path leading up to Alec's trash pile and shack. I could see Susie's and my footprints as they intersected the path at a right angle about two yards or so up the bank. Beyond, there were more footprints. I looked closely. There were two sets, one on each side of drag marks in the dirt. Both sets came down the path and then went back up. "Man's shoes," I thought to myself. The bank at the river end of the path was smooth, with a mixture of soft mud and silt. I looked at the boat. There were no unusual marks and no blood.

I took a deep breath and exhaled slowly. "Susie," I said softly; "can you go for help? There are houses on Main Street, just over there." I pointed to houses, not far away. "I'll wait here."

"Stay off the path," I added, and pointed to the footprints. Susie nodded; she understood.

"Yes ma'am," she said, as she swallowed convulsively. She scrambled up the bank next to the path, occasionally tripping over her untied shoelaces.

After Susie left, I glanced around at the evidence. First, the body: "It was stiff when Susie and I dragged it from the water; rigor has set in. What does that mean?" My mind raced: "Don't know the details, but I do know Alec was killed some time ago." I looked at Alec's head. "A hard blow to the head with a blunt weapon," I concluded. "Also, we have footprints and drag marks."

What should I do? "Think, think," I told myself. "Alec was my friend, and he was murdered. Can I trust the police to find the murderer?" Based on years of experience in my chosen vocation, the answer was a resounding "No."

I then remembered my camera. I also had a little closet on the houseboat that I used as a darkroom. In addition to snooping, photography was a hobby of mine. Sometimes my hobby came in handy with my customers, but that's another story.

I ran to the houseboat through the weeds beside the path; I didn't want to mess up the footprints and drag marks. Out of breath, I ran up the gangplank, across the porch and inside.

I found my camera on the shelf in my darkroom closet. I checked the film counter. Luckily, the camera was good for another dozen photos. As an afterthought, I picked up a 12-inch ruler that I used as a straight-edge when I sized prints. I also took a piece of blotting paper, which I normally used to soak up chemical residue from the print development process. "Good for a blood sample," I said to myself. I had read somewhere that people can be identified from their blood. By taking a sample from Alec and from a crime scene, I would have evidence that he was killed at a given location.

I flew out the door, down the gangplank and back to Alec's body, again through the weeds. I took photos of the drag marks and the footprints. I placed the ruler in each photo to serve as a scale. Grimacing, I also dabbed the blotting paper in the blood on Alec's face. I then raced back to the houseboat and stowed the camera, ruler and blood sample. Finished! I then caught my breath and walked slowly back to the crime scene to wait for the police to show up.

The wait wasn't long. First, Sam, a Clinton policeman, arrived. I showed him what I had found and explained what I had observed. He took notes, with occasional glances to Alec's bloody head and face.

Susie showed up a few minutes after Sam; she was as white as a sheet. "Go back to the houseboat, Susie," I said. Sam made no objection, and Susie complied. I noted that she walked off the path in the weeds, just like I had done. "Good girl, Susie!"

To my surprise, Sheriff Big Bill Johansson showed up about thirty minutes later. He glanced around at the scene. He also saw Susie on the porch of the houseboat, where she had been joined by Louisa, Maribel and Kathy. Bill saw them and tipped his hat. "Ladies," he said in a condescending manner. He barely acknowledged my presence, as I stood by Sam, with my arms folded.

"Has Miss Caroline given her statement?" He queried Sam.

"Yessir," replied Sam.

Bill turned back to me. "You can go now. I'm taking over."

I was startled, and it must have showed. We were in city limits, and the police should have taken the lead.

Bill saw my expression. "I'll manage from here, Caroline," he said brusquely. He turned to Sam, who nodded subserviently.

I opened my mouth to speak, thought better of it, and then closed my mouth.

Bill saw my expression and said: "I'm sure you have things to do to prepare for your evening's work." He smiled in a leering, condescending way. "Now go back to your houseboat." He then turned away and took no further notice of me.

"OK," I responded. I think my voice remained calm in spite of my resentment. "You big oaf!" I thought to myself, as I walked slowly back to my houseboat. Given my profession and social standing, I could hardly do otherwise.

On Tuesday, July 5th, the local Clinton newspaper had a short article about Alec. I clipped out, and it reads as follows.

WABASH RIVER DROWNING

Alec Feleovich, a local fisherman, died on Friday night, July 1. According to Sheriff Johansson, evidence suggests that Mr. Feleovich fell near his boat on the Wabash, hit his head on a rock and then drowned in the river. Dr. Speakwright, the Vermillion County medical examiner, confirmed that Mr. Feleovich's injuries were consistent with a fall, and his death was by drowning. Since no kin has come forward, Mr. Feleovich will be interned in the county section of Riverside Cemetery on Wednesday, July 6. The coffin will be closed due to the nature of the death. Friends may pay their respects at a brief graveside service. According to Sheriff Johansson, the case is closed.

I was dumbfounded. What happened here?

2

RIVER RAT DETECTIVES

Tuesday evening, July 5, 1921

The medical examiner's report in the newspaper was patently false. There were no rocks near the boat, and Alec's head was bashed in on the side, not the front or back, which would have been consistent with a fall.

"Alec will be buried in a pauper's grave," I thought to myself. I decided to investigate further.

Alec's shack was just a stone's throw up the river bank, along the back alley that paralleled South Main Street on the east side. Was Alec killed in his shack? The drag marks and footprints came from that direction.

Late this morning, I took my box camera with a new roll of film, my ruler and another piece of blotting paper. I also took a couple of "penny" brown paper sacks. With my gear in hand, I followed Alec's path toward his shack. I was alone. My girls were understandably scared, and they remained in the houseboat.

Although new footprints partially obscured the drag marks and the male footprints that I saw on Saturday morning, I could still make them out. They led past Alec's trash pile toward his shack. I took photos of the drag marks and footprints, making sure that the sunlight provided proper illumination. Again, I included the ruler in each photo for scale.

I stopped at the trash pile. Alec had an old rusty oil drum near the pile for burning refuse. I looked in. Something had been recently burned. I poked the ashes with a stick, and found a few shreds of a cotton sheet and what looked like an old army blanket. The shreds had dark reddish stains: blood? I lifted a couple pieces with a stick and placed them in one of my paper sacks.

I poked around the trash pile. There were no tins, just old boards, tree brush and assorted junk. However, I saw circular marks in the dirt under an old piece of canvas. Were Alec's tins placed there? It seemed likely. I took more photos of the contents of the refuse drum and the trash pile.

I followed the path to Alec's shack, past his ramshackle outhouse. Drag-marks were still discernable, right up to the door. There were many other footprints. I took photos, each with my ruler for scale.

The door to the shack didn't have a lock, and I pushed it open. It was dim inside and deathly still. I pushed the door wide to let in light.

I shivered, took a deep breath and stepped inside. I could smell the sour stench of unwashed clothes soaked with years of sweat and fish. However, the overpowering smell was of chlorine. "Bleach," I thought to myself.

Alec's one room had a small bed and a table with two chairs. A kerosene lamp rested on the table. A coal burning stove and a coal bucket stood about three feet out from the right-side wall; the stove pipe exited high on the wall to the outside. Shelves lined the left wall; these had a few canned goods, salt and pepper shakers, assorted utensils, a few hand tools and so on. A red A&P Eight O'Clock Coffee tin rested on a top shelf. I reached high and took it down. "One of old Alec's few luxuries," I muttered. There were a few coins inside, nothing else. I set the tin on the table.

A few wire clothes hangers were suspended from a short piece of baling wire stretched across a back corner of the room by the bed, about five feet up from the floor. I stepped forward and looked at the hanging clothes, which were mostly dirty shirts and pants. A winter coat hung at the back. The sour stench came from the clothes. There were no blankets or sheets on the bare, thin bed mattress. I pushed my hand through the hanging clothes. A few small insects skittered out and back inside. I shuddered and stepped back.

I turned around. The near left side corner at the front of the room had a wash basin on a tall stool and a bucket on the floor with a ladle sticking out. A used bar of brown lye soap lay next to the basin on the stool. The bucket had no water. "Bet the water was used with the bleach to clean up," I mused to myself.

I turned again, my back to the door, and looked down and around. The floor boards looked uncommonly clean, so did the side walls by the bed, as if they had been recently scrubbed. "Old Alec wasn't that tidy," I thought. Again, I noted the smell of chlorine. "Somebody scrubbed the back walls and the floor," I muttered aloud. "Who?" I took more photos, all around the room. The open door provided enough light.

As I looked back at the bed, the light from the open door behind me dimmed. I felt rather than saw a shadow on the far wall above the bed.

I spun around, sucking in a gulp of air. I vocalized a terror-driven squeak, much like, I imagine, a scared mouse. In the open doorway, I saw the silhouette of a very tall, broad shouldered man. My hands flew up to my mouth, and I stared.

I squeaked again, and then stuttered: "Who are you?"

The silhouette replied in a deep resonant voice: "And who are you?" There was a slight chuckle at the end.

"Caroline," I said, as I tried to regain my composure.

"Hannibal, Hannibal Jones," said the silhouette. There was a pause, and Hannibal backed out of the doorway into the sunlight. "Did you look at the ceiling by the bed?" he continued.

This was so unexpected that I involuntarily turned around and looked up. I saw specks in a thin spray of dark red.

"Blood," said Hannibal. "They didn't wash the ceiling." I remembered my camera and took two photos of the ceiling, close up. I also used blotting paper to take a blood sample. The blood was dried, but enough came off to make a decent sample.

Wheels turned in my mind as my fright subsided. Obviously, Hannibal wasn't going to hurt me, at least not yet. "Alec was killed here," I uttered.

"Yes," said Hannibal. "Alec's head was bashed in while he was in bed; he must have rolled off on the floor, and he was dragged outside and away, down the path to the river. Afterwards, the bed was stripped and the floor and walls were scrubbed."

My mind was working again. "It must have been very late last Friday night," I replied. "My last customers at the houseboat left just before midnight." I paused, and then continued. "If the killing had taken place before midnight, they would have noticed something; the path from my houseboat to Main Street follows Alec's path for quite a way. Also, Alec's body was stiff when Susie and I dragged it from the river."

"I agree," said Hannibal. "I think there were two killers, and they probably surprised Alec in his sleep."

"He didn't have a chance." I know my voice trembled a little, my imagination pictured Alec's last moments of terror, struggle, blows to the side of his head and then oblivion. I took a deep breath, and looked back to the bed. "I guess that the clean-up occurred right after the killing, otherwise I probably would have noticed visitors to the shack in the daylight after the Sheriff arrived," I continued aloud.

I then thought to myself: "My evening business on the houseboat almost always finishes about midnight; overnighters are not allowed. It's too dangerous; experience is a hard teacher sometimes." I ended my private thoughts and looked at Hannibal.

"Of course, the clean-up crew could have come at late at night on Saturday, Sunday or Monday," I mused out loud.

Hannibal nodded, and I looked up and noticed his face for the first time. He had chiseled features, with steely blue eyes. His short hair was dark, except for a touch of gray at the temples. His cheeks and chin had a stubble of a beard; he hadn't shaved for a few days. I looked him up and then down. He was tall, well over six feet. He had broad shoulders, a slim waist, long legs and work hardened hands. He wore a faded blue shirt, jeans and brogan work shoes. "A working man, yet not a coal miner," I thought quickly. "There is no telltale coal dirt under his fingernails."

A grin spread across Hannibal's face. "Do I pass inspection?" He queried gently.

I know I turned beet-red. "Ahem," I stuttered, and then recovered. "Would you like a cup of coffee?" I paused a moment. "I'm done here, and I have a pot on the stove." I stepped out the door and closed it. "Over there," I said, as I turned and pointed to the houseboat.

"That would be nice," Hannibal replied. "We have much to talk about." He stepped aside and motioned with his hand for me to lead the way.

I nodded, stepped past him, and walked slowly down the path toward my houseboat. "Hannibal Jones," I mused under my breath. "Mysterious, but not in a threatening way," I concluded.

All four girls were on the back porch of the houseboat: Susie, Louisa, Maribel and Kathy, the youngest. They were dressed for once. Besides, it was almost noon. Hannibal and I walked up the gangplank.

"Ladies," said Hannibal somewhat shyly, as we arrived on the porch.

I looked up at Hannibal. He looked slightly embarrassed. Apparently, he was not used to being observed by several women at the same time or possibly to my type of houseboat.

In the meantime, all four girls, especially the older three, gave Hannibal the once over. They looked very pleased with what they saw.

It was my turn to chuckle, and I enjoyed the moment. After a brief pause for effect, I said: "Introductions are in order: girls, this is Hannibal Jones." I looked up to Hannibal with a smile, and then said: "Hannibal, please meet Susie, Louisa, Maribel and Kathy."

Hannibal blushed, looked down, back up and then shuffled his feet. "Ladies," he repeated.

OK, enough, I had gotten even. In a kindly manner, I said: "Hannibal, please sit." I motioned toward one of the chairs.

Hannibal, with a couple of "pardon me" expressions, stepped gingerly around the girls and lowered his tall frame into one of the chairs.

"Susie, would you get us some coffee?" I then looked at the other three girls sternly. "Don't you three have something to do?" They took the hint and went back inside, with a few giggles.

I sat down in a chair, facing Hannibal on the other side of the porch. Except for the water gurgling under the boat and the occasional clatter in the kitchen as Susie prepared coffee, silence reigned.

I gave Hannibal a long look, and he returned it with a steady gaze. "Who are you, really?" I finally asked.

Hannibal watched me carefully for a few moments. I could tell he was weighing his words before speaking. "I like that in a man," I thought to myself.

Finally, he said: "Alec was my friend." He paused a moment, then continued. "We were in France together, during the war. Alec saved my life; he was a sergeant then."

"Wow!" I thought to myself, as I tried to keep my poker face. "So much I don't know about my friends!" There were so many questions; I didn't know where to start. Fortunately, Hannibal wasn't finished.

"I travel a lot," he continued mysteriously. "I stopped to see Alec on my way through town." He paused again, and then continued. "I arrived last Saturday, mid-morning. I watched from a distance as the coroner picked up Alec's body."

Silence reigned for quite a while. Susie came out to the porch with three cups of coffee. I gave her a long look. She got the point, gave Hannibal and me our cups and went back inside.

I could see that Hannibal wasn't going to reveal anything else for the moment, so I changed the subject.

"I took lots of pictures," I ventured.

"Yes," replied Hannibal. "But did you take pictures of the body?"

"No, I didn't think of it on Saturday," I confessed; I could see where this was leading. "Alec will be buried tomorrow."

"Still only one funeral home in town?" said Hannibal, with a slight smile.

"Yes," I replied. "Farris, over on Fifth Street; they take care of both county and private burials." I paused a moment, then said: "Alec will be there, but he won't have a public showing; county burials at taxpayer's expense never do. The newspaper said there would be a graveside service."

"Shall we pay our respects a day early?" Hannibal said. His smile broadened a little.

I got the drift. "Susie!" I called out.

Susie appeared in the doorway. "Yes ma'am?"

Together, the three of us hatched a plan. Action began late this afternoon, after most of the employees of the Farris Funeral Home were expected to go home to their families.

Susie and I arrived at the front entrance to the funeral home about five o'clock. Hannibal waited behind a nearby building, out of sight. As expected, we saw several employees leaving by a side door. After they departed, Hannibal slipped to the side of the home. He hid where he could see into a window to the front parlor. He had my camera.

Susie and I were dressed in demure dark clothes. For all the world, we appeared to be grief-stricken mourners. Susie's outfit was the best; her job was to be the sweet young niece of Alec. Her curves showed nicely from underneath her black dress. I was the respectable, prim but heart-broken older niece. Hats with veils and long black gloves completed our ensembles. After proper smoothing and primping, we entered the front door.

The front parlor was tastefully decorated but somber. Golden light glowed from sconces on the walls. Space along the left side of the parlor was vacant; coffins rested in the space during funeral viewings. "No funerals today," I thought to myself. "Good!"

Light glowed from an office on the right side of the parlor. We looked in. A small electric lamp rested on a large, dark wooden desk. A lone young man sat behind the desk in an expensive-looking leather chair. Papers lay on the desk, and the young man had a pen in hand.

He looked up as we entered. He rose and walked into the parlor. In a soft, soothing voice, he asked: "May I help you?" His cherubic face was clean-shaven, and his sandy hair was parted in the middle. He wore a black suit, conservative deep purple tie and black shoes. He also wore a sad, condescending, self-assured, somewhat weary smile. He held his hands together in a practiced, prayerful manner.

I surmised his thoughts: "What are these people doing here?"

I sighed, dabbed my eyes with a white silk handkerchief, and slipped into my role as a grieving niece.

"We were told that our dear Uncle Alec Feleovich is here." I paused, let out a deep sigh, and continued. "May we see him?"

Susie let out a stifled sniffle.

"Well," replied the young man, "Mr. Feleovich is here, but his service will be at the Riverside Cemetery tomorrow." He continued his sad smile.

"But, but," said Susie; her sweet voice was interposed with another sniffle; "May we see him?"

"Mr. Feleovich was not scheduled for a viewing," replied the young man, with a slight frown. He then looked at me with sad eyes: "His coffin will be closed due to his injuries."

"But, but, he was our favorite Uncle," responded Susie. "Oh, oh, how awful! We miss him so!" She let out a low moan for emphasis.

I could see that the young man instantly regretted his last statement.

I gave Susie a nudge with my elbow, which indicated: "Don't overplay it, girl." I then smiled sweetly. I also glanced out the window and saw a shadow move swiftly toward the side door.

Susie got back on track. "I feel so faint; may I sit down?" She sniffled and sighed and let her legs sag a little.

I gave Susie a deeply concerned look and supported her arm from the side as she sagged.

The young man instantly stepped to the other side and supported Susie's other arm and elbow. Susie leaned his way and let her body brush against his, slowly.

The young man did a sharp intake of breath. "Of course, of course!" He then looked around quickly; the only chair was the leather chair in his office; the parlor had not been set up for the next funeral. "In my office, please!"

Perfect! With the young man on one side and me on the other, we led Susie into the office and gently lowered her into the leather chair. I rested my behind on the desk top and let my dress rise up over my knees. The young man tried his best not to look.

Susie continued her fainting spell. Every minute or so, she gave out a low "Oh, oh!" sob.

The young man glanced at Susie, then to my legs, then back to Susie.

After the third "Oh, oh!" he looked up at my face and said: "I'll go to the back room and get her a glass of water." He started to step away from Susie's chair.

"Oh, my heaven!" I thought to myself. "He'll see Hannibal." My mind raced. "Perhaps later," I said, and I smiled sweetly. I then added: "After she has recovered a little."

The young man eased back; his face still had an uncertain expression.

"A man's presence is what we both need most now," I said, in the meekest voice I could muster. "Please don't leave us alone."

That did it. Hannibal was safe.

As Susie recovered in the office, I kept glancing out the window across the parlor. I finally saw a shadowy figure pass by. Mission accomplished! I gave Susie a look and a nod.

Susie's fainting spell abruptly ended, and she rose from her seat. I slipped off the desk top. We both smiled at the young man sweetly.

"Thank you so much for your kindness, sir," I said with a slight sigh. "We will be at the service tomorrow." This was actually true, we missed Alec, and we wanted to pay our respects.

"Of course, of course!" replied the young man, with deep solicitation. He then assisted Susie and me out of the office, through the parlor and to the front door. After appropriate goodbyes and thank yous, we crossed the street and walked toward Main Street. We met Hannibal about two blocks away, out of sight of the funeral home.

"Did you find Alec?" I asked.

"Yes, he was still on a table in the back," replied Hannibal. His face looked grim. "I took several pictures," he added. "Nothing had been done to restore his head. I overheard that the coffin will be closed, and that's a good thing."

The three of us said little as we walked the half mile or so back to the houseboat. Poor Alec!

As we approached Main Street, Hannibal turned to me and said: "Here is your camera." He handed the camera over with a smile. He then looked up and away toward the river. "Can you ladies make it back to your houseboat alone?"

"Yes, of course!" I replied. "What are you going to do?"

Hannibal didn't answer directly. After a moment, he said: "See you tomorrow?"

"Alright," I responded.

With that, Hannibal raised his right hand slightly as a goodbye, turned, and walked north on Main Street. Susie and I watched as he strode quickly away. Street lights came on as we watched.

"Let's go home," I said to Susie. She nodded.

We walked past Alec's now empty, sad-looking shack and down to the houseboat.

Wednesday evening, July 6

Sun beamed into the east window to my room this morning. I rolled over in my bed and looked at my clock on the nightstand. "Eight o'clock! Oh, my goodness!" I said out loud. I heard a clatter in the kitchen. I got up, quickly made use of our bathroom, and went into the kitchen, dressed in my robe.

Susie, Louisa, Maribel and Kathy were already there, dressed. Breakfast was on the table. My usual chair was vacant, so I sat down. Susie poured me a cup of coffee, which I accepted gratefully.

"Thanks!" I said.

"You're welcome," replied Susie. "Service today, at Riverside," she added. "Ten o'clock."

After breakfast, I quickly dressed. The five of us walked down the gangplank, planning a long walk to Riverside. As we approached Main Street, a hundred yards or so away, we saw a new, sensible-looking, black Model T sedan. Hannibal peered from the side window.

"Would you ladies like a ride?' Hannibal smiled warmly.

"Thank you, yes!" Louisa and Maribel responded, almost in unison. Susie, Kathy and I nodded vigorously. Riverside was a good two miles away, and it was already nine o'clock.

We piled in; the four girls were cramped in the back seat. I sat in front, next to Hannibal.

"Your car?" I queried.

"Yes," responded Hannibal. "I drove it from Chicago." He started the car; it had a new-fangled electric starter.

He didn't elaborate on the car, so I let it lie. "So much I don't know," I thought to myself.

Hannibal looked over at me as we headed north on Main Street. He smiled as if he read my mind. "I have a room at the hotel downtown," he said. He added: "Temporarily, of course." He paused, as if thinking things through. He then said: "I think I will stay a while."

The service at the graveside was brief. A kindly priest was there; it was known that Alec was Catholic. Mourners included about a dozen people, mostly river-folk.

Afterwards, we drove back toward the houseboat. Silence reigned for most of the trip.

Finally, Hannibal said: "I have something to show you."

"Would you like some lunch?" I responded.

"Yes, thanks," Hannibal replied.

Hannibal parked the car by the alley just above Alec's shack. He retrieved a brown paper sack from under his seat as he got out. The six of us walked past the shack down to the houseboat.

Susie and the other girls fixed lunch in the kitchen while Hannibal and I sat in chairs on the porch. Hannibal's sack rested next to his chair. I looked at it, waiting.

"Came early this morning," Hannibal said. "I made a search of the bushes and weeds that surround Alec's shack." He pulled a clean handkerchief from his back pocket and used it as he reached into the sack.

Using the handkerchief, he pulled a piece of two-inch pipe, about a foot long, from the sack. Dried blood and hair were caked on the pipe.

"Probable murder weapon," Hannibal said matter-of-factly. "I found it under some bushes by a tree next to the river." He paused, then continued: "Very careless; the murderer probably threw it toward the river, but it hit the tree limbs and fell to the ground instead."

I nodded and replied: "The murderer was in a hurry and it was probably dark. They did scrub inside the shack, except for the ceiling."

Hannibal nodded and replied: "I'm almost certain that the pictures of the crushing wounds on Alec's temple will match the size and shape of this pipe."

"Oh," I responded. I'm sure my mouth was open. I quickly recovered, thought a moment and then said: "We now have method, probable opportunity and a possible motive involving bootlegging." I paused again. "We also know that Sheriff Johansson was involved, but we don't know how or to what extent."

Hannibal responded. "What's more, we have evidence, including pictures. However, we have work to do."

"Oh, my!" This came from the doorway to the kitchen. Hannibal and I looked. Four faces appeared at the doorway: Susie, Louisa, Maribel and Kathy.

3

THE CHICAGO CONNECTION

Sunday, August 7, 1921

I have a box that contains photos of the crime scene and photos of Alec, the victim. The box also contains my notes, blood samples and a murder weapon. I run a red-light houseboat, which is tolerated by the local authorities. The county sheriff, who leaves me alone, covered up the murder of my friend Alec. What should I do? Going to the authorities does not seem like a wise move.

Fortunately, I have friends, including my girls and a few fellow river rats. Now there is Hannibal Jones. What do I know about Hannibal? Not much.

Here's what I do know. He was a friend of Alec, and they were together in France during the war. He is not yet thirty, but a little older than me. OK, that sounds about right. He also said he came here from Chicago. What is he doing there?

Hannibal apparently has money. He owns a car; he is staying in the hotel in downtown Clinton, and that can't be cheap. He doesn't have a job as far as I know, but he dresses in working man's clothes. He is always clean and neat, very different than old Alec. He is shy, and he doesn't talk much. My girls think he is handsome and the "cat's meow." I do too, but I will keep that to myself for now, thank you. Where does Hannibal get his money?

Most importantly, Hannibal helped me investigate Alec's murder. He is sharp as a tack, and he handles situations in a cool, calculating manner. He has observation skills, like a policeman. Who is this guy?

I will find out: carefully, of course. He came from Chicago. What if he is a gangster? That seems unlikely, but I really don't know.

I read about more killings in Chicago just last week, in the Sunday newspaper. Apparently, some sort of gang war is going on. Big Jim Colosimo was killed just last year. Rumor has it that Johnny Torrio was the brains behind it. And who is this new guy, Al Capone? He apparently works for Torrio. He came from New York by all accounts. And then there was the murder of Mossy Enright, who, according to the newspapers, was some sort of labor racketeer. The police made some arrests, but witnesses wouldn't talk, too scared.

The Chicago authorities seem to look the other way with regard to all the killings. Big Bill Thompson, the mayor, is apparently on the take, along with several aldermen. Gambling, labor racketeering, girls and now illegal booze: Sounds exciting! However, it also sounds very dangerous. I think I'll stay on the Wabash.

Sunday morning, August 14

Hannibal stopped by this morning. He said that he expects to stay in Clinton for a while. He also said he is looking for a place to live other than the hotel. Very mysterious, but I am glad he is staying.

Sunday morning August 21

Ogle McNabb stopped by this morning with a delivery of moonshine for my customers. Ogle took over Alec's still, which is back in operation.

Ogle said: "You get the firs' bottles of each run, Miss Caroline, which makes it the best." He grinned from ear to ear. "Nothin' is added," he continued. "It's the good stuff."

I tasted it, very carefully. Wow! It'll knock your socks off; just what my customers want.

Ogle said that he takes the rest of his stuff to a gas station on the Parke County side of the river. I was curious. I asked: "Where?"

"Jus' across the wagon bridge, Miss Caroline, on the road that heads toward the railroad bridge." He grinned. "I kin pull up my boat jus' below the station and walk right up the bank to the back door. It's only a hundred feet or so."

Ogle paused, and then added: "Lots o' boats make deliveries there." He chuckled. "One night I watched as trucks pulled up to the station; several guys loaded them up, and they took off, through the railroad overpass an' toward Lyford." He then added slyly, almost in a whisper: "Bet they head north, to Chicago."

That was news, and I said: "Be careful Ogle; you know what happened to Alec."

Ogle grew quiet, and his grin disappeared. "Yes'um, Miss Caroline, I know. I give 'um good stuff, not watered down, like Alec did." He paused, and his grin returned. "Not as good as yours, though."

I laughed. "OK, Ogle. But you be careful, just the same."

"Yes'um," he replied. After appropriate goodbyes, he left.

OK, what do I know? Apparently, our local booze goes to Chicago. That explains the sinister-looking guy in the suit that visited Alec that day in the spring. Bet he came from Chicago; local folks don't dress like that. I'll mention this to Hannibal the next time I see him. I'll also tell him about the gas station in Parke County.

Sunday morning, October 2

Fall has arrived. The stove burns all night now; it's not just for cooking. The leaves on the trees by the river are beautiful, and I love to sit on the porch in the mornings, sipping hot coffee.

One morning a couple of days ago a camp was set up along the river, where Alec used to keep his boats. I watched off the stern of my houseboat as two men cleaned their steel traps for the upcoming trapping season.

They walked over to the houseboat when they saw me watching.

The older man introduced himself and his partner. "I'm Joe, ma'am, an' this here is Cliff: proud to be your neighbors for at least a while." Cliff touched his cap and smiled.

"Hello, Joe, Hello Cliff," I responded with a smile. "I hope you don't mind if I watch; your work seems very complicated!"

"You go right ahead, ma'am, pleased to have your company," replied Cliff. The pair then touched their caps, turned and went back to work.

"River Rats can be very nice," I thought to myself: "Better than most folk." I watched their progress the rest of the day, looking up occasionally as I worked on my account books on the porch.

Preparing steel traps is an interesting process. Joe and Cliff built a fireplace out of old bricks. They set a galvanized tub over the fire, and filled it with a mixture of river water, reddish colored logwood chips and leaf mulch. They cleaned traps with a wire brush and adjusted the triggers and pans with plyers. They then placed about a dozen traps in the boiling mixture in the tub.

An hour passed. Joe dipped into the tub with a stick and lifted the traps out, one by one. The traps were all black. He draped the blackened traps over a nearby wire line, strung between two trees, where they dried. Cliff added a new load of traps to the tub.

This process was repeated until they had about a hundred traps on the line. The pair then emptied the tub into the river. They set the tub aside and placed a smaller galvanized bucket on the fireplace. They put a couple of blocks of paraffin and a couple of balls of beeswax into the bucket.

After this concoction melted, the two men lifted traps off the line, one by one, with a stick. They dipped each trap into the melted wax bucket. Each trap, coated with wax, was then draped back on the line.

By 11 o'clock, over a hundred fully prepared traps hung on the line. Joe and Cliff then donned heavy rubber work gloves and loaded the finished traps into boats, which were tied up nearby.

About midday, I called out and asked Joe: "Why this long process?"

"To get rid of human scent, Miss Caroline," he replied. He paused and grinned. "We'll use some old muskrat meat from last year, which we keep in fruit jars, for smelly bait, for mink sets." He then added with a chuckle: "We also have some fox pee from last year; we'll use it for fox sets." He then laughed: "The foxes love it!"

"Good heavens!" I exclaimed. I could never be a trapper. A little later, I made some sandwiches and lemonade and took it to Joe and Cliff. They thanked me profusely. The day ended on a cordial note.

Sunday morning, December 4

Fall has passed; winter has arrived, and ice has formed along the river banks. Trapping season began in mid- October along the river, and this lasted until the heavy rains in mid-November. The water rose and ice jammed up. Trapping on the river ended due to the rising water. Trapping continued in the swamps, creeks and drainage ditches on the Parke County side of the river; folks had to make a living. Fortunately, the river hinterland was bountiful, and trapping was good.

As the water rose and the ice jammed in the main channel, I was very busy. I constantly had to move my houseboat up the bank as the water rose. Hannibal, Ogle, Joe and Cliff helped; we used small boats, ropes and pulleys to move the big houseboat. I finally ended up in some cottonwood trees just below Alec's old shack, which remained empty. It looked very forlorn, and I tried not to think about it. Oh well.

Sunday, December 25

Christmas! Business has been uncommonly good this winter, in spite of the ice on the river. It is now Christmas evening, and I have time to write. It has been a wonderful day, worth writing about.

Hannibal stopped by Christmas morning. He brought gifts for each of the girls and a very nice gift for me. We all sat around the kitchen table and had breakfast. Afterwards, we opened gifts.

The girls each got a set of warm gloves and a very tasteful woolen scarf, perfect for the season. They all oohed and ahhed, and gave Hannibal big hugs. He looked very uncomfortable, and we all laughed.

I gave each girl an envelope with twenty dollars inside. They all thanked me profusely.

The girls gave me a set of crocheted doilies for my dresser and nightstands. I know they made them by themselves during the summer, but at the time, I pretended not to notice.

I unwrapped my gift from Hannibal last, just like a big kid. I hadn't received a gift from a man in a long time. Tears came to my eyes, and I tried not to let it show. The girls all smiled, and so did Hannibal.

After much fussing with the wrapping paper, I found a beautiful small jewelry box. It was dark brown, with gold-painted trim.

"Open it," said Hannibal.

I lifted the lid. Inside, pearls gleamed. It was a necklace. "Oh my!" I exclaimed. The girls oohed and ahhed again.

I had a lump in my throat. I finally muttered: "Thank you!" I got up from my chair, walked around the table and kissed Hannibal on the cheek.

"I then said: "But we have no gift for you!" I felt really terrible, we hadn't expected his visit.

He smiled and his eyes twinkled. "Merry Christmas," he said. He then added: "Being with you ladies on Christmas is more than enough."

Tears came, I couldn't help it. My heart tells me that Hannibal, for whatever reason, did not expect favors in return. What a nice man!

The icy river, bootlegging, gangsters and troubles of every kind were forgotten for this day. It really was a Merry Christmas, in the year 1921.

Sunday, January 8, 1922

The winter is passing slowly, but New Year' Eve is over, thank heaven! What a night! Booze flowed, the girls were busy, and profits soared. Reality returned late New Year's Day.

Tuesday, February 14

Valentine's Day has arrived. Hannibal stopped by, with some chocolates for the girls and me. He also had some news.

"I bought a house," he said.

"Where?" I was genuinely surprised.

"At 840 South Main Street, just across from the county hospital," he replied. "It's not far away." He then added: "I'll need help furnishing and decorating it; I don't know much about such things."

"Of course!" I then thought a moment. "Do you think the neighbors will mind if I stopped by?" I was alluding to my "reputation," and I could tell that Hannibal understood my meaning.

"You are always welcome," he replied. I could see from his smile that he meant it.

Hannibal had other news. "There was trouble at the gas station across the river, between the bridges," he said. He paused, and then continued: "Ogle was involved. I know he is your friend."

I opened my mouth and exclaimed: "Oh! Is he OK?" My mind raced. Not again! Not another Alec!

"Just a few cuts and bruises," responded Hannibal. "Ogle gave better than he got. The other guy was a tough looking character in a suit. Bystanders broke it up; coal miners, I think. The other guy got in an expensive-looking car and left, with several others."

I thought a few moments, and then said: "I would like to see the gas station across the river; would you drive me over?"

"Yes," Hannibal replied slowly. He leaned back in his kitchen chair, with an appraising look in his eyes. We were alone; the girls had gone shopping for groceries, wearing their new gloves and scarves. "What do you expect to see?"

"I don't know," I responded. "When do the Chicago people pick up their cargo?"

"Fridays usually," said Hannibal. He saw the question in my eyes, and continued. "I have made it a point to stop by the station for gas every week, and I have heard talk."

He then added: "I saw two men lounging around the station, both dressed in suits, on several occasions."

He paused; I could tell he was weighing his words before speaking. "Last Friday, I also saw Big Bill, the sheriff. He was having words with one of the men in suits."

Hannibal looked at me carefully, and then continued. "They were outside, out of earshot. However, the conversation seemed friendly."

This was news. More than ever, I wanted to visit the station myself.

Hannibal smiled, and said: "How about this Friday? I'm sure I will need gas about then."

"How does he do that?" I thought to myself. "He knows my question before I ask." I finally responded: "Sounds good." I then remembered to close my open mouth.

Hannibal just smiled. "See you Friday about noon? We can stop by my house; I'll give you the dime tour. We can then go get gas." He added: "I'll have you home at your convenience."

There he goes again! He knows I have to be back at night for business. Very perceptive!

"OK," I responded, a bit flustered. Hannibal grinned openly, got up, waved goodbye and left.

What is it with Hannibal? He is kind, and he gives friendship without guile or expected favors in return. Why does he care about me? I don't know, but he does, and I'm glad. I can hardly wait until Friday!

4

ALL POLITICS ARE LOCAL

Evening, Friday, February 17, 1922

What a day! Earlier, I watched from the porch as Hannibal's car rolled up and stopped near Alec's old shack. Hannibal got out, lifted a watch from a side pocket on his dress pants, looked at it and then put it away. I glanced back in the kitchen; my clock said five minutes to twelve.

"Hi Caroline," said Hannibal as he approached my houseboat at exactly 12 o'clock. Hannibal was wearing a heavy leather jacket, nice shoes and a hat with the brim turned down. His outfit was very different than his usual jeans and work shoes. I liked it.

I responded with: "Hi," as I walked down the gangplank.

The weather was cool and damp. I also wore a heavy coat over my dress, gloves and so on.

"You look very nice today," said Hannibal as he smiled.

"Thank you," I responded.

Hannibal politely assisted me as we walked to the car. "Hannibal has learned old-fashioned manners somewhere," I thought to myself. "Very nice."

The drive to Hannibal's house at 840 South Main Street took only about ten minutes. I looked at the house as we turned into the driveway on the south side.

The house was white with gray trim. It looked relatively new. It had a broad, open front porch, a double front door made of varnished oak and a large window on each side of the door. A golden light gleamed from inside. A concrete walkway led from the porch steps to the sidewalk that paralleled South Main Street. Dormant flower beds lined the porch and the walkway. A few patches of old snow lay in shadowy places. Smoke rose from two chimneys.

We drove along the south side of the house on a smooth gravel driveway, which led to a garage at the back of the lot. I could see a coal shed and outhouse to the left of the garage, along an alley. Like the house, these outbuildings were white with gray trim. It was all very neat and totally consistent with what I know, which isn't much, of Hannibal's personality.

We stopped short of the garage door. Hannibal got out, walked around the car to my door, and opened it.

"Welcome to my home," said Hannibal with a smile and a look that said: "I would very much like your opinion." He then continued in a soft voice: "Inside or outside first?"

"Outside," I replied and glanced around. I then looked closely at Hannibal and thought: "What does he hope to find here, in this simple house? An anchor?"

"Well," responded Hannibal, "garage, coal shed and other necessaries." He pointed to emphasize his words. "The house gutters drain to a filter and then to a cistern over there." He pointed again and I nodded.

"The cistern water doesn't freeze, and there is a pump for cistern water in the kitchen." He waved his hand to the large window at the back of the house. "Kitchen," he emphasized.

"My neighbor on the south side is Henry Draper; he's a painter." Hannibal paused a moment, then continued. "I had Henry fix and paint everything, inside and out." He added with a grin. "Henry is a bachelor, like me."

"Nice paint job," I responded, and I meant it. I reached over and touched Hannibal's gloved hand. To myself I thought: "Hannibal provides direction, others respond."

Reassured, Hannibal continued. "The garage is big enough for my car, a workbench and a little storage." He then pointed to the coal shed. "Coal deliveries come through the alley, and the Wabash is just down the hill on the other side, across a small field."

He then pointed to the house to the north. "My neighbors on the north are Ollie and Mary Anderson. Ollie is a coal miner; he works in the New Goshen mine south of town." He paused a moment, then added: "Henry, Ollie and Mary are nice folks."

"You seem to know a lot about your neighbors," I observed. I was a little surprised; Hannibal seemed shy during my previous encounters with him. "So much to learn," I thought to myself.

"Yes, well, they came over and introduced themselves." He shuffled his feet a little.

"OK, shy," I re-adjusted my appraisal.

"There's room for a small garden over there," Hannibal pointed to the space between the house and outbuildings. "Vegetables or flowers," he added. Almost to himself, he mused: "My mother had both." For a moment, his eyes had a faraway look. He quickly recovered and smiled at me. "Inside?" he said.

"Yes, of course," I responded.

We walked across the back yard to the north side of the house. A neat open porch was cut into the back corner of the house. An ice box rested against the house wall on the porch. A door provided an entry from the porch to the kitchen.

"Ice deliveries in the summer," said Hannibal, as he pointed to the ice box. He then walked up the steps, opened the door and motioned me in.

I walked into the kitchen. I saw a sink under the back window. Like Hannibal said, a pump was mounted on the left side of the sink. The back of the sink had a water tap.

Hannibal noticed my glance. "City water as well as cistern water," he said.

A large cook stove rested about three feet from an interior wall across the room. A stove pipe led from the back of the stove to the wall, about five feet up. Heat came from the stove; Hannibal obviously had built a fire earlier.

"Wood and coal," explained Hannibal. 'There's a bathroom on the other side of the wall behind the stove." He pointed to the doorway on the right side of the stove. "The bathroom just has a galvanized tub, some shelves, a dresser and a washstand." Somewhat defensively, he added: "still have to heat water in a tank built into the stove and in a kettle."

"Better than my houseboat," I replied truthfully. To myself, I thought: "Hannibal is using this house to show me a direction, but where does he want to go?" As usual, I had to tell myself: "patience, Caroline."

Re-assured again, Hannibal continued. "Want to see the rest of the house?" He paused and looked carefully at me. "It's not furnished yet, but it has a dining room, living room and three bedrooms." He paused, and then added: "There are two more coal stoves, one in the living room and one in the biggest bedroom."

We walked through the house, room to room. I looked into the large bedroom; a bed rested near a small heating stove. "Hannibal's staying here," I concluded to myself.

We continued our tour. Walls were either freshly painted or covered with tasteful wallpaper. The windows were neatly trimmed in light oak wood; they matched the newly varnished oak front door and also the doors to the two bedrooms.

Hannibal observed me as I looked around.

"Henry's handiwork," he said. "He has an eye for detail."

"Like you," I responded. "It's very nice."

After pointing out a few more details, Hannibal ended the tour. We walked out on the front porch. As Hannibal closed the front door, I noticed an open box by the step.

"Milk deliveries," said Hannibal, as he noticed my glance; "I can set out the empty bottles and the milkman will replace them with full bottles. There's also a card in the window with a pointer and a color code to show the days I want ice deliveries in the summer. It can be seen by the ice delivery man as he passes on the street."

Hannibal led the way as we walked around to the car on the south side of the house. As he opened the car door for me, he looked long at me, waiting.

"Hannibal, it's wonderful," I said. "This has been the nicest afternoon that I have had in a very, very long time." I meant every word. I reached out and touched Hannibal's hand for a second time.

Hannibal's eyes twinkled, and he smiled warmly. "I'm glad," was all he said.

I got in the car. Hannibal closed my door, walked around to his side and got in. He pulled out his watch, checked the time and put the watch back in his pocket. He then looked at me carefully, with that appraising look that I had come to expect.

"Want some lunch?" he inquired. "It's only one o'clock, and I know a nice lunch restaurant on Ninth Street."

"That would be very nice," I replied. There was a catch in my voice. I couldn't remember the last time a man had asked me out to lunch. I almost melted on the spot.

We had a long, wonderful lunch at a family Italian restaurant. Hannibal seemed to know the very friendly "Mom and Pop" who ran the place. They were so very nice.

After a sumptuous meal of spaghetti and meatballs, homemade bread and "grape juice," I leaned back in my chair, looking at Hannibal. "You are full of surprises!" I thought to myself. Lunch ended at three o'clock.

Finally, I thought to myself: "Time to end our trip to La La Land." I could tell from his expression that Hannibal had the same thought.

"Shall we inspect a gas station?" He said it softly, as he paid the bill.

"Yes, of course," I said, as I reluctantly re-oriented my thoughts to the task ahead. Two last fleeting thoughts of today's events touched my mind: "Where does he get the money for this, and where is this leading?"

Hannibal saw my expression. I could tell he was reading my mind again. He just smiled.

The drive from Ninth Street to the wagon bridge was uneventful, except that we saw Sheriff Johansson's car coming from the Parke County side as we crossed the bridge.

"A little out of his jurisdiction," I stated as we passed his car.

"Yes," responded Hannibal. "I don't think he recognized us, though."

It dawned on me suddenly that we were taking a risk. Why would Hannibal Jones, a relative newcomer, be driving with a local madame over to a gas station on the Parke County side of the river? We couldn't just walk in and start asking questions.

Again, Hannibal seemed to read my thoughts. "Some couples drive their cars just past the railroad bridge in the evenings," he said with a smile. "There are several pull-offs from the road that provide privacy."

I got the drift. "Wanna go park?" I giggled. "I hear it's the latest thing!"

"Of course!" said Hannibal with a chuckle. "It's a perfect cover story if we're spotted."

We continued driving in silence until we turned left on the river road just over the wagon bridge. Hannibal reached under his seat and pulled out a worn but expensive-looking set of binoculars.

I opened my mouth in surprise, and then closed it. "Where did you get those?" It was all I could think of at the moment.

"One of my military souvenirs," Hannibal responded mysteriously. His eyes had a far-away look for a couple of seconds, but then he returned to the present. "We can see who comes and goes for a few hours." He then gave me a quizzical look. "Can your girls manage if we come back late?"

I nodded. "Susie doesn't expect me until eight or so; they'll be fine," I replied.

Hannibal nodded approvingly. "Good job," was all he said.

I felt proud of myself. The only surprises were the lunch, the "invitation" to park and the binoculars. I had already planned to snoop until after dark.

After a quarter-mile drive, Hannibal passed the gas station on the left, drove through the railroad embankment underpass just off the railroad bridge and then turned off the road to the left, just past the underpass. Our parking spot was secluded, with trees on both sides. We could see the turbulent river about 20 feet in front of the car, down a drop-off. The water level was high, and chunks of ice drifted by in the current.

We got out of the car and climbed the railroad embankment near the underpass. We had to be careful; we were still in our good clothes. Fortunately, my shoes had low heels. Hannibal helped me up the embankment. Finally, we peered over the top. I shivered; there was a cold evening breeze. The gas station was in plain view, about one hundred-fifty yards away. Hannibal gave me the binoculars.

After some adjustments, I could plainly see three men lounging in chairs in front of the station. Two were dressed in suits. The third wore slacks and a cap. He looked familiar. "Sam the cop," I whispered.

"I think so," said Hannibal, as he squinted his eyes. "In civilian clothes," he added. "The other two are Carlo and Louie; I heard their names when I got gas last week. Carlo is on the left, Louie is on the right."

I focused the binoculars on the two men in suits. They were talking, smoking cigarettes and laughing. Sam joined in. Suddenly I recognized the man on the left. "Carlo, the one on the left, he was with the pick-up driver before Alec was killed!"

"Are you sure?" Hannibal looked first at me and then back toward the station.

"Yes!" I whispered hoarsely.

As we watched, an expensive-looking car drove up to the gas pump, a Packard, I think. Two attendants, who I didn't recognize, came out of the station. They checked with the driver and began servicing the car; one pumped gas and the other cleaned the windshield, checked the oil, and so on. I couldn't see the driver very well, but he was a large man. I also saw another figure on the passenger side: shadowy and indistinct.

As I watched, Louie and Carlo got up from their chairs. Carlo waved nonchalantly to the driver of the car, took an envelope out of his breast pocket, gave it to Louie and motioned with his head toward the car. Louie sauntered over to the driver's side and handed the envelope to the driver.

Briefly, I saw a face in the open car window: a fat and smiling face, with a cigar. I gasped. "It's the mayor," I uttered aloud.

"Let me see," whispered Hannibal.

I handed the binoculars to Hannibal. As he focused, Louie walked away from the car, back toward Carlo, who had resumed his seat. The attendants soon finished servicing the car, stood back, and touched their caps. No money was paid by the driver; he simply waved his hand, started the car and drove off. He made a U-turn and headed back toward Clinton.

Hannibal lowered the binoculars and looked closely at me. "Fat man with a cigar?" he queried in a low voice. "There was a passenger, a woman, I think."

"Yes, and I'm sure the fat man was Mayor Benito Nuardi," I replied. I then added: "He visits my houseboat on occasion." I then blurted out: "Services are free to the mayor, just like Big Bill." I instantly regretted my statement. I lowered my eyes. Somehow, I felt ashamed; Hannibal's opinion of me mattered.

Hannibal looked at me for a few moments; it seemed like an eternity. Finally, he just nodded his head. I know he understood.

Hannibal turned to me; his blue eyes seemed a little sad. "We better go; we might be spotted."

"Yes," I responded. "It's getting dark." Indeed, the lights around the station had just flickered on. We climbed carefully down the embankment, got in the car and left.

Hannibal followed the road north and then east, away from the station. The road soon turned south, joining the main highway between Lyford and Clinton. Hannibal turned right at the junction and headed toward the wagon bridge.

I felt as if I had to say something; the silence was very uncomfortable. Finally, I ventured: "Let's review what we know."

Hannibal looked over at me briefly and then turned his face back toward the road ahead. He reached forward and turned on the car lights just as we reached the bridge. "OK," he replied.

I took a deep breath. "Mayor Nuardi, Sam the cop and the gas station people are friendly with Carlo and Louie, the two out of towners," I stated slowly; my thoughts were still forming. "You also saw Big Bill at the station last week."

Hannibal nodded and replied: "Yes, and you said earlier that you saw Carlo at Alec's shack before Alec was killed."

I sighed; I was so glad Hannibal had responded. I just couldn't stand a silent treatment. "Yes," I said; I tried to sound analytical; I think I succeeded.

We continued our discussion until we reached the stopping place near Alec's shack.

Hannibal shut down the car and turned the lights off. He summed up our joint conclusions as we sat for a few moments. "There is a connection between those two gangsters, Carlo and Louie, and local politicians," he said slowly. "I'm pretty sure the two gangsters are from Chicago; I saw Illinois plates on a car parked by the station last week. He paused a moment, then continued: "The mayor, the sheriff, and Sam the cop are involved, and probably the county medical examiner. What's his name again?"

"Eben Speakwright, according to the newspaper," I replied.

"How far does this go?" Hannibal replied. "Bootlegging is big business, and Chicago is a big market."

Hannibal turned to me and smiled. "It's time for you to get back to your boat." We could both hear laughter coming from the houseboat.

"Come, I'll walk you down." With that, Hannibal got out of the car, came around to my side and opened the door.

I got out. Slowly, carefully, Hannibal bent down and kissed me lightly on the cheek. I sighed deeply. I felt relieved, flattered and happy all at the same time.

We walked to the boat. Hannibal left me at the gangplank, turned, and walked up toward his car. My day had a good ending.

5

DEATH OF OGLE

Friday evening, June 30, 1922

Spring came slowly this year. As promised, the girls and I helped Hannibal pick out furnishings for his house. It ended with a very tastefully decorated home, if I do say so myself.

Hoffman's Furniture Store had a very nice selection, and Hal and Mary Hoffman were very cordial to my girls and me; such behavior doesn't always happen. I suspect that Hannibal scouted out several stores first, but I don't know for sure. I do know that he paid cash for the furniture.

The girls and I were rewarded with a steak dinner in Hannibal's newly furnished dining room. Hannibal cooked the steaks on a grill he had made from an old oil drum and a grate; the heat was provided by coal, which he let burn down to glowing embers before putting the steaks on the grate. What an interesting way of cooking! The girls and I prepared potatoes, other vegetables and two cherry pies. It was a merry evening.

Hannibal was away for about a month in June; I don't know where. He said goodbye of course, but added no details. "I'll be back in a few weeks," he said.

I didn't pry; I didn't want to spoil our relationship.

Ice drifted away on the Wabash, along with the spring floods. The water level subsided by early summer. With the help of Ogle, Joe and Cliff, the girls and I gradually worked the houseboat down to the normal river channel. Joe and Cliff used their boats, which were equipped with powerful motors, to pull the houseboat up to Montezuma for a month in June. Business was slow there, so we returned to Clinton in mid-summer.

Saturday, July 8

There is a rhythm to Wabash Valley life. Summer has brought the mussel season; the button factory in Terre Haute is buying again. Catfish are easier to catch in nets as the river level lowers and fish follow narrower channels. Trotlines have also appeared, and the Wabash is busy. Local coal mines have started stockpiling coal for fall and winter; yet coal consumption is maintained at a lower level by the electric power plants and by home cook stoves. The local economy prospers, along with the rest of the country, according to the newspapers.

Bootlegging is big business. Local consumers do their part with enthusiasm. Gary, Hammond and Joliet, steel towns all, add to the demand. Chicago, apparently, has an unquenchable thirst. Every week, the newspapers have headlines on one gangland killing after another. The Bureau of Prohibition, an agency of Internal Revenue, has established permanent offices in Terre Haute. Local folks call the agents "revenooers." Raids are made in the Valley, but local officials often warn bootleggers ahead of time, and few arrests are made. Booze continues to flow.

Saturday, July 29

According to local gossip, the gas station across the river has become a major shipping point. Caravans of trucks, guarded by sinister looking men in cars, make weekly runs north. I don't snoop anymore; the risks are too great; attention is the last thing I need, given my own business.

Ogle has become my prime source of inside information. Like Alec before him, Ogle has more money than ever before in his life.

Hannibal and I cautioned Ogle to be less talkative about his activities, to no avail.

Saturday, August 5

Yesterday Susie and I found Ogle's body. It was a chance discovery; Susie and I were walking along the single lane dirt road that led along the river, just north of our houseboat. We were taking a short stroll; you know, girl talk, relaxation, and so on.

The sun had dipped behind the summer clouds to the west, the moderate breeze along the river was cool, and the mosquitos couldn't land on us. The late afternoon was pleasant enough, until we saw Ogle's body.

"Oh my heaven!" exclaimed Susie. Her hands flew to her mouth, she backed up a few steps, and she stopped. "Oh, oh!"

Thoughts raced through my mind. "Not again! This can't be happening!" But it was. I looked around. No one was in sight; we were alone, except for Ogle.

We were about a hundred yards or so from our houseboat. Ogle had a small house about a half-mile up the road, to the north. His body lay face up, in the weeds just off the road, on our right, between the road and riverbank.

I looked back at the body. It had started to bloat in the summer heat; the face was turning dark purple. The shirt was stained all over the front. Blood! There were many buzzing flies. I saw two holes in his chest. "Bullet holes," I thought to myself.

I stepped back from the edge of the road and looked down. Tire tracks: a car had stopped at this spot. I could see spin marks from the right rear drive tire as it took off from a dead stop. From the dirt spray caused by the spin of the tire, the car came from the direction of Ogle's house, then continued south, past our houseboat. "Ogle's body was dumped from a car," I surmised. "Based on the bloating, it was dumped last night."

My thoughts continued in logical sequence. "Since the car came from the north and Ogle was dumped on the east side next to the river, he had been in the back seat; the driver would have been in front on that side." My thoughts continued: "A driver and probably at least one other person," I concluded.

My thoughts raced. "Why here?" I looked up the road. Had Ogle been taken from his home, killed and then dumped here? "Most likely," I concluded.

My inspection had taken only a few seconds, but it seemed forever. I looked at Susie. She still had her hands to her face. Her mouth was open in an "oh" shape. She was still staring at Ogle.

"Susie!" I said in a hoarse voice. I sounded like a frog. I tried again. "Susie!" My voice was clearer. Susie slowly pulled her gaze from Ogle and looked at me with wide eyes.

"Susie!" No reaction. "Susie!" my voice finally made an impression; reason returned to her expression. "Go get my camera. Also, bring a ruler, blotting paper and a couple of brown paper sacks; they should be in the darkroom on the shelf next to the camera."

"Yes," Susie responded. "A camera, ruler, blotting paper and sacks?" She asked with a puzzled expression.

"Yes," I said rather sharply; I didn't have time for explanations. We both looked quickly around; we were alone. Susie took off like a shot, racing back the way we had come.

I was alone with Ogle's body. I began to look for more details. Except for the two bullet holes in his chest, Ogle had no other signs of injury. Ogle's hands lay open, nothing there.

Gingerly, I walked into the weeds to the right of the body and peered closer. I saw nothing, except blood around the body in the dirt, where Ogle had bled out. "Exit wounds in the back, most likely," I mused to myself. "Given the amount of blood around the body, not much time passed between the shooting and dumping of the body."

The buzzing flies swarmed up as I moved. The body had a sweet-sour stench. My stomach began to react. I quickly retraced my steps back to the road. I was standing there when Susie appeared in the distance.

Breathless, Susie ran up and stopped in front of me, camera, ruler, blotting paper and sacks in hand. She had taken only a few minutes to complete her errand. Good!

"Film?" I asked. I had forgotten to mention it before Susie left.

"Yes," Susie replied. I put in a new roll."

"Good girl!" Given the circumstances, Susie had done well. I tried to smile. Susie's gaze returned to Ogle's body.

Again, I looked quickly around. We were still alone. I began to take photos, quickly and efficiently: body, tire tracks, footprints, everything. One set of footprints was made by dress shoes; the other set was made by boots. The right boot print had a distinct mark, as if the owner had stepped on something that made a diagonal cut, or groove.

I laid the ruler down for scale in each photo. I finished the whole roll of 24 photos. I also took a blood sample with the blotting paper.

Susie had not been idle. She had found a leafy horseweed stalk on the other side of the road, pulled it up from the ground and brought it to me.

I got the idea; no words were needed. Between us, we brushed out our tracks around the body and down the road for some distance. We then continued back to the houseboat.

Inside, I sat down at the kitchen table and looked at the clock. As best I could tell, the whole operation, from leaving on our walk until our return, had taken less than 30 event-packed minutes.

Susie went to the other rooms and told her story to Louisa, Maribel and Kathy. Soon all four were seated at the table, their eyes on me. The question was obvious. What should we do next?

After a few minutes of silence, Susie said: "We have to tell Hannibal."

On that we all agreed. Louisa volunteered to walk to Hannibal's house; neither of us had a telephone. "Go!" I said. Quickly, she left. "I hope he's home," I thought to myself.

Susie then said: "Shouldn't we report it to the police?"

That was a more difficult question. I looked at the clock. "Only five o'clock," I mused. "Folks who live on South Main Street will be coming home for dinner." I knew only one family that had a telephone; we had been allowed to use it several times in the past: nice family. I made a decision.

"Maribel, go to the Mackey's house, you have used the phone there before." Maribel nodded. "Ask the Mackey's if you could use their phone for a private call." I paused for effect. "They are nice people, I'm sure they will." Maribel nodded again.

The next part was more complex. "Make a call to the police station; you'll have to go through the switchboard operator." I paused, and then continued: "The operator will be sure to listen in, and she will know where the call is coming from."

My mind raced. "When you get the police on the phone, just tell them that you heard suspicious noises from the river road, just up from our place, late last night." Then ask: "Would someone please look?" I then looked closely at Maribel: "Don't volunteer, but if asked, give them your name. If the police check, they will find out anyway."

I then looked at all three girls, one by one. "If the police come by, just stick to the story; we heard suspicious noises late last night, that's all." I paused for effect. "Understood?" They all nodded. "I will fill in Louisa when she returns." Maribel took off.

As Maribel was leaving, Louisa returned. "Not home," she reported. Rats! I filled Louisa in on events during her absence.

Maribel soon returned; mission accomplished. We all had a quiet meal, and then prepared for the usual Friday night business.

I looked at the clock again. "Seven o'clock," I noted to myself. Three hours had passed since Susie and I found Ogle's body.

Sheriff Johansson and Mayor Nuardi were our only customers that night, no one else. The pair just showed up at our houseboat. Other than a good time, the pair didn't seem to be concerned.

I did notice, however, that Big Bill occasionally gave me long, searching looks. I pretended not to notice. From the police report, he suspects that I know about Ogle's body. He also knows that I know about Alec's death and that both Alec and Ogle were murdered. What else does he know? Was he involved with Ogle's death? Bill and the Mayor left about ten o'clock, after they had satisfied their particular fantasies. So many questions!

Several days passed: Saturday, Sunday, and then Monday. Nothing appeared in the newspapers, no visits from the police, nothing at all. Events unfolded as if Ogle had never existed. Susie and I walked the river road on late Monday afternoon. Ogle's body was gone.

"I will get Hannibal to take me to Ogle's house when he returns," I decided. Hannibal has a car and more freedom of action without arousing undue comments.

Saturday August 26, 1922

Hannibal stopped by this morning. I was having coffee on my porch when I saw him pull up in his car and get out. He was dressed in his usual jeans, faded blue shirt and work shoes. He waved as he walked toward the houseboat. I raised my coffee cup in recognition.

I could hear Susie in the kitchen. "Susie," I called out. "Hannibal's here; put on a fresh pot of coffee."

"OK," Susie responded. I heard the other girls stirring inside. Soon we all were seated on the porch with Hannibal and coffee.

We girls filled Hannibal in with regard to Ogle. Each of us contributed to the story. After the tale of events, I suggested that we visit Ogle's house with my camera. I showed him my photos of Ogle and the crime scene. He studied them carefully, but said nothing.

I asked the obvious question: "Hannibal, we tried to find you on the day we found Ogle," I stated. "Where were you?"

Hannibal sighed, and then looked in my eyes. "I had business in Terre Haute." His gaze remained steady, but he didn't provide details.

I didn't know what else to say. Clearly, Hannibal wasn't going to volunteer more information. Patience, Caroline!

Hannibal then shifted in his seat as well as in our conversation. "I think," he said slowly, "that Ogle's body was dumped near this houseboat as a warning."

I thought a moment. It dawned on me that Hannibal was right. The visit by the mayor and the sheriff that same night was no coincidence. "Oh," was all I said; I'm sure my expression said much more; I was scared. I looked around at my girls. I could see the impact of Hannibal's words. They were scared too.

"I suggest that you all keep a low profile for a while," Hannibal stated, as he looked around at each of us. "We know what those gangsters and their local political friends, including the mayor and sheriff, are capable of doing." He paused for effect, and then added: "Please, no visits to Ogle's house." He paused, and then mused, almost to himself: "I'll see what I can find out." He then smiled, and continued: "I'll keep you posted."

Hannibal got nods of agreement from each of us, as well as continued frightened expressions.

Hannibal finished his coffee, stood up and said: "I best be going; I'll be in touch." He then looked at me with his steady gaze: "You will find me at home if you need anything." He paused for a moment, and then said: "By the way, can I borrow your camera and some blotting paper?"

I got my camera out, put in a new roll of film, and handed it to Hannibal. I also handed him a couple of sheets of blotting paper from my stock that I used during the film developing process.

With that, Hannibal said his goodbyes and left. We girls looked at each other. The unspoken question was: "Who is Hannibal, anyway?"

Sunday evening, September 3

Hannibal returned this morning for a few minutes. I was drinking coffee on the porch when he arrived. "Always perfect timing," I thought to myself. "He knows my routines."

Hannibal waved as he walked down the path. He was carrying my camera. Soon he was on the porch.

"Photos of footprints and tires at the gas station," he said with a grin. "I also got a couple of photos of Louie and Carlo, their shoes and footprints, and the inside and outside of their car." Hannibal paused again, and he chuckled a little. "I also collected a couple of samples of what looked like blood on the running board under the back door on the driver's side. As you will see when you develop the film, everything fits together quite nicely."

"How did you do it?" I asked incredulously.

"My secret," said Hannibal. "Don't worry; Louie and Carlo don't know that they were my star attractions." He thought a moment, and then added: "Keep the photos and negatives in a safe place."

"I will," I replied. My mind raced. How did Hannibal know to check out Louie and Carlo? Of course! Hannibal saw my photos. The footprints by Ogle's body were not from work shoes. Tire tracks can be compared to tires. Very smart!

"One other bit of information," Hannibal stated. "I stopped by Ogle's house on Friday, August 25, just before my visit to the gas station."

"And what did you find?" I queried.

"Not much," replied Hannibal. "It turned out that Ogle's house was rented from the Anderson family who lived next door. I talked with old man Anderson, and told him Ogle was missing. Anderson agreed; he hadn't seen Ogle since Friday morning, August 4th. Anderson and I went into Ogle's house, looked around, and found nothing, not even personal papers. We did find a half-eaten sandwich on the table with a bottle of beer. The chair by the table was turned over."

"That's consistent with our finding Ogle's body on Saturday August 5th," I replied.

Hannibal nodded, got up from his chair, said goodbye, and departed. "What a strange man," I concluded: "Lots of secrets."

The days of summer passed. I refined my notes and developed my remaining photos. I had quite a stash, all in a cardboard box, which I kept under my bed. I began to realize that my bed was not the best hiding place. "I will have to find a safer place for this," I decided.

Monday evening, September 18

This morning, I rented a safety deposit box in the First National Bank, downtown Clinton. I already had accounts there, so adding a safety deposit box was not an unusual request. Except for my most recent notes, I put the contents of my cardboard box in the bank.

I also started buying a mix of stocks and bonds, mostly treasury bills, with some of my savings. The bank helped; they had stockbrokers on staff. They were quite happy with my purchases, since they got commissions; never mind the source of my funds. They were a little dismayed that I chose conservative investments; they had a range of speculative stocks available, with much greater returns, they said. I politely declined and stuck with my conservative approach. OK, they still got commissions. Business is business.

6

BLUFF AND COUNTERBLUFF

Saturday, November 4, 1922

Cold! Ice has formed in the swollen river; we will have to move the houseboat soon.

According to the newspapers, Al Capone is a rising star in the Chicago mob. Apparently, he is now Johnny Torrio's right hand man. Capone exercises personal control over several brothels, gambling joints and speakeasies in Chicago's first ward. According to editorials, he has also moved into the suburbs, including Cicero. His base of operations is the Four Deuces Club at 2222 South Wabash Avenue.

Al enjoys talking to the press. He often gives "Quotables" to newspapermen, who hang on his every word. "I just give the people what they want," was one quote. Another was "You can get much farther with a smile, a kind word, and a gun than you can with a smile and a kind word." He's quite an entrepreneur, and by all accounts, a very dangerous man.

Illegal booze is readily available at the Four Deuces and in just about every neighborhood in Chicago, its suburbs and in Gary, Hammond and Joliet. The demand is insatiable. Supply sources include legal distilleries and breweries in Canada and small operator stills across the Midwest, including the Wabash Valley.

The demand for booze and other illegal activities goes hand in hand with political corruption. In Chicago, Mayor "Big Bill" Thompson leads the pack, along with Alderman "Bathhouse" John

Coughlin from the first ward. However, a reformer candidate, William Emmett Dever, may run for mayor next year. We'll see how that turns out; even elections, by all accounts, have been bought.

We have our own local corrupt politicians. Obviously, this includes our Mayor "Fat Benny" Nuardi and Sheriff "Big Bill" Johansson. Bootlegging has become an essential part of our local economy, and our mayor and sheriff, along with others, are clearly on the take. I'm not sure about politicians in Parke County, but the gas station between the wagon and railroad bridges is on the Parke County side of the river. Small truck caravans, with armed guards in black cars, make almost weekly booze runs from pick-up points in the Valley, including the gas station between the bridges.

How do I know all this? In addition to newspapers and customer gossip, I have Hannibal. Last week, on Thursday, October 26th, Hannibal stopped by the houseboat. The evening was pleasant and cool, just right for sitting on the porch with a cup of hot coffee. The girls were busy inside, and we two were alone.

On several occasions, Hannibal advised that we should stay away from the gas station across the river, even though the gas station is within easy walking distance from our houseboat. He's right, of course, and the girls and I keep a low profile. However, he still stops for gas at the station every week, and on the 26th, he told me what he observed the previous Friday.

"The station doesn't appear to sell much gas; I never have to wait in line," said Hannibal last week. "But it always has people around."

"What kind of people?" I asked.

"Well," Hannibal replied, "Carlo and Louie are almost always there on Fridays when I get gas, and boats come and go on the river behind the station."

Hannibal paused, thinking. He then added: "There's a new large shed behind the station; I think the moonshine is stored there, waiting for pick-up." Hannibal paused again, and then continued. "Last Friday, I was at the station when two cars and five trucks pulled into the parking area to the side of the station. As they drove up, one car was in front, the other behind."

I'm sure my eyes widened. "Oh," uttered.

Hannibal continued. "The truck drivers were average looking working men, but the two men in each car were gangsters, and I'm pretty sure they were armed." Hannibal's eyes gleamed as he recalled the scene. "The four gangsters from the cars talked with Carlo and Louie as they walked around behind the station. I got my gas and left."

I watched Hannibal's eyes as he seemed to weigh his words before speaking. "I like that in a man," I thought to myself.

Finally, Hannibal spoke again; he was smiling this time. "I often walk from my house to the wagon bridge in the evenings," he said. "It's not far, and I enjoy watching river traffic from the wooden walkway on the bridge."

I looked at Hannibal. He then said: "Perhaps you would walk with me some evening."

"I would like that," I replied and smiled in return.

"Anyway," said Hannibal, as he returned to the subject at hand, "I watch men and boys in boats as they arrive at the landing behind the station; I get a good view from the bridge." He paused a moment, thinking, and then continued. "One evening I counted seven boats, mostly from up river. The men and boys unloaded tins and a few wooden barrels."

This was news; I hadn't realized how much bootlegging activity had blossomed on the Wabash. I gave Hannibal a questioning look.

Hannibal recognized the look and continued: "I could see activity behind the station," he said. "I saw tins being emptied into barrels."

I thought a moment. "Barrels would be easier and more efficient to transport on trucks," I replied.

"Yes," responded Hannibal. "The new shed behind the station is more than just a storage facility." He paused, thinking, then added:

"The Chicago buyers probably do a little mixing as well, to standardize their product."

There was a long pause; Hannibal had finished with the news. I began to think about evening walks.

Hannibal watched me with his steady gaze. He then said: "Would you like to go for a walk to the bridge with me tomorrow evening?" He said it with a knowing smile.

Rats! How does he know what I'm thinking? I regained my composure, smiled in return and answered: "Love to: how about four o'clock? I have to be back by seven."

"See you tomorrow," Hannibal replied. He then rose from his seat, nodded goodbye, and walked to the gangplank.

I watched as he walked up the path, headed toward home. He whistled as he disappeared into the evening shadows.

In addition to Hannibal's reports, I get information from Jimmy McDonald, known to just about everyone as "Scottie." We have a business relationship, and we meet every week or so at his place.

Scottie is an insider. He lives on the west side of town with his wife Edith. The middle-aged pair do not have children, as far as I know. Scottie runs a speakeasy from a big house just off North Main Street. He has a roadhouse in Lyford, just north of the "Y" in the roads, which is about two miles across the river from Clinton. The North Main Street house is upscale, but the roadhouse has working class customers, mostly rowdy coal miners, who, not surprisingly, feel entitled to drink what and when they want, legal or not.

According to Scottie, business is good, but prices of bootleg whiskey and gin have increased dramatically due to the Chicago demand. To supplement his income, he has opened back rooms in his Lyford roadhouse for two of my girls several days each week. In addition to the increased customer flow, he gets a cut of the take from the girls. We have talked about expanding our mutual business.

I visit Scottie often to divvy up the profits. Scottie loves to talk, so I get the latest gossip from an informed insider.

Scottie hears a lot of talk when he picks up his bootleg whiskey at the gas station across the river. During our meeting yesterday in his establishment on North Main Street, Scottie said: "Carlo and Louie, the Chicago gangsters, have become arrogant. Business is booming, and local politicians and police, for the most part, look the other way."

"Louie brags a lot," Scottie continued: "I overheard Louie talking at the gas station about taking a local no-account on a short ride." Scottie paused a moment and looked at me with sympathy: "I think he meant Ogle, the timing was about right."

Scottie then added: "Louie went on to say: "it should be a warning to others about snooping." Scottie paused, then said: "Louie laughed, and Carlo said: "shut up, Louie, you talk too much!" Scottie added: "Carlo's the boss, and Louie did what he was told, with a few more sniggers."

I struggled to keep my feelings of rage over Ogle and fear of Louie and Carlo under control. Hannibal's suspicions about Louie were now confirmed. After a moment, I replied: "What happened to Ogle's body? It just disappeared, and there was nothing in the newspaper."

"Yes," replied Scottie. "Well, I'm not exactly sure, but later, I also heard Louie brag: "Dere's two corpses in the same hole now." Scottie's face showed a touch of fear. "I pretended not to hear, moved away, got my own deliveries and left the station."

I waited, but Scottie turned to his books. Clearly, he didn't want to say anything else. My mind raced. I could check the newspaper obituaries for burials during the week after August 4th, the day Susie and I found Ogle's body.

After going home, I told Susie what Scottie had said. We still had all of the local newspapers of the week of August 6 through 13 in the stack we kept for starting fires in the kitchen stove. We found only two funerals that week in the obituaries. One was a prominent businessman with an ostentatious obituary and a grand funeral. The other was more interesting. A Mrs. Emily Blackburn, age 86, had been interned in Riverside Cemetery. A lone widow, she had died of natural causes at home. Her internment was handled by the county, through Farris Funeral Home.

"Wow!" Susie said. "Any bets on where Ogle' body went?"

"We need to be careful, Susie," I replied. I was silent for a while, thinking. "We can't go digging up a grave, and Carlo and Louie know about us." Finally, I said: "We need some insurance."

Susie gave me a questioning look. I continued: "We have a camera, and Fat Benny and Big Bill are frequent customers."

The light came on in Susie's eyes, and she grinned.

Tuesday, December 26, 1922

Hannibal invited us all over to his house for Christmas Dinner yesterday. So nice! We had a wonderful time, with simple gifts and a sumptuous dinner. Hannibal prepared the turkey; the girls and I prepared mashed potatoes, green beans, dressing and gravy. We had pumpkin pie for dessert, baked by Hannibal. A man with many talents!

After dinner, conversation turned to our activities since Ogle's disappearance. Hannibal listened carefully as each of us girls added bits to the conversation. He didn't say, much; he mainly nodded as he got each element of the story.

Finally, I explained our planned next move. "The mayor and the sheriff usually show up at the houseboat over the holidays," I stated. "We will take some pictures during their visits."

Hannibal's eyes widened a little. After a few moments, he said: "I understand," he paused, then continued: "Insurance."

I nodded. Susie giggled, and said: "A compromising photo or two might be of interest to wives or even the newspaper."

"Of course, we will just let Fat Benny and Big Bill know we have photos, that's all," I emphasized.

"You might lose two customers," responded Hannibal, with a chuckle. "Do you think you might be taking too big a risk?"

"No," I responded. "Both the mayor and the sheriff already know that we could tell on them; that's why they leave us to our business." I paused for effect. "The knowledge that we have photos will just emphasize the point." I then added: "If it was just one person who could disappear, the risk would be too great, but there are five of us."

Silence prevailed for a long minute. I know we were all weighing the risk in our minds, and we all hoped I was right.

Finally, Hannibal said: "Be careful." We girls all nodded. The rest of the day was spent celebrating Christmas.

Monday, January 1, 1923

Guess who showed up last night? Fat Benny and Big Bill arrived about 9 o'clock, and both had already been drinking. I got several great photos from a convenient hiding place. They left about 1 AM. I just smiled and wished them well. The pair staggered off the houseboat, nearly falling off the gangplank.

Tomorrow, I will make prints of a couple of the best photos, place them in an envelope and mail it to the sheriff at his office. The envelope will be marked personal, of course. The negatives will go in my safety deposit box at the bank.

Tuesday, January 2

Envelope sent and mission accomplished! I'm sure Big Bill will consult with the mayor about the photos. I don't think the mayor will do anything, but Big Bill might. "Keep your nerve, Caroline," I tell myself.

Sunday, January 7

The society page of the local newspaper had an interesting article today. Anna Nuardi, the mayor's wife, gave an interview to a reporter. Mrs. Nuardi was quoted as saying: "My husband is concerned about vice in our community; I'm sure he will take appropriate action."

I laughed: "He already has, my dear."

I continued to read. When asked what action the mayor had in mind, Mrs. Nuardi said: "You will have to ask my husband."

I laughed again. "Well, he might stop coming to my houseboat." I thought a moment: "Wonder what wifey knows?" I continued to read.

The article also showed a photo of Mrs. Nuardi at her tea party for "notables" in the community. "She's an attractive lady, in a prim sort of way," I thought to myself. "Lots of jewelry: look at those diamonds!"

I thought a moment. "Still, the mayor owns a car dealership and he gets a small salary for being mayor." I then recalled the scene at the gas station the previous February. "The mayor supplements his income," I concluded. "The little hoity-toity wife can afford diamonds."

I then thought about the mayor's periodic visits to my houseboat. "Wonder what she knows or suspects about her fat husband's extracurricular activities?" I mused. I know I chuckled a little as I wrote this down; I recalled the mayor's rather unusual tastes when he was liquored up.

Monday, January 8

I went shopping at the grocery store this morning, you know, flour, sugar, coffee, vegetables, canned goods and so on. Hannibal drove me downtown; I couldn't carry it all home myself.

While in the store, Hannibal wandered off on his own while I looked at canned goods on a shelf. No one else was in the aisle. Suddenly, I felt a presence at my back. I quickly turned, and there was Big Bill, glowering down at me. He was in civilian clothes. I could smell his fetid breath, like whiskey and cigarettes. My heart skipped a beat. I looked wildly around, I was alone with Bill.

"I got your message," said Bill in a menacing tone. "You have a lot of nerve!" He clenched his fists.

"I swallowed the lump in my throat. "Yes, I do," I retorted, trying to keep my composure.

Suddenly a tall form stepped into the aisle and moved quickly between Bill and me. Bill stepped back.

"Hello," said Hannibal in a soft voice. "Do you have official or personal business with this lady?"

Big Bill turned and faced Hannibal directly. "None of your business, Mister." In a menacing voice, he continued: "Who are you?" Bill's fists were still clenched, and he raised his right fist.

There was a blur of motion and a whoosh sound as air escaped Bill's collapsing lungs. He doubled over, gasping.

Hannibal stood there, quietly, ready.

After a long minute, Bill regained his breath and painfully stood erect.

"I think the lady has more shopping to do," said Hannibal. He paused, and his steady, steely blue eyes squinted as he stared at Bill's eyes. "Your business with the lady is over, don't you agree?"

Bill nodded; there was fear in his expression.

"I didn't hear you," said Hannibal. There was another blur of motion, and Bill doubled over again. It took another minute, but Bill finally straightened.

Hannibal said: "Did you have something to say?"

Bill got the message. "Yes," he said, with a wheeze. He saw Hannibal's eyes narrow again. "Yes, my business is over," Bill said in a clearer voice.

"Oh good," responded Hannibal. "You can go now, and have a nice day."

With a slight stagger, Bill walked down the aisle and out the door of the store.

Hannibal then looked down at me with a smile and said: "More shopping?"

Wow! I couldn't help myself, my mouth was wide open. Finally, I responded: "I'm nearly finished, thank you." The "thank you" meant more than just polite conversation.

Hannibal grinned and offered his arm. I took it and smiled up at him. My knight in shining armor! Or, more precisely, my knight in a leather jacket and hat with the front brim turned down. What a day!

7

BRAWL AT THE ROADHOUSE

Sunday morning, October 7, 1923

Scottie's roadhouse in Lyford was a bloody mess Saturday night. I got the story from Louisa and Maribel. Both girls were at the roadhouse when it happened.

I found out about it just after nine o'clock last night. I was in the houseboat when I heard a car drive up to our spot at the edge of the road. I looked out the porch door. Louisa raced down the path; I could see that she was in tears. Maribel followed, and her face was as white as sheet. The car quickly drove away. "What's going on?" I muttered to myself; "it's too early!"

I stepped out on the porch as Louisa and Maribel hurried up the gangplank. Two customers were in the back rooms of the houseboat; Susie and Kathy were busy. "What's wrong?" I said in a low voice. I didn't want to disturb the customers inside.

Louisa sat down in a porch chair, sobbing softly. Maribel sat in a chair beside her. After a few minutes, Louisa regained control. "You better sit down, Miss Caroline," she finally said, between hiccups.

I looked at her closely. There were spattered bloodstains on the front of her white blouse. I sat down, pulled my chair close to both girls. "Are you hurt?" I asked.

Louisa took a deep breath and said: "No, but there was a shooting at the roadhouse tonight; two men were killed." She paused; I could see that the scene was replaying in her mind. "Johnny Swift was shot in the face, but I think he's still alive."

"Oh!" I exclaimed, a little too loudly. I then waited.

Louisa continued: "About eight o'clock, I was at a table near the bar. Maribel was in one of the back rooms with a customer." Louisa paused and took another deep breath. "Drinks had been poured at my table; I had my usual tea in a Schott glass."

I nodded. The colored tea looked like whiskey, the customers paid for whiskey all around, and my girls stayed sober. It was our standard practice.

Louisa continued: "Johnny Swift, a regular, had just bought our drinks, when I saw two well-dressed men walk in the front door. They had guns; one had a handgun and the other had a short double-barreled shotgun."

"Chicago gangsters," the thought raced through my mind. I nodded for Louisa to continue.

"Well," she said, "Apparently they were after a man at the bar, because I heard someone yell, "Look out!" from that direction. I turned to the sound of the voice, and I saw another well-dressed man at the bar."

Louisa stopped. I looked at her closely. Her chest was heaving from sharp intakes of air. This went on for a full minute. I waited.

In a choking voice, Louisa then said: "There was a bang, then a loud boom, then several sharp bangs. I think there were four of five, and they came from several directions. I heard loud screams." Louisa paused, and then continued. "Some screams came from the direction of the bar, but one came from Johnny."

"Oh no," I said in a hoarse whisper. I waited.

Louisa then said: "Johnny fell to the floor, still screaming. He had his hands to his face. Blood was everywhere." She looked down at her blouse and brushed her hands over the bloodstains, as if that might make them go away.

Louisa choked again and put her hands down. She then added: "I jumped up; I was horrified. I looked toward the bar; the screaming from that direction had stopped. The well-dressed man was on the floor, twitching. I know he was dead. A handgun lay next to him on the floor."

"Oh, good heavens!" I exclaimed, again a little too loudly.

I heard stirrings and voices from inside the houseboat. I could hear Susie and Kathy as they entered the kitchen behind me. I also heard the voices of two men. I looked at Louisa and then Maribel.

"Wait here," I said, and then I stepped inside.

I finished up the business with the two men and ushered them on their way. We five girls were left alone. Louisa and Maribel came in from the porch, and we sat around the kitchen table. Louisa brought Susie and Kathy up to date on her story.

Louisa then picked up from where she had left off while on the porch.

"I turned from looking at the bar and saw one of the two men who had just come in the front door. He was on the floor, lying very still. His shotgun was on the floor nearby. The front door banged shut, and the other man was gone."

Louisa was quiet for a few moments, recalling events, and then continued. "Someone came over and wrapped a towel around Johnny's face; he was still screaming. They took him away. I went to the window. I saw a car roar off: someone had Johnny in the back seat. I turned and ran to the back room, found Maribel, and we ran out the back door. Billy, Scottie's driver, brought us home."

She stopped again and looked at me. Fright was still in her eyes. "That's all I know," she concluded.

Maribel then added: "I was in the back room, but I heard the shots and the screams."

I heaved a deep sigh and looked around the table. "Alright," I said. "Kathy, you and Susie help Louisa and Maribel clean up and go to bed. In fact, we all should go to bed. We'll close up for tonight."

And we did. Morning would come soon enough.

Monday, October 8

Scottie sent word by his driver this morning to cancel our usual meeting on Wednesday this week. He's probably scared to death. This morning's newspaper has a headline and a story on the front page about the shooting. I cut it out; it reads as follows.

MURDER IN LYFORD

Two men were killed and another seriously injured in a blaze of gunfire last Saturday evening. The incident took place at a popular nightspot in Lyford, across the river from Clinton. Parke County Sheriff Dave Potts, in an exclusive interview, said the following: "The names of the two dead men are not known. According to eyewitnesses, they were travelers on the main road toward Rockville. The gunfight was apparently over a personal issue between them." The sheriff went on to say that the injured man was a local resident named John Swift. He was caught in the crossfire, and he is being treated in the Vermillion County Hospital. Sheriff Potts also indicated that attempts were being made to identify the two dead men so that next of kin can be notified.

The brevity of the article was astounding; yet I was not surprised. Popular nightspot my foot! It's a speakeasy fronting as a roadhouse. Based on Louisa's description, the two dead men were Chicago gangsters. I thought a moment: "Wait, Louisa said three shooters were involved. What happened to the third man?"

I showed the article to Louisa and the other girls. Louisa was most concerned about Johnny.

"Johnny is in the hospital?" Louisa asked.

"That's what the article says," I replied. "The hospital is over on Main Street; please go see him."

"Oh, thank you," responded Louisa, tears came to her eyes.

Louisa left shortly afterwards; Maribel went with her. I resolved to find out details of who and why. "My girls are involved, for heaven's sake!" I thought to myself. "They may be in danger, especially if they go back to Scottie's roadhouse."

Tuesday, October 9

Louisa and Maribel saw Johnny in the hospital yesterday. He was blinded in both eyes. How horrible! Louisa was in tears most of the day; she is sweet on Johnny.

Saturday October 13

Scottie's roadhouse finally re-opened; I guess his fright has subsided. I will try to meet with him next week.

Monday, October 15

I finally cornered Scottie, in the grocery store of all places. It was early, and not many people were in the store. Scottie and I moved to the back, away from the few other shoppers.

He was very subdued, but he was still interested in having two of my girls for Friday and Saturday nights. "They are good for business," he said.

I agreed; I will send Maribel and Kathy; Louisa will not be up to it.

In whispers, Scottie also confirmed Louisa's story. He also added useful details. As he talked, he looked and sounded like a frightened rabbit.

"There's a war going on," Scottie whispered hoarsely. "We get protection from the Torrio and Capone people, but they are being challenged by the O'Banion Gang."

I knew about Torrio and Capone of course; Chicago newspapers were full of stories. "Who is O'Banion?" I asked.

"Dion O'Banion runs the North Side Gang in Chicago," whispered Scottie. "He and Capone are on the outs."

A couple of shoppers walked down the aisle toward us. Scottie looked at them nervously.

I wanted more information, but a grocery store wasn't the place. I whispered: "Let's talk at your place." In addition to money, I wanted answers on security at the roadhouse; my girls worked there, but getting shot wasn't part of the bargain.

Scottie nodded. "Wednesday, North Main, about ten o'clock," he whispered in response. We parted company.

Wednesday, October 17

What a meeting! I walked up to Scottie's place this morning and got an earful. We made the usual cut, twenty-five percent to Scottie and seventy-five percent to the girls and me. I then asked about security at the roadhouse; Louisa's blood-spattered blouse was seared in my memory.

"I want protection for my girls," I stated flatly.

Scottie understood. "I talked to Carlo," he responded. "Carlo will have someone at the roadhouse every evening."

"OK," I replied. "Who?" I then added: "Not Louie, I hope!" For obvious reasons, Louie scared me.

"Oh, no," said Scottie. "I don't want Louie either." He paused a moment, then said: "Carlo hired a local man, an off-duty Clinton cop. His name is Sam."

I laughed. "Yes, I know Sam," I said. Scottie looked a little puzzled, but I didn't elaborate. Based on my encounter with Sam after Alec's death, I knew Sam was in cahoots with Big Bill. I then said: "Sam will be fine."

I then turned to the shooting at the roadhouse. "You said there was a war going on when we talked at the grocery store," I ventured.

"Yes, responded Scottie. As if he were still afraid someone would hear, he started to whisper. "Capone controls the bootlegging trade in the Valley now." He paused, collecting his thoughts. "But O'Banion's people have been hijacking shipments from the Valley." He added: "last month, they hit Capone's trucks just outside Chicago; people were killed, and Capone's shipment was stolen."

"What do you know about O'Banion?" I asked.

"He's a kingpin on Chicago's north side, replied Scottie. "He supplies the good Canadian stuff, the bathtub gin and the moonshine to the speakeasies along the Chicago's northern lakefront. He looked at me knowingly. "Lots of rich folks there, and they want their booze."

I waited. I knew Scottie would add more details. "Scottie is a big gossip," I thought to myself. After a short moment, sure enough, Scottie continued.

"I think O'Banion owns an interest in a flower shop near the corner of West Chicago Avenue and North State Street," said Scottie. "Rumor has it that O'Banion runs his operations from there."

"A flower shop?" I asked incredulously.

Scottie nodded and said: "I think its call Scofield's, but I'm not sure." After a brief pause, he continued: "Anyway, O'Banion and his boys have been hijacking whiskey and gin convoys owned by Torrio and Capone, which ain't too smart. Capone, especially, won't stand for it."

"Is that what the shooting at your roadhouse was about?" I asked.

"Yes, yes," replied Scottie, as he leaned back in his chair. His brow furrowed and his eyes stared off into space. "O'Banion's gangsters tried to highjack a couple of Capone's trucks about five miles north of Lyford on the road to Rockville that night."

Scottie paused, and he looked back at me. "The road gets lonely north of Lyford, and the trucks had to slow down for a steep grade. O'Banion's men put a big tree limb across the road and pulled up in cars and trucks. There was a shootout."

"Who won?" I asked.

"Capone's men were ready," replied Scottie. "O'Banion's men took off." He paused, and then added: "At least one showed up at my roadhouse. He was the gangster at the bar. Two of Capone's men walked in and shot him. One of Capone's men was also killed; the other ran out and drove off."

"How do you know all this?" I asked. "Surely you have a source." Scottie hasn't been to Chicago lately, as far as I know," I thought to myself.

"Louie," replied Scottie. "Louie talks a lot." Scottie leaned forward and added: "And Carlo doesn't like it."

I suppressed a chuckle. "Pot calling the kettle black," I thought to myself. However, I simply stated: "Johnny was shot in the face."

"I'm real sorry about Johnny," replied Scottie. Scottie was quiet for a moment. "This ain't over."

Sunday, October 21

Whew! Friday and Saturday nights are over and no more shootings! I want to talk to Hannibal. Where is he anyway?

Wednesday, October 24

It's uncanny; whenever I think about Hannibal, he shows up. I saw his car this morning about eight o'clock as I was having coffee on the porch. He got out of the car and walked down the path toward my houseboat. He waved in an off-hand manner as he approached.

I motioned to him with my coffee cup. He nodded. I slipped quietly into the kitchen, the girls were still asleep.

Hannibal was waiting on the porch when I returned. I made his coffee fresh and black, just like mine. "Learning the man's tastes," I thought to myself. To Hannibal, I just smiled as I handed him his cup.

"Thanks," said Hannibal with a return smile. He waited until I sat down before taking a seat.

After we both settled in, Hannibal sipped his coffee and then said: "Understand you had some excitement over the last two weeks."

He took another sip and watched me with steady blue eyes over the rim of his coffee cup.

I nodded. "You've been away again," I stated.

"Yes," Hannibal replied, "Just got back two days ago."

I waited, but there was nothing else about his absence. "You are so mysterious!" I thought to myself. To Hannibal, I just smiled and said: "Glad you're back."

"Thank you," Hannibal responded. "How are the girls doing?"

"Well, Louisa is still very upset about Johnny Swift," I said. "He was blinded in the shootout at the Lyford roadhouse." I paused, and then added: "She told me they were sweethearts." I continued: "The other three girls are OK."

"I heard about Johnny," responded Hannibal. He took another sip of coffee and watched me for a moment. "I also heard that the shootout was between two of Capone's men and an O'Banion hijacker."

"Yes," I replied. Obviously, Hannibal knew the story of the shooting. In my private thoughts, I added: "Two days! How does he do it?"

"Do you have any plans with regard to Louisa?" Hannibal asked.

"That was nice," I thought to myself. To Hannibal I said: "Well, I think she really wants to be with Johnny, especially now."

Hannibal nodded. "Maybe I can help out," he replied. "There's a small house out on Ninth Street, owned by the Valenti's." He paused, watching me. "Papa and Mama Valenti own the Italian restaurant that we visited last year, remember?"

"Yes, that was a wonderful evening," I said and meant it.

"Mom and Pop Valenti are my friends," Hannibal continued. "I told them about Louisa's experience and gave her a good reference. They said they would offer her a job, waiting tables at their restaurant." He paused, and then added: "They also said they could offer to rent their little house, which is currently vacant, at a very reasonable rent."

I was astounded. "Hannibal, I don't know what to say," I finally managed. "That's wonderful!" I thought a moment. "Do the Valenti's know about Louisa's background?" I'm sure I frowned a little, because Hannibal smiled knowingly.

"They know about Louisa," said Hannibal. "It's not a problem."

"I will have to replace Louisa, but that can be done," I thought to myself. "It's time for Louisa to move on." My thoughts summarized many reasons for this conclusion.

Again, Hannibal smiled and sipped his coffee.

"We will have to ask Louisa, but I can't imagine why she would refuse," I said to Hannibal.

Hannibal nodded. "One other thing," he said. "I also told Mom and Pop Valenti about Johnny." He paused a moment, then continued with a smile. "They might be able to find work for Johnny, in spite of his blindness."

"What nice people!" I exclaimed. "And you too, Hannibal." I paused, and then added: "You constantly amaze me!"

Hannibal blushed, looked down, and then looked back at me. "Well, don't tell anyone; that would ruin my reputation." He grinned a little.

Saturday, December 1

Fortunately, things have been quiet in town for a while. Also, some good news: Louisa has a new job.

Louisa is in the process of setting up a household in the little house near the restaurant. Hannibal supplied her with some furniture; he is the nicest man!

Saturday, December 8

Hannibal has invited everyone over for Christmas dinner. I am determined to help make it a great success; it is good to forget our troubles for this season.

8

SCHOOL OF HARD KNOCKS

Sunday, January 27, 1924

Karla joined our little houseboat crew last night. We call her Kitty.

Maribel and Kathy found her at the Lyford roadhouse, just drifting. She was with some men on a survey crew for the new highway that will follow the road from Terre Haute through Lyford to Rockville. Rumor has it that the new road will be paved. Anyway, Kitty confided in Maribel and Kathy. After hearing her story, my girls brought her home: a stray kitten, so to speak.

Like me, Kitty came from the wrong side of the tracks. She has no clear idea of her birthdate, but she thinks she is 20 years old. Her earliest memories are of a dingy house near Twelve Points, just at the north end of Terre Haute, not far from the railroad freight yards. Since she came to us on Saturday, January 26, we all decided that January 26 is her birthday. Happy birthday, Kitty!

An interesting observation: on Christmas Day at Hannibal's house, we had all just finished dinner. The girls were cleaning up, and Hannibal was taking out the trash. I took a break to freshen up in the bathroom behind the kitchen. The side door from the bathroom into the master bedroom was open. Kathy came into the bathroom from the kitchen, so I stepped into the bedroom to finish up.

The bedroom closet door was open. When I turned on the bedroom light, I could see a military uniform hanging in the closet. Curious, I walked over and looked. I had seen many uniforms during the Great War, and I recognized the insignia.

Apparently, Hannibal was a Major! The uniform had a number of ribbons for medals and service. I finished up my toilet and walked back into the bathroom and out the door to the kitchen. Snooping, I know: I will keep this to myself for now. Hannibal is full of surprises.

Business is good, coal miners mostly. I keep Kitty and Susie with me on the houseboat, and Maribel and Kathy work at the roadhouse. Billy, Scottie's driver, picks them up on Friday morning. Since the winter weather is bad, the two girls come back to the houseboat on Sunday morning now.

Scottie wants me to add more girls. I told him I would think about it. If I do, we'll have to move into town; the houseboat isn't big enough: decisions, decisions.

Saturday, February 16

The Capone and O'Banion war is heating up. According to the newspapers, a gangster named John Duffy was murdered in Chicago. He was last seen at the Four Deuces, Capone's club. However, the police suspect that O'Banion did the killing. I doubt that witnesses will testify one way or another. Bad blood!

Booze production and shipments from the Valley continue at a growing pace. According to Billy, Maribel and Kathy, Carlo has two more men in addition to Louie. As far as I know, the hijackings have stopped, at least locally. My girls at the roadhouse seem safe enough.

I haven't seen Hannibal since Christmas. He is away on another of his mysterious trips. I miss him.

Saturday, February 23

Hannibal stopped by the houseboat today. He brought woolen sweaters for the five girls. How nice! I glanced at the labels. The sweaters were made in Toronto, Canada. How did Hannibal know to buy five? I introduced Hannibal to Kitty, and the pair had a long conversation. Kitty liked Hannibal immediately.

Later, Hannibal asked me if I wanted to have dinner with him at Valenti's Restaurant. "We could visit with Louisa," he said.

"Of course," I replied. "We could go next Thursday; Friday and Saturday nights are busy." I then added: "I would love to see Louisa again."

"See you about six o'clock on Thursday," responded Hannibal. He then said his goodbyes, left the houseboat and headed back to his car, whistling as he walked along the path.

Friday, February 29

Dinner with Hannibal was bittersweet. My time with Hannibal was sweet, of course, but our conversation with Louisa was sort of sad.

Louisa had broken up with Johnny. We got the story as Louisa waited on our table.

"Johnny is trying to adjust but he just can't," confided Louisa. "He's very bitter, and he took it out on me."

"Louisa, Johnny's blindness is not your fault," I replied.

"I know, Miss Caroline," Louisa responded. "Johnny is angry at everyone."

Hannibal then said: "Louisa, perhaps you should move on." Hannibal's eyes expressed sympathy. "Only Johnny can come to terms with what happened to him."

"You think so?" Louisa's eyes were moist. "I just wanted to help," she added.

Hannibal's right, Louisa," I said. "Johnny can't change his blindness, but he can change his outlook." I paused, thinking, then added: "I hope he takes advantage of the job the Valenti's offered."

"He hasn't so far," said Louisa. "The Valenti's offered twice, but Johnny doesn't seem to care."

Hannibal then asked: "How are you doing with the Valenti's?"

"They are so nice," replied Louisa. "I work hard, and they have taught me many things."

Just then Mama Valenti walked up to the table, smiling. "We find you a nice Italian boy," she said; first she looked at Louisa, then to Hannibal and me, adding a wink for good measure. She turned back to Louisa, and said: "You work hard; I like you!"

Hannibal and I couldn't help but chuckle.

"Oh, thank you," replied Louisa. She wiped away a tear and tried to smile. She then bustled about and made sure that our table was just right.

As Louisa walked away with several empty dishes, Mama Valenti poured us each another glass of "grape juice."

"So sad about that Johnny," said Mama, and shook her head. She paused a moment, reflecting, then added: "What else can I get you?"

"Nothing Mama," replied Hannibal. "The dinner was wonderful, as usual."

And so, the evening passed. Louisa will do fine, I think. Johnny? Well, we'll have to wait and see. Maybe Mama Valenti will find Louisa a nice Italian boy. I hope so.

Monday, May 19, 1924

Yesterday was quite a day! I found another stray cat; or more accurately, a stray boy.

As usual on Sunday mornings, I sat in my chair on the porch of my houseboat, coffee in hand, watching the river. All was quiet inside. Maribel and Kathy had returned late on Saturday night; we were back on a summer schedule.

The morning was beautiful: rising sun, soft breeze, new spring leaves on the cottonwood trees and a quiet, brown river flowing by. Occasional boats slipped back and forth in the main channel.

One boat caught my eye. It angled across the river from the Parke County side. The oarsman was a slim, tall figure, and he rowed the boat with steady, practiced strokes.

I watched as the boat approached the bank about fifty feet away. As it eased up on the bank, I could see that the oarsman was a boy, probably in his mid-teens.

"Very unusual," I mused. "Most river rats are older men." The boy had sandy, tousled hair, a slim but muscular build and a complexion browned by the sun. "Nice looking boy," I observed. "Wonder what he's up to?"

I could see three wooden crates in the bottom of the boat. "Whiskey!" I muttered out loud: "the good stuff." I recognized the crates; they were just like the pre-prohibition crates that came from distilleries. "Probably Canadian," I surmised to myself; "no legal distilleries exist in the U.S. nowadays, and moonshine and bathtub gin don't come in wooden crates."

The boy tied up his boat, looked around and spotted me observing him. His eyes squinted as he gave me a long, steady look. He stood on the bank, watching me for a long minute.

I raised my coffee cup, acknowledging our eye contact. The boy smiled, and his eyes twinkled. He raised his hand in a brief wave and turned to his work. Soon the three crates were on the bank. The clink of glass as the crates were moved supported my earlier analysis.

"The boy has decided that I am not a threat," I thought to myself: "very perceptive." My thoughts continued: "He also knows that I know what he's doing."

The boy then made three trips from the landing to the road, about a hundred feet up the path from the river bank. As he carried up the last crate, a car pulled up. It was Billy, Scottie's driver. Billy and the boy loaded the crates in the car. Billy then gave the boy an envelope and drove off.

I had already heard that Scottie's place has acquired a wide reputation as a "safe" place for upscale drinking, gambling and titillating encounters. "Scottie sells the good stuff," I mused to myself. "Good for Scottie."

I watched as the boy stuffed the envelope in the front of his jeans and tightened his belt. He then walked slowly, yet with purpose, down the path toward my houseboat. His eyes were on me the entire trip.

I rose from my chair as the boy approached. He stopped just short of my gangplank.

"Want some coffee?" I called out.

The boy smiled, then replied: "Yes, Ma'am, that would be nice; black please."

"Come on board then," I responded.

The boy walked up the gangplank and stood before me.

"Please have a seat," I offered.

"Thank you, Ma'am," he responded and waited.

"Manners," I thought to myself. I then said: "I'll pour you a cup; the pot's in the kitchen." I turned, opened the door and stepped inside. I poured a second cup, returned to the porch and handed it to the boy.

"Thank you, Ma'am," the boy said, as he took the cup. He stood until I sat down; only then did he take a seat.

I eyed the boy over the rim of my cup as I sipped my coffee. "Making a delivery to Scottie?" I asked.

The boy nodded and smiled. His blue-gray eyes twinkled.

"I could tell from the crates that you delivered the good stuff." I paused, smiled and asked: "Canadian?"

The boy nodded again. After a moment, he said: "Scottie has a few high rollers at his club on North Main Street." He then added: "Scottie told me about you; that's why I landed here."

"Ah," I replied, then asked: "Do you have a name?"

"Yes Ma'am, the boy replied. He then waited a few moments, and his eyes twinkled again, as he toyed with me. "I'm Frank Gardner."

He waited another moment. I swear he was reading my mind, anticipating my next three questions.

"I will be fifteen in October," he stated. "My folks live in Indianapolis," he continued. "I'm adventuring on the Wabash this summer."

The way he said "adventuring" indicated a good education; he was not a street urchin from the city. "Runaway?" I queried.

"No, my folks know I'm here," he replied. His eyes gave a brief troubled look.

"His folks know but do not approve," I concluded to myself. "OK for now, I will not pry."

I had never met a boy like this before. My mind made the obvious connection: "Frank Gardner, you are a younger edition of Hannibal Jones," I thought to myself.

"Why deliveries by boat?" I asked.

"Scottie doesn't get this product through the people at the gas station between the bridges," Frank replied. "We have to be careful."

"O'Banion?" I queried.

"Not sure," Frank replied. He then added: "Scottie hired me because I deliver by boat, and I'm not very noticeable." Frank smiled; I could tell that he knew that Capone's gangsters, Carlo, Louie and the others, would be watching for men, not a boy.

"OK," I said. "However, it's also dangerous for you."

Frank smiled and stated: "I'll be careful, Ma'am."

"I bet you will," I thought to myself. I then asked: "Where are you staying?"

"Up river," Frank replied.

I waited, but Frank didn't elaborate. "Smart boy," I concluded; "very smart."

"You're always welcome here," I stated, then added: "for a cup of coffee."

"Yes Ma'am," replied Frank with a grin; he clearly understood my meaning. "I best be going now." He stood and drained his cup in a couple of gulps. He said again, for the umpteenth time: "Thank you Ma'am," as he handed me his cup.

Frank then turned and walked down the gangplank. I watched as he untied his boat, waved and started rowing across the river. He angled the boat northeast to compensate for the current. I watched until he reached the far side, turned north and headed up river.

"How interesting," I muttered to myself. Just then I heard giggles from the kitchen. Susie, Maribel, Kathy and Kitty had been eavesdropping.

"Girls, shame on you!" I stated firmly. More giggles.

Friday morning, May 23

Hannibal and I had dinner at Valenti's again last evening. This is becoming a regular thing! We visited with Louisa of course, and she's doing better. She prattled on about how she's fixing up the interior of her "new house." Mom and Pop Valenti prepared a wonderful meal, as usual. I got no news about "a nice Italian boy" yet.

I told Hannibal about Frank Gardner. He listened carefully as I related the details of my encounter with Frank the previous Sunday.

When I finished, Hannibal asked: "Scottie's getting supplies from both Capone and O'Banion?"

"It seems so," I replied. "Young Frank is in a very dangerous position." I paused a moment, then added: "So is Scottie." I thought a moment, and then added: "I think my girls will be safe enough, as long as there are no more roadhouse shootouts."

"I'll look into it." responded Hannibal. The rest of the evening was spent in pleasant conversation.

Friday, Jun 13

Had dinner with Hannibal at Valenti's again last night. Louisa and Hannibal both had news; Louisa's news was good; Hannibal's news was more somber, except for his report on young Frank Gardner.

Louisa first: Mama Valenti fulfilled her promise; Louisa has a boyfriend.

As soon as we were seated, Louisa came up to our table with a handsome young man in tow.

"Hannibal, Miss Caroline, this is Antonio," Louisa bubbled. "Antonio sells cars," she added.

Antonio smiled, shuffled his feet a bit, and said: "Hello, Miss Caroline, Mr. Jones." He paused, and then continued. "Louisa told me that you are her good friends."

"Why yes, Antonio," I responded. "And Louisa is very special to us."

Hannibal stood and offered his hand. "Pleased to meet you, Antonio," he said. "Just call me Hannibal." He smiled warmly.

Antonio responded: "Call me Tony."

The four of us had a very pleasant conversation, while Mama Valenti watched from the kitchen door, beaming from ear to ear. Even Papa Valenti peered out from behind Mama with a big grin on his face. After a while, Louisa and Tony said their goodbyes. Louisa's eyes were shining as the pair walked out the front door.

Mama walked up to our table and confided in a whisper: "My Louisa has the night off." She added: "I take care of you tonight; Papa made spaghetti and meatballs: you like?" She waved a big spoon about for emphasis; she had forgotten to leave it in the kitchen.

We all laughed. "Of course!" said Hannibal. "If Papa made it, it has to be good!"

"Wonderful!" replied Mama. Then she whispered "It's my sauce on the meatballs." We all laughed again. The dinner was even better than advertised.

When we were alone, Hannibal turned the conversation to more somber issues.

"The war between the Torrio-Capone gang and O'Banion's North Side Gang is getting worse," he confided. "According to the newspapers and rumors that I overheard at the gas station, O'Banion double-crossed Torrio on an illegal brewery deal. Torrio lost half a million dollars and got arrested."

"Wow!" I replied. "Capone won't stand for that."

"Probably not," Hannibal agreed. "Anyway, I suggest that you tell Scottie and young Frank Gardner to be very careful."

"I will," I responded. The conversation then turned to Frank Gardner.

"I know a few people in Indianapolis," said Hannibal. "They said that Joseph Gardner, Frank's father, is a well-respected businessman." Hannibal thought a moment, and then added: "From what I can tell, young Frank is a bright, very adventurous sort. His parents, with some trepidation, let him travel to the Wabash on his own for the summer."

"At fourteen?" I responded. "Seems a little young, don't you think?"

"Perhaps," said Hannibal with a grin. "It depends on the boy, or in your case, the girl."

I had no argument to refute Hannibal's statement, so I just said: "OK, OK," with a sheepish smile.

"Still," said Hannibal, "I will keep an eye on him."

"Please do," I responded, "I like him."

The evening continued, and Hannibal took me home about eight o'clock. Susie had done just fine in my absence.

Wednesday, June 18

I had my usual meeting with Scottie this morning. I warned him about the Capone-O'Banion war. "Be careful, Scottie, with your purchases of booze supplies from both gangs."

Scottie seemed a little surprised that I knew about the source of the Canadian whiskey, but I didn't elaborate.

Scottie went on to say: "Now don't you worry, Caroline; Carlo and Louie don't know where I get my Canadian whiskey, and I am one of their best local customers for moonshine and gin."

"Well," I replied, "you best keep it a secret." I paused, and looked him squarely in the eye. "Please don't put that boy Frank Gardner in danger."

"Yes, yes," responded Scottie. "Don't worry, everything will work out." He then turned to our usual business matters.

Sunday evening, July 6

Every other Sunday morning since May 18th, young Frank has made deliveries of Canadian whiskey to the landing spot by my houseboat. Each time, Billy picked up three crates, and Frank received an envelope.

I watched and waved from my porch as Frank made his deliveries. Once, Frank joined me on the porch for coffee. He didn't say much about the nature of his business, and I didn't pry.

This morning, Frank arrived in his boat, as usual. I watched as he unloaded his cargo. Suddenly, four figures moved from behind trees above Frank's landing spot. The figures were young men, and they were all dressed in jeans and shirts. "Not Chicago gangsters," I thought to myself. They approached rapidly. Two carried clubs.

"We'll take that!" yelled the lead man. He brandished a club, which turned out to be an axe handle. He was the first to reach Frank at the landing spot, the other three were a few yards behind.

Frank did not back down. The first man swung his axe handle. Frank ducked. I could hear the swish as the axe handle passed over his head.

Frank's fists flew. His right uppercut caught his opponent in the gut, and the man doubled over. Frank grabbed his opponent's shirt with his right and the back of his belt with his left. He heaved. Then man half stumbled, half flew down the bank and into the river, banging his head on Frank's boat in the bargain.

"Not bad for a fourteen-year old," I thought to myself. I scrambled back into the kitchen for a weapon.

As I emerged with a heavy iron skillet, I could see that the other three men were all over Frank. As I was running down the gangplank, one man hit Frank across the knees with another axe handle. Frank went down. In spite of his fighting spirit, he really didn't have a chance.

I didn't see Hannibal arrive; he was just there. Frank's three assailants turned in surprise.

In a practiced, efficient fashion, Hannibal dodged the punches and the axe handle of his opponents. He administered crushing blows of his own. In a flash, two men were on the ground. Hannibal faced the remaining man, fists ready.

I arrived with my skillet. The remaining man turned toward me with a surprised expression. I can still see his face as my skillet cracked his head with a resounding "bong!" Lights out, fight over.

Hannibal looked at me. "Nice job!" he said with a grin.

I was wound up pretty tight, so I just stared at Hannibal, then to Frank on the ground, then back to Hannibal.

"See what you can do for Frank," said Hannibal. "I'll take care of the others." After a quick glance to the three on the ground, Hannibal walked down the bank to the man in the water. The man was face down and probably would have drowned if Hannibal hadn't fished him out.

I helped Frank stand. He was a little wobbly, and his face expressed pain, but nothing appeared broken.

In a few minutes, Hannibal had all four assailants in a pile, high up on the bank. They were a sorry looking lot.

Hannibal looked sternly at the four young men; fire was still in his eyes. "What are your names?" Hannibal looked at each one, in turn. Each gave a name. "Where's home?" Each said: "Clinton." "Do you know anyone from Chicago?" The response was negative; but the four exchanged scared glances. Hannibal's eyes squinted; I could tell that he thought the four young men knew more than they were admitting. Hannibal gave me a knowing look, and I understood.

I ran through the possibilities in my mind. The four might just be local toughs who had spotted an opportunity. On the other hand, the fact that they went after a delivery boy for O'Banion whiskey was suspicious; perhaps they were local hires connected to Capone's gang. If not Carlo and his Chicago crew, perhaps some local mastermind? My thoughts raced. Big Bill and Fat Benny were possibilities, but they had never hired local tough guys before. Who else could it be? I turned my attention back to Hannibal, who was addressing the culprits on the ground.

My attention focused; Hannibal was saying: "I don't expect to see you around here again," and he gave each culprit a long look. His hands flexed from open to closed fists. He added: "I know you now, and I can find you." He paused for effect, and then said: "Leave the boy alone, understood?"

The four on the ground all muttered "Yes sir."

"Now get out of my sight," responded Hannibal. The four got up, fell a few times, groaned a lot and made their way up the bank. We watched as they disappeared behind the trees along the road.

I heard a car drive up. "Oh, no," I muttered. Then I saw Billy get out. I breathed a sigh of relief.

Billy came down the bank toward us. He looked at the three crates still on the bank and then at each of us. His eyes expressed a whole range of questions.

Frank broke the silence. "You're late," he said. Billy opened his mouth, then closed it, and then said: "What?" Hannibal and I laughed, both at Billy's expression and in relief. Frank joined in.

Soon all was settled. Billy drove off with the crates. Frank got his envelope and departed in his boat. Hannibal and I returned to the houseboat.

I put away my trusty skillet. Susie, Maribel, Kathy and Kitty all emerged on the porch, oohing and ahhing over Hannibal and recent events. I ordered more coffee and collapsed into a chair.

After a few minutes, the girls went inside. Hannibal and I were alone. Soon we could hear the girls working on morning chores, and we could talk in relative privacy.

Hannibal began. "We need to do something about that boy." He eyed me over the rim of his coffee cup.

"Yes," I agreed. "What do you have in mind?"

Hannibal was silent for a few minutes. Finally, he said: "We could offer him a job that is much less dangerous."

I nodded and waited.

Hannibal said: "We could use an inconspicuous snoop," he grinned at me.

I pretended to be offended and said: "Humph! I take it that as a snoop, I'm not inconspicuous." I couldn't help it; the pretense ended, and I laughed. Hannibal joined in.

We then got down to details. Our discussion lasted for over an hour. When we finished, we both had our assignments. What a day!

9

THE COMMITTEE

Sunday, July 20, 1924

I made a point to be on my porch early this morning. Hannibal and I had a plan, and it was time for action. I waited for young Frank to show up. He did, right on time.

Coffee cup in hand, I watched in the early morning light and mist as Frank approached in his boat. He was very cautious. He held his boat stationary, well offshore, sculling with his oars to compensate for the current. This lasted for several minutes. He scanned the shoreline as he maneuvered the boat. Finally satisfied, he brought his boat to the landing, got out and tied it to a tree. No unwelcome greeters appeared.

"Good!" I said to myself. "Caution based on lesson learned."

Frank saw me, of course. He waved briefly, and then went straight to work. He had four crates instead of just three like before.

"Scottie's business must be improving," I thought to myself. I stood as Frank finished unloading, and then motioned with my cup; it was an invitation. Frank understood.

A car drove up to the pull-off along the road above at the usual spot. Billy got out. Soon the pair had the crates in the car; Frank got his envelope, and Billy drove away. Frank walked back down the path to my houseboat. I had his coffee ready and waiting.

As we settled in our chairs, Frank eyed me with a curious, expectant, yet confident look.

I got right to the point. "You did well two weeks ago in the fight," I began. After a pause, I added: "however, you were lucky that Hannibal and I showed up."

"Yes, Ma'am," Frank replied, between sips of coffee. His expression did not change.

"Two of my friends have been murdered as a result of the booze business," I stated softly. There was a catch in my voice; I couldn't help it. I added: "You could very well meet the same fate."

Frank's eyes widened a little. I could tell that he had expected fights, and he was confident in his abilities, but murder was a whole new level.

I pressed the point home. "Even with those local boys two weeks ago, you were in over your head," I stated matter-of-factly. "You might not be so lucky next time."

"Yes, Ma'am," replied Frank, and he gulped a little on his coffee.

I could tell that his self-assurance was taken down a peg, which was precisely what I intended.

I watched Frank for a full minute. He squirmed a little under my gaze.

Finally, I said: "I think Hannibal and I might have a job for you." I paused to let this revelation sink in, and then added: "it would replace your delivery business." I could see that Frank's curiosity was aroused. "Your new job would still be adventurous." I gave this last word the same emphasis that Frank had given it during our first meeting.

"Pay?" Frank responded.

I chuckled a little; the boy had his wits about him. "We can give you as much as you are making now, and your job would be less dangerous."

"What about Scottie?" asked Frank.

"Integrity," I thought to myself. "Good!" I replied: "I'll talk to Scottie." I paused and then added: "Scottie will make do, he always does."

This was certainly true. Scottie was a shrewd businessman, in spite of his tendency to talk too much. I let my thoughts run to a logical conclusion. "Scottie's mouth will get him in trouble one day."

"Are you busy later this week?" I asked. Without waiting for a response, I added: "Would you visit me here, say about noon on Thursday?"

Frank thought a moment, and then answered: "I can be here at noon on Thursday." He smiled; I could see that I had piqued his curiosity.

"Good!" I replied. I stood up and added: "See you then."

Frank took the hint. "Thank you for the coffee, Ma'am," he replied.

He got up, gave me his cup and departed. I watched him untie his boat; get in, and with expert strokes of the oars, row across the river.

"That went well," I mused to myself. "I like that boy."

I heard stirrings in the kitchen. I looked in the door. It was Susie. "Have you been eavesdropping?" I asked sternly. Susie giggled.

Wednesday, July 23

I had my usual business meeting with Scottie today. He was full of enthusiasm.

"Business is great," he said. "Have you given any thought to adding more girls for the roadhouse?" He added: "We can do the usual twenty-five and seventy-five percent split."

I had already decided on this topic. "Yes," I replied. "I will recruit four girls who can work the roadhouse, but I will have to find a home for them." I didn't want my girls living full time at the roadhouse for many reasons: safety, down time and privacy for the girls, sanitary conditions, control, and so on.

"Good," responded Scottie: "When?"

"I should be set up in time for the holiday season," I replied. "I need to recruit, buy a house, and provide for salaries and so on." To myself, I reflected: "Things will be different with a house; Clinton will be a more permanent base of operations." I carried this thought to a logical conclusion: "Maybe it's time to sell the houseboat."

"OK," Scottie responded. "You know your business, Caroline." He paused, thinking, then added: "I can be ready for them by November; I'm adding an extension to the back of the roadhouse as we speak; your girls will each have a room upstairs."

I nodded; the girls had told me about the new construction.

Scottie continued. "Have you heard about the new road?" Without waiting for an answer, he said: "The new road will be paved from Terre Haute, through Lyford, up through Rockville, and on to Chicago." He paused, grinning from ear to ear. "I think it will eventually go all the way south to Florida; it's part of the new national highway system, and it will be called U.S. Highway 41." He added the obvious conclusion: "Great for business!"

This revelation was news. "It will certainly increase the traffic in moonshine to Chicago," I thought to myself.

I then took a deep breath and turned my thoughts to the topic of Frank Gardner. I eyed Scottie carefully, and he got a puzzled look; he knew something was coming.

"You use Frank Gardner, a fourteen-year-old boy, to obtain your Canadian whiskey from the O'Banion gang. The boy makes deliveries from the Parke County side of the river to a landing near my houseboat."

"Yes, yes," replied Scottie. I could tell he was surprised that I knew so much.

I pressed on, stating: "I have offered Frank a job that is much less dangerous." I looked Scottie in the eye and continued: "You need to find a new person to do your deliveries." I then added: "I suggest that you find a man, not a boy."

Scottie's mouth opened, then closed, and he stuttered a little. "I suppose I could," he finally replied. I could see that he was thinking. Finally, he said: "Frank told me about the fight at the landing two deliveries ago." He paused again, and then stated: "You're right of course."

So, it was settled with Scottie. Now I had to close the deal with young Frank.

Thursday, July 24

Hannibal and I waited on the porch of the houseboat for Frank to show up. I had already sent the girls off on errands. Kathy, Kitty and Maribel had left for the grocery store. Susie had a more complicated errand; she would go with Billy in his car to Terre Haute on a recruiting mission. The pair would not return until Friday evening.

Hannibal had brought a small brown leather case, which rested on the floor beside his chair. I was curious, but I didn't ask about the contents. "Hannibal will let me know when he is ready," I had concluded. Besides, I had come to enjoy Hannibal's little surprises.

Young Frank crossed the river in his boat right on time. Hannibal grinned, took out his watch and verified the time. "Ten minutes to twelve," he said. "Good!" Soon Frank was on the porch. We exchanged the usual greetings, and we settled in chairs with cool sun tea.

I got right to the point. "Hannibal and I are investigating the murders of two friends: Alec Feleovich and Ogle McNabb." I gave Frank a long, steady look. "We need your help."

Hannibal picked up the narrative. "Alec and Ogle were casualties of war," he stated. He paused a moment, and then continued. "The Capone and the O'Banion gangs are fighting over the illegal booze trade in the Wabash Valley."

Frank nodded, he knew about the war. Capone's men were buyers of moonshine whiskey and gin for the Chicago area markets, and O'Banion's men had hijacked Capone shipments. O'Banion was also the main supplier of illegal Canadian whiskey to Wabash Valley speakeasies. A war was inevitable.

I picked up the story and said: "Local politicians and law enforcement people, among others, are on one or more gang payrolls." Frank's eyes widened a little, and I continued: "We therefore cannot take our murder case to the local authorities."

Hannibal added: "We already have strong evidence that the murders were covered up by Big Bill Johannsson, the sheriff, and probably Fat Benny Nuardi, the mayor." Hannibal took a deep breath, and then continued. "We need to establish motive, method and opportunity for the murders, and obtain evidence for political corruption."

Frank looked back and forth to Hannibal and me. Finally, he stated: "Why?"

Hannibal and I waited; we could tell that Frank was thinking things through.

Frank looked directly at me and added: "Your business is also illegal, and you benefit from the booze trade." He then drove the point home. "Are you after revenge?" He then looked at Hannibal. "I appreciate your help during the fight, but I really don't know you."

Wow! Smart kid! I smiled in spite of myself; so did Hannibal.

After a few moments of careful thought, I said: "No, it's not just revenge."

I looked directly into Frank's eyes and continued: "I have reason to believe that my girls and I are in danger. Big Bill and the Capone men are certainly aware that the girls and I know that Alec and Ogle were murdered. They might put us out of business or take even more drastic action."

"Proof of murder and corruption can be effective blackmail tools to keep the gangs and local officials at bay," added Hannibal. "Also, I have my own reasons, which I will keep to myself for now."

I looked at Hannibal with surprise, and not for the first time. Who is Hannibal, really?

Frank looked at Hannibal and then back to me several times. Finally, he said: "How do I fit in?"

"We need an inconspicuous snoop," I stated with a wry smile.

Hannibal chuckled at our private joke.

I then stated: "If you want the job, we can give a more high-falutin' title. How does "Field Investigator" sound?"

Frank grinned: "Yes, I want the job, and "Snoop" as a title is just fine." We all laughed.

Hannibal reached down into the leather case on the floor beside his chair and carefully removed a beautifully crafted camera. He set the camera on my small coffee table between our chairs. He then reached into the case again and produced a second camera, and he placed it by the first.

I said: "Oh, my!" I couldn't help myself. A glance to Frank showed that he was also suitably impressed; his eyes grew wide.

Hannibal grinned. "For the snoop," he said, with obvious pride. "You may borrow these," he hastily added.

"How do they work?" asked Frank. I had the same question; both cameras far surpassed my little Kodak.

Hannibal smiled and said: "This first camera is an Ermanox, made in Germany just this year. It takes pictures on four and a half by six-centimeter plates. It has a very fast shutter speed and a 100-millimeter f/2 lens, which means it can capture fast-moving subjects without blurring the photo."

He paused a moment to let Frank and me think about the implications. He then continued. "The camera essentially looks through a kind of low power telescope, which means that distant objects can be made to look close up." He then added: "It also works well in low light situations, which means you can take good, clear photos in the evening or in low-light indoor environments."

"Wow!" exclaimed Frank. "May I hold it?"

I was envious; I wanted to hold it too. Frank was just faster than me. Oh, well.

Hannibal handed the camera to Frank, who proceeded to inspect it from all possible angles. I looked on with obvious envy.

Hannibal looked at me, grinned and then continued: "The downside of the camera is that it takes photos on plates, not film. This means that you must carry extra plates in the case and set up with a new plate after each photo."

I nodded and replied: "Not fast, like my Kodak camera with film."

"Right," responded Hannibal. "That's why we have a second camera." He then picked up the second camera and handed it to me.

I took the camera gingerly; I didn't want to break it.

Hannibal smiled as if he knew precisely what I was thinking. "This camera is a Leica, also made in Germany. It is one of only 31 prototypes; production will begin next year."

Frank said: "Wow! How did you get it?"

"My secret," Hannibal replied. "Anyway, the Leica uses 35-millimeter film, which means you can take many photos quickly. However, it has only a 50-millimeter f3.5 lens, which means you have to be relatively close to the subject to gain detail. Also, the subject has to be stationary or moving slowly, otherwise the photo will blur, and you need good lighting."

"One slow camera for distance, low light and fast-moving subjects, and one fast camera for close-up, good light and stationary subjects," I summarized, as I looked closely at Hannibal.

"Right," responded Hannibal with a smile.

I could tell Hannibal was pleased with himself. "So full of surprises," I thought, and tried, probably without success, to not show my wonder at the cameras, and of course, Hannibal's obvious mastery of camera technology.

"I will show you both how the cameras work," continued Hannibal. "Also," and he looked at me, "we will need your darkroom services."

The next two hours were spent discussing the cameras. Hannibal was a wealth of information. Frank and I learned how to take quality photos and to apply new darkroom techniques; how fascinating!

When all photography questions were answered, I turned the conversation to our physical evidence. "What can we do with the probable murder weapon for Alec and our blood samples for both murders?" I asked.

"Hannibal nodded and replied: "I know some people who work in a laboratory suitable for forensic work."

"Fore – en – sic?" asked Frank.

"Forensics is the application of science to criminal investigations, replied Hannibal. "The people I know can use the probable murder weapon, the blood samples, photos and your documentation." Hannibal looked first at me then at Frank. "We want to establish place, cause of death and maybe time of death." He paused a moment, then added: "We also want to obtain evidence to place the suspected murderers at the scene of the crime."

After Frank and I nodded, Hannibal continued: "Forensic analysis supports criminal prosecution in a court of law." He then smiled, looked at me and added: "If not criminal prosecution, at least blackmail."

I looked at Frank. His mouth was wide open. After a bit, he closed it. I was also amazed, but I think I covered it better, well, maybe. Hannibal had a knack for touching on motivations.

Hannibal then summarized our discussion. "Our little committee has three main tasks: first, gather intelligence and evidence, second, analyze the information gathered and third, assess the risks to us and our friends. We can seek outside scientific help as needed." He then looked carefully at both of us, and said: "The risks are already high, and if we are discovered in our work, they may be very high." He added: "Understood?"

Frank and I both nodded. How exciting!

"We have one other task," said Frank with a big smile. "What should we call ourselves? A "Committee" doesn't sound very adventurous."

I thought a moment, and then said: "How about "The River Rat Detective Agency?"

Frank and Hannibal both laughed, and then said, almost in unison, "Done!"

Sunday morning, August 3

And so, we formalized our little group. Later, we will bring my girls into the fold as needed; they could be a big help. They were also at risk even now, and they had a right to know what was going on, at least at a certain level.

Frank will go back to school in Indianapolis in late August, but he promised to return in May, with his parent's permission. I hope we can make better arrangements for his place of residence; a camp on the Wabash seems a bit too "adventurous."

Later, after Hannibal and Frank left, I had more sober thoughts. "Risks," I said to myself. "And danger." In my mind, the path ahead was shrouded in a pale mist.

10

STRICTLY BUSINESS

Wednesday evening, November 12, 1924

Big news! Scottie showed me the Chicago newspapers during our meeting this morning. On November 10th, Dean O'Banion was murdered in his North Side Chicago flower shop. Capone allies are suspected, but of course, no one is talking. According to Scottie, Hymie Weiss, Vincent Drucci and Bugs Moran are now the key players in the North Side Gang. The war goes on.

Wednesday evening, January 28, 1925

I had another meeting with Scottie, and the newspapers report more shootings in Chicago. On January 24th, Johnny Torrio was struck by a hail of gunfire near his apartment on South Clyde Avenue. Torrio is in the hospital, and he is expected to survive. However, Capone is effectively in control of the Torrio's operation. What a bloodthirsty bunch! Even Scottie seemed a little scared. We are dealing with these gangsters for our booze, and the risks are high.

Sunday, May 10

Whew! The winter was busy, and I have a booming business! I now have eight girls; I bought three houses, and I sold my houseboat. In addition to Susie, Maribel, Kathy and Kitty, I'm now the "den mother" to Clara, Sandy, Emily and Maria.

I live in one resident house with the new girls, and Susie manages Maribel, Kathy and Kitty in the other resident house. The two resident houses are side by side, just off South Main Street, in a quiet neighborhood, not far from Hannibal's place.

The third house is an ornate Victorian, very suitable for our line of work. It is located south of town, just outside the city limits, for obvious reasons.

The new owner of the houseboat is a railroad executive and former customer. I do miss the old boat; it was my home. However, the river itself was a constant worry and moving the houseboat from town to town was expensive. Now, with the booming, free-wheeling economy, moving is unnecessary. I have no idea how the railroad executive plans to use it, and I'm trying not to care.

My capital outlay was considerable. The two residences cost six thousand each, plus another two thousand for furnishings. The old Victorian cost ten thousand, with an additional two thousand for re-modeling, including a full-service bar, and two thousand for furnishings. I sold the houseboat for four thousand, so my net outlay was twenty-four thousand.

I raised the twenty-four thousand by selling some stock and drawing down my cash reserve. I did not pick up any debt. Given the nature of my business, I did not want to explain about my income sources to bankers or even to private lenders. Even if I had gotten a loan, a paper trail could be a disaster.

In addition, Scottie and I have become business partners. Four of my girls work in the Lyford roadhouse, and I buy all of my booze for the Victorian from Scottie, including the good Canadian whiskey. I don't ask where he gets the booze; but it is clear that he deals with both Capone and the North Side gang.

I invested fifteen thousand in Scottie's Main Street speakeasy; I now own a 30 percent share. On paper, I own 30 percent of a large, expensive private residence on North Main Street; we didn't document the "business" use of the residence, for obvious reasons.

Scottie used my money for improvements. On the outside, the place appears to be a large private mansion. On the inside first floor,

Scottie has a beautiful bar, a small stage for entertainment and tables for about thirty or so people. Entertainment includes a small band and occasionally a singer, all the way from Chicago. There is even a coat check room and ornate restrooms, one for ladies and the other for gentlemen. Upstairs, Scottie has rooms for private gambling, a large room with a roulette wheel and four blackjack tables and two small overnight rooms.

Scottie's place has acquired a wide reputation. The clientele is definitely upscale, very different than the Lyford roadhouse. Wow!

My revenues from all my enterprises exceed my operating costs, and I make a substantial profit. I continue to invest profits into conservative stocks and bonds, and I keep a tidy amount of cash in my safe deposit box for unexpected expenses. I may start investing in local legitimate businesses soon; why not?

Sunday, May 17

Frank is back in town; school is out for the summer. He took several great photos at the gas station between the two bridges. He got several of the car used by Carlo and Louie, including more close-ups of the tire treads. Combined with Hannibal's earlier photos, we can definitely tie the car to the scene where Susie and I found Ogle's body. Frank also managed to capture Big Bill talking to Carlo, and Fat Benny taking an envelope from Louie. How resourceful!

Hannibal, Frank and I continue to gather and analyze evidence concerning the murders of Alec and Ogle. Frank has become particularly adept at taking photos without being seen. I gather information from business contacts, especially Scottie, as well as customers who become talkative. Hannibal has laboratory contacts who provide "forensic" assistance; I like that new word!

The three of us set up operations in one of Hannibal's two spare bedrooms. He equipped the room with a portable chalk board, a large table with chairs and a filing cabinet. We moved my darkroom equipment from my houseboat closet to a roomy storage hallway between two of Hannibal's three bedrooms. Hannibal installed proper lighting, a door and a venting system to get rid of chemical vapors. Very nice! Money doesn't seem to be a problem for Hannibal, again, more questions: patience, Caroline!

My main source of information remains Scottie. He confirmed that he is paying Big Bill and Sam, the Clinton cop, for "protection." I am trying to figure a way of getting photos of actual payoffs, but so far, I don't know how to do this.

Saturday, May 23

I haven't had visits from Big Bill and Fat Benny at my place of business since the confrontation with Bill in the grocery store in January two years ago. I can only assume they have found another place to indulge in their particular fantasies.

Susie, Kathy, Maribel and Kitty hear lots of bar talk at Scottie's roadhouse. I have yet to figure out how to follow up on their leads. Is photography an option?

Sunday, June 7

Hannibal got lab results back on the blood samples and the probable murder weapon for Alec. The type of blood from Alec's body and from the shack matched the type of blood on the short piece of pipe that Hannibal found in the bushes. Also, the lab found fingerprints on the pipe; now we have to get fingerprints of our suspects to see if we can get a match. Hannibal also got back the blood type from Ogle's sample, but we have nothing to compare it to. Over three years have passed since the murder, would there be viable blood spots in the car used by Carlo and Louie? I doubt it, but we'll see.

Friday, June 12

Scottie has completed the expansion of his Lyford roadhouse. Susie, Kathy, Maribel and Kitty now have nice rooms upstairs and free access to the bar and potential customers downstairs. Nice!

Scottie and I settle accounts in his office at his speakeasy on North Main Street every other Wednesday. He also re-modeled his speakeasy; including his now plush office just off the bar. Scottie proudly gave me a complete tour. The office even has a private "water closet" on the left side from Scottie's desk. The door to the water closet has a transom above and the wall at the back has a vent, both for ventilation.

I like his office, but he has only one door which opens to the bar area and no windows. I mentioned the lack of an escape route to Scottie, but he didn't seem to care. Oh, well.

Sunday, June 14

Surprise! Big Bill and Fat Benny showed up at the Victorian, drunk as skunks, on Friday night. I'm not sure whether their visit was a scouting expedition or just a spur-of-the-moment thing. They seemed to like the new girls, the full-service bar and the good Canadian whiskey. I didn't take photos, there wasn't any point. Careful, Caroline!

Sunday, July 5

Happy Fourth of July, I think. Things are a little hazy after last night. Business was the best ever on the Fourth, both at the Victorian and Scottie's roadhouse. The North Main speakeasy was reserved the entire evening for a "private" party of local notables, but attendees included many out-of-towners. Today we recover; tomorrow we go back to work.

Wednesday evening, July 8

Scottie and I had our usual meeting this morning in his new office. I arrived about 10 o'clock. Scottie already had a dozen or so customers, in from the heat, no doubt. One man caught my attention immediately.

The man sat at a table in a dim corner. He was young, but thin and haggard. His face had pockmarks and his empty eye sockets were covered only by shriveled eyelids. I couldn't help myself; I stared.

Scottie came out of his office, saw me staring, came over, and whispered: "That's Blind Johnny Swift."

"Oh," I responded, and turned toward Scottie with a questioning look. I had not met Johnny before, even during the days of Louisa's infatuation.

"I let him sit at that corner table," continued Scottie. He then shook his head, and continued: "My bartender has instructions to give him a couple of free drinks and to let him sit."

I watched Johnny for a few moments in silence. He faced a nearby window; it was if the sunlight through the window gave him pleasure. As Scottie and I were whispering, Johnny cocked his head a little; I could tell that he heard us.

Scottie's voice interrupted my thoughts. "I owe him that much at least; he was blinded in my Lyford roadhouse."

"Does he have money?" I whispered. "Where does he live?"

"He gets a small allowance from the county," replied Scottie. "I think he lives in a squatter's shack by the city dump, but I'm not sure." Scottie shook his head again; his face had a sad expression. "At least in here, Johnny is out of the weather." Scottie then motioned toward his office and said: "Come on in, we can settle up our accounts."

We went into Scottie's office and sat down. Scottie droned on about business, but I hardly heard what he was saying. I couldn't help but think about Blind Johnny. Finally, I had an idea.

I turned to Scottie and blurted out: "Do you think Johnny could work for us?"

Scottie was caught in mid-sentence on an entirely different subject: "Who? What?" he stuttered.

I let my thoughts run to a logical conclusion, and then said: "I understand that blind people have an acute sense of hearing."

"Yes, so?" replied Scottie.

"Johnny can listen to bar talk for us," I responded. "We can get names, gossip and insight from and about people who come into this place."

I looked intently at Scottie for a long moment. Scottie's brow furrowed, then the light came on. His face brightened and he smiled.

"I see," Scottie replied: "Intelligence and insurance!" He paused as his mind worked it out. "We will have a pulse on the community; we will find out the goings on around town." He then smiled broadly and said: "Good idea!"

Scottie leaned back in his chair. "We could pay him a little, see that he gets fed, and I also have a small room upstairs where he could stay."

I smiled. Scottie tries to be a hard-nosed businessman, but he's really an old softie.

"Better than a shack on the dump; he'll be safer here," I replied.

Scottie then looked closely at me and said: "With regard to Johnny, let's do a fifty-fifty cost share." He harrumphed and tried to look businesslike.

I smiled and said: "Of course." I then continued: "Now we have to convince Johnny."

"Let's call him in and ask him," responded Scottie.

Soon it was done. Johnny came in; hat in hand, moving his cane about, touching walls, the doorway, and so on. Scottie and I explained our proposition. Johnny understood; there was nothing wrong with his mind. We watched as tears came to his empty eye sockets as he realized that he could be useful again. I must admit that tears came to my eyes too, and I think Scottie felt the same.

Johnny began work immediately. The three of us went out to the bar area, and Scottie turned him over to Jim, the bartender, with a complete explanation. Jim caught on, and said: "Johnny, I'm going to have a lunch break, would you join me?" Soon all was settled, and Scottie and I returned to his office.

After we were seated, I looked long at Scottie.

Scottie eyed me cautiously. "OK, Caroline; What else?"

"Your water closet has a transom," I stated, as I pointed to the door to the water closet across from his desk.

"Yes, so?" replied Scottie.

I think photos of your payoffs to certain politicians would be good insurance," I stated. "Young Frank Gardner is very good with a camera, and your water closet would be a perfect hide."

Scottie caught on instantly. However, this time he frowned and said: "Yes, but I would be in the photos, handing over money."

"True," I replied," but so what? You are being shaken down by local strong-arm politicians." I paused a moment, then continued: "You run a speakeasy and a brothel, Scottie, both of which are illegal."

Scottie's frown lessened a little; then he brightened. "Far worse for the upstanding sheriff, the city policeman and the mayor," he said with a grin; "and others," he added.

Scottie's last statement was a revelation. I knew about Big Bill and Sam the cop, and I suspected Fat Benny. Who are the others?

11

BLACKMAIL

Sunday evening, July 12, 1925

Frank is the perfect snoop. He looks innocent, moves quietly and acts in an unobtrusive, efficient manner. He is also an excellent photographer. He understands lighting; he knows how to "frame" a photo, and when appropriate, he includes items of known measurement in photos to provide scale.

This morning, with Scottie's permission, Frank and I scouted out the speakeasy on North Main Street. We need to understand the layout so Frank can take photos of persons of interest with regard to our investigations.

Note to myself: Blackmail? Careful Caroline, the objective is to gather incriminating evidence with regard to the murders of Alec and Ogle, remember? Oh, well.

The front door of Scottie's North Main Street speakeasy opens to a beautifully decorated main salon. The salon can easily accommodate forty people. Customers see two rows of four tables per row; each table with four chairs. The tables are spaced along the left side of the salon. On the right, a long bar with a dozen stools stretches from the front to the back of the room. The space behind the bar has plenty of room for a bartender, glasses, liquor bottles and beer taps. A large, ornate mirror lines the wall behind the bar, which makes the already spacious room look even larger.

The back of the salon has a partition wall that stretches from the bar on the right more than halfway across the room. A small, backlit stage rests against the partition wall at its left end, and a space between the stage and the bar provides room for a five or six person band.

Scottie told me that during his remodeling, he added materials to deaden the sound of the band. Outside the speakeasy, little sound can be heard. No noise, no neighbor complaints, no reason for police visits. Wow!

Customers can walk around the left end of the partition wall and turn right into a long hallway. Five doors exit off the hallway. The first door on the left provides an entrance to Scottie's plush office. On the right, the second door provides access to the space behind the bar. The next two doors, also on the right, provide entrances to the ladies' and gentlemen's' restrooms. The fifth door exits the building at the end of the hallway.

Scottie's office has a desk and chair in the center at the back of the office, a small bar and liquor cabinet along the back wall to the right of the desk and a private "water closet" restroom along the left wall to the side of the desk.

I had scouted out the private restroom on an earlier visit; it provides a perfect "hide" for Frank and his camera. Frank plans to use a short step ladder to see out the transom above the restroom door into Scottie's office. A linen closet inside the restroom has enough space to hide the ladder. Frank will have to find a way to mask the sound of the click of the camera when he takes photos, but this should not be an insurmountable problem. Perhaps an electric fan in the office will do the trick; we'll work this out later.

Wednesday, August 5

Frank and I met with Scottie this morning in his office. Scottie was full of enthusiasm. Business was good, his upscale speakeasy customers loved the North Side gang's Canadian whiskey, and the local moonshine controlled by the Capone gang provided a titillating experience, never mind its nefarious source and contents. Scottie also gets pretty good beer from the Capone gang; I'm not sure where it's made; probably it's from Chicago. In sum, Scottie has full service for every thirsty, otherwise law-abiding citizen with money to spend. What a business!

Scottie escorted Frank and me into his office, with obvious pride. Soon we were seated. Scottie relaxed in his big leather chair behind his desk, and Frank and I sat in comfortable chairs in front.

"So, Caroline, what do you have in mind for young Frank?' Scottie began, with a smile and a wink at Frank, who grinned in response.

"Well, we need photos of you with the mayor, the sheriff and Sam the cop," I replied. I collected my thoughts, and then added: "Can you put the cash in an envelope and hand the envelope to each during their respective visits?"

"Yes, I can do that," replied Scottie. "I get the point; you want two photos of each transaction, one showing the cash going into the envelope and the other showing the envelope being handed to each of our local esteemed officials."

I nodded in response, then said: "Right; we need to know when each of the three plans to visit, so Frank can be set up in your water closet, ready for action."

"Well," said Scottie, "all three usually stop by on Friday afternoons just before we open for business." He paused a moment, thinking, then added: "They usually arrive at separate times, with no particular schedule."

I nodded and waited for Scottie, as he leaned back in his chair. I could tell he was reviewing past visits in his mind.

Finally, Scottie continued. "They come into my office separately; I think they each don't want the other two to know how much he is getting. They usually lounge about together in the bar area for drinks after their separate transactions with me." He smiled broadly, and added: "You know, free Canadian whiskey."

I thought a moment, and then asked: "Since I'm now a junior partner, how much are we paying these turkeys?"

Scottie laughed, and replied: "More than I would like, but we really have no choice if we want to stay in business. Fat Benny gets two hundred a week; Big Bill gets one-fifty, and Sam, the little turkey, gets fifty." He paused, and then added: "Their free bar tab, combined, runs about thirty to forty bucks a week."

Frank whistled softly, and said: "Even at cost, that's a lot of booze."

Scottie and I both looked at Frank with appreciation; for a fifteen-year-old, the boy had excellent business sense.

"OK, Frank, tell us your plan for snooping," I said with a smile. I was not in the least condescending, I really wanted to know. Scottie also looked at Frank, waiting.

Frank took a deep breath, let it out, and then replied: "I can be here Friday about noon, enter the back door, and set up with a ladder in the water closet." He paused, thinking, and then added: "Sir," he began, as he looked at Scottie, "please make sure lights in your office shine from the water closet side toward your desk." He looked at me and said: "I will use the Leica; it has 35 millimeter film, and I can take photos quickly. The downside is that it requires good lighting." He looked back to Scottie for emphasis.

Scottie and I nodded, and then Scottie said: "I'll have a ladder for you in the linen closet inside the water closet on Friday. The lights won't be a problem; there is a tall standing lamp in each corner on the water closet side."

"One other thing," said Frank with a grin, and he looked at Scottie; "please put an "out of order" sign on the door to the water closet; I don't want one of our turkeys opening the door and knocking me off the ladder."

Scottie and I both laughed. "Done!" replied Scottie

"Are we all set?" I said.

Frank nodded, and Scottie rose from his seat. After appropriate goodbyes, our little meeting ended. We're ready to catch, on film, three upstanding turkeys taking bribes!

Thursday, August 6

I visited the speakeasy again early this morning; I wanted to work out a plan with Johnny, our blind investigator.

Johnny was waiting for me in the main salon; I had left word with Scottie yesterday. Johnny's appearance had changed dramatically since our first meeting. He wore a nice suit and tie and his shoes were polished. His damaged face was clean-shaven, and he looked well-fed. "This is Scottie's doing, I thought to myself: "the old softie."

Johnny's face brightened as I arrived around the corner of the partition; I had entered through the back door. "Good morning Miss Caroline," said Johnny, as I moved past the partition. Johnny rose from his seat at the back corner table.

"Good morning Johnny," I responded. "How did you know it was me?"

"Footsteps," he replied. "I have memorized the sound of your footsteps."

"What a unique talent," I said, with genuine surprise. I thought a moment as I walked to his table, pulled out a chair and sat down. "Do you know the sounds of the footsteps of others?"

"Oh yes," replied Johnny, as he took his seat. "I know the footsteps, voices and preferred seating of nearly everyone who visits here. If I concentrate, I can also keep track of where certain people are, by name, in the room."

"Wow!" I replied. "That's impressive!" I thought a moment, and then added: "I would like for you to take notes on certain individuals and keep a record for me; can you do that?"

"Yes, of course," responded Johnny. "Do you want anyone in particular?"

"Yes," I said. "I would like a record of the visits and any useful conversations of the mayor, the sheriff, Sam the cop and any members of the Capone and the O'Banion gangs." I thought a moment, and then added: "And anyone else who, in your opinion, merits my attention."

Johnny gave a low whistle. "OK," he responded. "My writing may be a little shaky, but I can do it."

"Johnny, you've just earned a raise," I said. "How does four dollars an hour sound, for every hour you work? Of course, you also get a room upstairs and meals." I paused, and then tried to sound stern: "I expect a written report every Wednesday when I visit Scottie and keep a record of your time. Susie can help you with the writing."

Johnny smiled with obvious pleasure and said: "Yes Miss Caroline, I'll be on time with my reports, and you won't be sorry you hired me."

After some additional pleasantries, I left. Johnny remained at his table. I had a lump in my throat; I couldn't help it.

"So that's settled," I told myself. "It's just good business."

Wednesday, August 12

Wow! What a day last Friday! According to Johnny and Jim, the bartender, Fat Benny arrived at the speakeasy first, just after lunch. Right on que, the big oaf walked through the front door as if he owned the place.

"Good day, gentlemen," he said to Johnny and Jim. Both Johnny and Jim responded with a polite: "Good afternoon, Mayor." Jim added: "Scottie's in his office."

"Yes, yes, replied Benny, as he waddled across the room, around the partition corner, and according to Johnny, six steps to Scottie's office door. Without knocking, he opened the door and made his grand entrance.

Scottie was waiting, cash on his desk. Frank was also waiting, but of course, Benny didn't know this. Cash was transferred, photos were taken, and the mission with regard to Fat Benny was accomplished.

After a few minutes, Benny appeared from behind the partition, waddled to a central table and sat down in a creaking chair. He motioned to Jim and said: "The usual, please, my good man." Jim complied, and soon Benny was sipping his good Canadian whiskey.

Sam, the little turkey, arrived next, also through the front door. Sam said "Hello," and glanced furtively around the room.

Johnny and Jim responded with: "Hello, Sam." Fat Benny merely nodded; Sam was beneath his continued notice, and he took another sip of whiskey.

Sam disappeared around the corner of the partition and six steps later, knocked on Scottie's door. Soon his business with Scottie was finished and Frank had his photos.

While Sam was in Scottie's office, two unscheduled visitors arrived. Carlo and Louie walked in the front door. The pair stepped up to the bar and Louie said to Jim: "We want to see Scottie." He paused and then added: "Is he in?" Carlo just glared.

"Yes, replied Jim, and his voice quavered a little. "He's with someone at the moment."

Fat Benny tried to carry the situation in his usual bluff and hearty way. "Good day, gentlemen."

"Mayor," responded Louie, with a nod. Carlo just looked at Benny with a steady gaze for a moment, and then turned away.

"Harrumph," uttered Benny, and sipped his whiskey.

"We'll wait," growled Carlo, to no one in particular. The pair sat down at a table next to Johnny, where they could see the front door and part way down the hallway behind the partition.

Scottie was soon finished with Sam. Frank was also finished with Sam; second mission accomplished.

According to Johnny and Jim, Sam walked back around the partition into the salon, saw Carlo and Louie at their table, turned around, and headed back down the hallway, twenty-two steps to and then out the back door.

Big Bill arrived next. He entered the front door, glanced around and greeted the occupants. "Hello, boys," he said.

Jim and Johnny both responded with "Hello Sheriff." The others in the room said nothing.

Bill walked directly across the room, around the partition, and to Scottie's office door. Carlo and Louie waited at their table; apparently they did not want to interfere with Bill.

Bill finished his business with Scottie in a few minutes. Frank got his photos. Bill left Scottie's office, walked around the partition, sauntered over to the center of the salon and joined Benny at his table. Jim brought over a large tumbler of Canadian whiskey.

Carlo and Louie got up and walked around the partition. This time, Johnny heard a knock on Scottie's door.

"Yes, yes," Johnny heard Scottie say. "Who is it?" The door clicked and opened.

At the same time, Johnny heard Carlo's voice. "It's Carlo," was the reply. The door closed and clicked.

After the door closed, Johnny heard muffled voices. Scottie's sound proofing was working, so the voices had to be loud.

Frank was still in the water closet. He supplemented Johnny's account with details of the conversation. He also took four photos.

According to Frank, Scottie began the conversation. "What can I do for you gentlemen?

Louie got right to the point. "Where do you get your Canadian whiskey?"

Frank peered over the transom. He saw Scottie standing behind his desk. Louie was standing in front. Carlo was by the liquor cabinet with a bottle in his hand. He was reading the label.

"Yes, well, I get it from a local man," Scottie replied. "I'm not certain where he gets it."

Louie and Carlo could easily discern that Scottie' voice was apprehensive; they also knew that Scottie wasn't telling the whole story.

"If we could supply the good stuff, would you buy it?" said Louie.

"Yes, I might; I'm a businessman," replied Scottie. "I pay five dollars a bottle."

"Our price is higher," growled Carlo; "but it would be in your interest to buy from us." The implied threat in his voice was sinister and very clear.

Unfortunately, Scottie bristled. "I don't like your tone," he said. "Now get out!"

"Sure, sure," responded Louie. "By the way, we'll make a delivery tomorrow. How many cases do you need?"

"Get out!" Scottie replied loudly.

Carlo put the bottle he was holding on Scottie's desk. The pair then turned, and without another word, walked out Scottie's door, around the partition, through the main salon and out the front door.

As Carlo and Louie walked out the front door, an angry Scottie came out of his office. He walked directly over to Fat Benny and Big Bill.

According to Johnny, Scottie said: "That pair just threatened me over my source of Canadian whiskey."

Benny harrumphed and said nothing.

Bill replied: "So?"

Scottie was fuming. "Perhaps others in this town would like to know about our business," he said loudly. "I have evidence!"

Later, Jim told Johnny that Benny's face turned white as a sheet. Bill's face turned an angry red.

Bill stood and towered over Scottie. "You better keep your "evidence" to yourself and your mouth shut, Scottie," Bill growled.

Scottie did not back down, which was very unwise.

Bill shoved Scottie down into a chair, grasped his shirt front and tie with his huge right hand and pulled tight. He then said: "Understand?"

At that point, Benny said: "Now Sheriff, I'm sure we can work this out." He leaned back and added: "I'm sure Scottie won't do anything rash, right Scottie?"

Bill released Scottie and stepped back, glowering.

Scottie's anger had turned to fear as he gasped for air. Reason had returned, and according to Jim, he seemed to realize that he was in over his head.

"Yes," he finally uttered: "nothing rash." He then got up, turned and went back to his office. Big Bill and Fat Benny glanced at each other and then finished their drinks in a quick gulp. Benny stood, and he and Bill walked out the front door.

As I write this, I am deeply concerned. I must talk to Hannibal. Where is he anyway?

12

BACK ON TRACK

Saturday, August 15, 1925

Frank returned to school in Indianapolis; I will miss him. He promised to return in May.

Sunday evening, August 16

Hannibal stopped by my home just off South Main Street this morning, about eleven o'clock. I was so glad to see him! Clara made some coffee and Sandy had just finished baking some cinnamon rolls. Emily and Maria busied themselves, picking up the place. Soon they were done, and the girls discretely found other things to do.

Hannibal and I were left to ourselves, at the kitchen table, with coffee and cinnamon rolls. Hannibal eyed me over the rim of his coffee cup as he sipped and waited; he could see, no doubt, that I was fairly bursting with news.

"I'm so worried about Scottie," I began. Soon the whole story of recent events at Scottie's speakeasy poured out. Hannibal listened and nodded occasionally, but he didn't say a word. Finally, I finished, almost out of breath.

Hannibal put down his coffee cup and looked out the large kitchen window for what seemed like forever. A robin perched in the little cherry tree just outside; we could hear him chirping away.

Finally, I said: "Well?"

Hannibal returned from his reverie and looked at me with his steady, blue-eyed gaze. "I think we should develop Frank's photos and read Johnny's notes," he stated matter-of-factly. "Let's also talk to Scottie and Jim; I want to get fingerprints from glasses and bottles handled by Benny, Bill, Carlo and, if possible, Louie." He paused for a few seconds. "We may have to wait for a future visit, but Jim is the key, if he's willing."

Hannibal took another sip of coffee, and then continued: "My lab friends can compare these prints to the prints from the murder weapon used on Alec." He paused again, took another sip, and added: "With Jim's help, we will build a file, or "data base," to use a new term, of fingerprints for future reference."

I sat with my mouth open for a full minute. Hannibal's logic was impeccable, and he had a plan. "I'm so glad you're back," I finally responded.

Hannibal smiled and said: "By the way, next summer, Frank will move in with me. I've already talked to his father, and got his permission." He paused and then said: "I encouraged Frank to do well in school this winter, and I think he will."

"Oh, Hannibal, that's wonderful!" I replied. "I have been so worried about Frank living at some remote camp on the river."

Hannibal smiled and then said: "I plan to re-model the empty third bedroom for Frank. I will also re-model the bathroom and add a bathtub, shower, sink and toilet. A septic tank will be buried out back, near the alley." He grinned and added: "By Christmas, we will no longer have to use the old privy by the alley."

"Very modern," I replied. "I understand that the town will soon have a new sewer system, and everyone who can afford it will be hooked up."

"Times change," stated Hannibal. "But we have work to do. Can you explain to Scottie and Jim what we need with regard to fingerprints?"

"Yes, I will meet with Scottie on Wednesday anyway, and I'm sure we can get bottles and glasses for your lab guys."

Hannibal nodded, finished his coffee, and left.

I watched him as he walked down the street toward his house. He whistled as he walked. "So much I don't know about that man," I mused.

Wednesday evening, August 19

Scottie and I had our usual meeting this morning. Once I explained the fingerprint idea, he was quite pleased. He clearly holds grudges against Fat Benny, Big Bill and the gangsters from Chicago. I cautioned Scottie to be discrete.

"Yes, yes," he said. "I will make sure Jim understands; he's very smooth with all our guests."

I also said: "please, Scottie, keep your mouth shut." Scottie huffed a little, but he got the point, I hope.

Jim was brought into the office, and we worked out the details. Each Wednesday, I would get a box of assorted bottles and glasses, each labeled with the name of the user. I will deliver the box to Hannibal the next day. The River Rat Detective Agency is on the job!

Friday evening, Christmas Day, 1925

Hannibal had my girls and me over to his house on Christmas morning. We asked Louisa and Tony, of course, but they were spending Christmas with Tony's folks. Good for them!

As we entered the front door, we saw that Hannibal had been busy. In addition to a wreath on the door, he had a decorated tree, and candles glowed on side tables. Coffee and tea in silver pots and little holiday cookies on silver trays rested next to the candles. He had placed cups and napkins next to the cookies. We could see the dining room table; it was set with beautiful china, silverware and glassware. White linen napkins were folded and laid under two forks on the left of each place setting. The centerpiece on the table was made of evergreen and red ribbon, with two red candles. A glance into the kitchen showed us a large turkey in a pan and lots of veggies, potatoes, rolls, and pies, all in various stages of preparation. The kitchen stove radiated heat, ready and waiting for action.

"Hannibal, what a lovely setting!" I exclaimed. The girls all made similar comments. Hannibal assisted as many of us as he could with our coats, gloves and so on. Soon everything was put away, and we all sat on soft chairs and the sofa near the tree. Suzie and Emily served cookies, coffee and tea.

Hannibal had gifts for everyone. Each of my eight girls got beautiful pearl earrings set in gold. Each had a different design, and each was in a little box wrapped in silver-colored paper. Expensive! Hannibal was shy, and he blushed rosy pink, as the girls oohed and aahed over their gifts. None of my girls had ever received such a gift before.

For me, Hannibal had a very large box, all wrapped in gold paper with a red ribbon. I soon made a mess with the paper, just like a big kid.

It was a white mink cape in the latest style. "Oh Hannibal, it's wonderful!" I exclaimed. I stood and hugged and then kissed him, this time on the lips. Hannibal responded; he put his arms around me and gently massaged my shoulders.

Suddenly, Hannibal realized he had an audience. Eight girls were watching, each with a smile as big as a crescent moon. He put his hands up and away; palms open, and stepped back. His face turned beet red. "Oh," he said, "I'm glad you like it." He shuffled his feet a little as he glanced around at the girls.

Everyone, including me, burst out laughing; we couldn't help it. I could tell my girls were happy with the growing fondness between Hannibal and me. Yet there was more; Hannibal was a man so different than the others we dealt with every day. He was, in every sense, a gentleman. What a wonderful experience!

I reached out to Hannibal and hugged him again, with my head against his chest. "Hannibal," I said, "You are the nicest man I have ever known." I meant every word.

"Yes, well," he responded. "You ladies are family." His eyes had a misty look; I could tell that emotions were churning inside him. After a few seconds, he regained his composure.

The girls and I also had a gift for Hannibal. He got a smoking jacket, all the way from Chicago. We insisted that he model it for us. He did, with a big grin, blushing all the while. How handsome!

After a merry hour or so, the girls and I fixed dinner. During and after dinner, I took pictures of everyone at the table and by the Christmas tree, and they all laughed as I fiddled and fussed with Hannibal's Leica camera. We had a wonderful time. Merry Christmas!

Sunday morning, December 27

I am alone in the kitchen with my coffee; the girls are still asleep.

I can't help but reflect on the wonderful Christmas day the girls and I had at Hannibal's home. He obviously wanted to please us; and he certainly succeeded. His home is beautiful, and he clearly knows about style and genteel entertaining. Money seems to be absolutely no problem. Yet he has sadness sometimes, as if old memories are touched when we girls are with him. I want to know more; I want to assuage that sadness and make it better. Is this love? I don't know.

Friday evening, January 1, 1926

We had a busy night on New Year's Eve, as expected. My head hurts. Scottie's speakeasy and roadhouse and my Victorian had full complements of happy, carousing and usually drunk men and not a few liberated women.

Fat Benny and Big Bill showed up at the Victorian. Benny was drunk as a skunk, as usual. Bill was still working on it. Benny passed out in the men's room, and it took my bartender and three customers to haul his big butt out the door and into his Packard. Bill, only half-drunk, got in the car with Benny and drove. I can only guess what happened after that. I managed to collect the glasses Benny and Bill used: lots of fingerprints.

I hope Scottie and Jim collected fingerprints and Johnny wrote down snippets of conversation from Carlo, Louie and any other Chicago gangsters; I'll find out next Wednesday.

Wednesday evening, January 6

Good news from Scottie today, we now have bottles and glasses with fingerprints of both Carlo and Louie. Johnny also gave a report; Carlo and especially Louie had discussed "the boss."

Apparently a local person manages all of Capone's affairs in the Wabash Valley. The obvious question is who? No answers yet, but based on hints in Carlo's and Louie's conversation, Big Bill and even Fat Benny acknowledge the authority of, to use their term, "the boss."

On a more immediate note, Scottie is buying his Canadian whiskey from both Capone and the North Side Gang. Capone, through the local person called "the boss," and eventually through Carlo, charges double the North side gang's price. However, Scottie really has no choice. So far, demand has been high enough to satisfy both suppliers. Scottie sends my share for the Victorian every Friday, a whopping three cases of 12 bottles per case!

Friday evening, January 8

I sent Susie and Emily over to Hannibal's house with two boxes of empty bottles and glasses. When we get a report back from the lab, we might know who handled Alec's murder weapon. In any case, we have expanded our data base of fingerprints.

Wednesday evening, January 13

Scottie and I had our usual meeting this morning. Business is great, and the money flows in.

I have continued to invest my profits in conservative stocks and bonds through the bank. I may follow up on my idea of investing in local businesses; I just found out from a client that a car dealership in Terre Haute wants to expand. I will check it out.

I have assigned Susie the task of organizing and editing Johnny's notes. She has become a very efficient secretary. I may train her to keep my financial books; accounting is such a pain. However, if I give her a new job, I will have to hire another girl for the roadhouse. Personnel decisions, decisions: oh well.

So far, our crime data collection activities remain a secret known only to insiders. None of our suspects, gangsters or locals, know about the fingerprints and our other evidence. If any of them find out, we will be in extreme danger. Keep your mouth shut, Scottie!

Of course, Fat Benny and Big Bill know we have photos of them taken during their indiscretions with my girls. The unspoken agreement between us is that Scottie and I continue to operate without interference from local authorities; otherwise the photos will be leaked. I think the photos also keep Benny and Bill under some control with their demands for protection money. As far as I can tell, Benny and Bill know nothing about our photos of their extortion of money from Scottie.

Monday evening, February 15

Hannibal stopped by the house yesterday with a big box of chocolates. The girls got most of them, I got two. However, he also brought me a little rosewood jewelry box. It's beautiful. I kissed him again, this time without the girls watching. He responded tenderly, and then left. Where is this going?

Sunday evening, February 21

Hannibal stopped by this morning for coffee and to give me big news.

After we were seated at the kitchen table, he said: "The lab was able to match the fingerprints on a glass used by Carlo to the fingerprints on the pipe used to murder Alec." He paused, and then added: "Also, the blood type on the pipe matches the blood type from the ceiling in Alec's shack and the blood type from Alec's body."

"That's the confirmation we've been waiting for, I responded. "Our photos show that the pipe could have made the wound on Alec's head."

"Yes," responded Hannibal. "Other photos show drag marks from the shack to the river and two sets of male footprints." After a brief pause, he added: The photos of one set of crime scene footprints match the photos of footprints and shoes worn by Louie at the gas station. The other set matches Carlos' shoes."

"We have enough evidence to confirm our suspicions," I agreed. "Carlo and Louie murdered Alec."

"We also know that Big Bill the sheriff and Eben Speakwright the medical examiner produced a death report that called Alec's death an accident," replied Hannibal. "At best, their report shows negligence and at worst, a cover-up."

I nodded. "Going to the local police is not an option," I stated matter-of-factly. "For many reasons," I added.

Hannibal was quiet for a long while. Finally, he said: "Keep the evidence, photos and reports in a safe place for now."

"I know just the place," I agreed; "my safe deposit box at the bank."

Hannibal nodded, and then said: "Times will change, and perhaps we can eventually bring Carlo and Louie to justice."

"Yes, and in the meantime, we still have to solve the Ogle's murder," I replied.

Hannibal nodded, and smiled grimly. "The lab guys are looking carefully at all of the photos of the crime scene, the tire tracks, the footprints and the car. They are also looking at the photos and the samples I took at the gas station."

He then stood up, drained his coffee cup, said his goodbyes, and left. We didn't kiss; somehow a show of affection didn't seem appropriate. I watched Hannibal walk down the street toward his home from my window.

Sunday evening, March 7

Hannibal stopped by my house this morning, just as I finished perking a pot of coffee. The girls were still asleep. "Perfect timing, as usual," I said to myself as I padded over to the door in my slippers.

Hannibal smiled as I opened the door. He held up a large manila envelope for me to see. "We have new information," he said.

After we moved into the kitchen, poured coffee and found some cinnamon rolls left from Saturday, we spread the contents of the envelope out on the table.

Hannibal's face expressed satisfaction. "We now have enough evidence about Ogle," he began. He pointed to the photos. "Remember these? I took them with your camera nearly four years ago." He paused a moment and then continued: "The lab guys have just made some enhancements."

I looked at the photos. I could tell that they were of a car, but some of the images had been cropped and expanded. The expanded images were less sharp, but they focused attention on important details Instead of the whole car, some showed only the back seat. Others showed only the tires. One showed the running board below the back door on the driver's side.

Hannibal explained: "Look closely at the back seat in this photo," and he pointed.

I looked and saw two small holes in the fabric in the center of the seat back. The holes were surrounded by a dark stain. "Bullet holes and a blood stain?" I queried.

Hannibal nodded and replied: "Of course, the photo is black and white, not color, but yes, the two holes are consistent with holes made by bullets, and the dark stain is consistent with a blood stain."

"But there are other plausible explanations," I responded.

Hannibal's face expressed a grim smile. "Yes, but I have something else." He pointed to the photo that showed the running board. "See that spot?"

I looked closely. I could see a smear that could have been blood. I looked up at Hannibal; I'm sure my eyes expressed the obvious question.

"Yes, it's blood," Hannibal stated. "I used a clean piece of your blotting paper and swiped a sample, remember?" He paused, and then added: "the blood type matches the blood type of the sample you got from Ogle's body."

My mind raced. "We already know that the tire treads on that car match the tread marks on the road where we found Ogle's body," I stated. After another moment, I added: "The evidence places Ogle in the center of the back seat of the car, where he was shot twice in the chest. The bullets passed through into the seat back."

Hannibal nodded, and said: "We also have Carlo's footprints at the scene of the crime and we have one other set of footprints that until now have not been matched, remember?"

"Yes," I replied. "What have you got?"

Hannibal leaned back in his chair and took another sip of coffee. I waited and fidgeted. Hannibal just grinned.

"Well?" I finally said.

"We have a match," Hannibal replied. "Remember the photos you took of Bill and Benny on New Year's Eve, 1922?"

I thought a moment, and then replied: "So?"

Hannibal grinned. "In addition to Bill, caught indisposed, your photo shows his boots." Hannibal pointed to two other photos.

I looked. My mouth opened, then closed, then I uttered: "Wow!" One photo showed Bill on the bed, naked as a jay bird, and his boots on the floor. The right boot was lying on its side. The sole had a diagonal mark, just like the second photo, which showed a set of boot prints next to Ogle's body.

Hannibal waited a moment, and then said: "Carlo and Bill were in the back seat with Ogle in the middle." He paused, and then added: "Louie was probably the driver, but he didn't get out of the car; his footprints were not at the crime scene." Another pause, and then Hannibal concluded: "Bill or Carlo shot Ogle while in the back seat of the car, and then the pair got out with Ogle's body between them. They dragged it a few feet off the road, where you found it."

I nodded, and then asked: Does the lab report document the evidence shown by the photos?"

"Yes," replied Hannibal. "Carlo and Bill definitely murdered Ogle and a third person, probably Louie, drove the car."

Nearly four years have passed," I mused, "but now we know." I reached back in my memory. "We also strongly suspect that Ogle was buried in a grave with Emily Blackburn in Riverside Cemetery the week after his murder."

"That's true," replied Hannibal. "My conversations with his next door landlord and a search of Ogle's possessions in his small rented house provided no record, verbal or on paper, of his birth or anything else." He paused, and then added: "His boats and other possessions just disappeared in the weeks after his death."

"It is as if Ogle had never existed," I said, with a catch in my voice, "and we can't bring the killers to justice."

"Not yet," Hannibal responded grimly.

Hannibal finished his coffee and picked up our cups and the dishes from our cinnamon rolls. He walked over to the kitchen sink, got out some soap powder and a towel, and washed and dried our cups and dishes.

I watched with amusement. "Very domestic," I said to myself. "He would make a great husband." After a moment, my thoughts added: "Careful Caroline!"

When Hannibal finished with the dishes, he turned to me and said: "Keep all this in your safe place," as he pointed to the photos and papers on the table. He then walked over, kissed me lightly on the cheek, picked up his coat and hat and walked out the kitchen door.

I heard a sound behind me, and turned. Clara, Sandy, Emily and Maria were peeking in the kitchen doorway that led back to the rest of the house.

"Nosy!" I stated sternly. The four girls all giggled.

13

GHOSTS FROM THE PAST

Sunday morning, May 23, 1926

Frank stopped by the house yesterday. School is out in Indianapolis. Frank is 16 now, and my girls all think he is a very handsome young man. So do I, for that matter.

I gave the girls stern looks, which said: "hands off!" Frank grinned with all the attention. He didn't blush, very different then Hannibal!

Frank still has his boat. He plans to keep it on the river near Alec's old shack. Adventure is still on his mind; I could see it in his eyes.

During coffee around the kitchen table, I told Frank about our solution to the murders of Alec and Ogle. It was a somber conversation.

Frank listened, and then had one question: "What can we do about Carlo, Louie and the sheriff?"

"Nothing at the moment," I replied. "But I will keep our evidence and written analysis in a safe place."

Frank nodded, he understood. He finished his coffee, got up, and boldly said goodbye to Clara, Sandy, Emily and Maria. The girls all giggled. I gave them another stern look. They stopped giggling.

Frank glanced at me; then back to the girls. He gave a sigh, looked back to me, and said: "Thank you for the coffee, ma'am." He turned and backed up all the way to the kitchen door. I got up and followed him.

"Goodbye, Frank," I said again in a formal tone.

Frank fumbled with the door, opened it, and left. As soon as the door closed, all four girls started giggling again. I could hear Frank whistling as he walked down the street.

"I'm so glad he's staying with Hannibal," I thought to myself.

Sunday morning, June 6

Business remains steady. Scottie has managed to stay out of trouble, and Frank has busied himself setting and running trotlines on the river. He has done quite well; he sells his catch to Bob Stultz's fish market, just a few blocks from his small boat dock.

Hannibal was kind enough to drive me to Terre Haute last Thursday and Friday. I am now thirty percent owner in a Ford dealership. Hannibal helped me with the paperwork, the banker, and the majority stockholders, who are all members of the wealthy Conklin family.

Dividend income from my shares will amount to about twenty five to thirty thousand per year: a tidy sum. Prospects for the future are good; people want and can afford cars. As a major shareholder, I also sit on the board of directors. Quite a change! I am beginning to like this legitimate entrepreneur role.

Sunday morning, July 25

Hannibal remains mysterious. He was out of town for three weeks in early July. Where does he go?

Saturday evening, August 14

Frank has finished up his fishing enterprise for the summer, and he turned a tidy profit. Hannibal and I both encouraged him to do well in his junior year in school. Hannibal also mentioned college, but Frank, I think, has other ideas. He mentioned his elderly Uncle Jim and Aunt Mary, who own a large farm south of Terre Haute. Frank the farmer? We'll see; the boy has time to decide.

Sunday morning, September 5

Clara and Emily came down with the grip last week. Hannibal calls it influenza, or the flu. At Hannibal's insistence, old Doc Loving stopped by the house on Friday. Hannibal's face showed grave concern. According to Doc Loving, many folks in town are sick.

Saturday evening, September 18th: Maribel and Kathy have also come down with the flu. Susie, Kitty, Maria, Sandy and I are staying home; nursing has become a full time affair. Business has stopped. I closed the Victorian. Hannibal has been a lifesaver; he buys groceries, does laundry, watches over the Victorian and sits with the sick girls.

Scottie's customers have dwindled to a handful. There are no parties. Even the booze trade has slowed to a fraction of what it was during high summer. People are frightened; I can see it in the faces of my neighbors.

Sunday morning, October 3

According to the newspapers, the sickness has spread to many cities and towns. Several editors have compared the epidemic to the outbreak in 1918, just at the end of the war.

Hannibal, Susie and I remain healthy, but very tired. Sandy, Kitty and Maria have joined Clara, Emily, Maribel and Kathy on the sick list.

Saturday evening, October 9

Doc Loving stopped by both of my houses this morning on his way to County Hospital. Clara and Emily seem a little better, but they still cough a lot. Sandy, Maria, Kathy, Kitty, Maribel and now Susie are ill. Chills, severe headaches, back pain, sore throats, fever, and vomiting, in varying degrees, affect all six girls.

During his visit, Doc Loving swabbed out throats with iodine. He also recommended bed rest and cool bathing to mitigate high fevers. He gave me an oral thermometer and taught me how to use it.

Before he left, Doc Loving turned to Hannibal and me and said: "Keep them warm, feed them hot tea, mild soup or broth, crackers and fruit juices if they can keep it down. Give them salt water to gargle, and then a teaspoon of whiskey. Also, make sure they drink lots of water; we don't want them to dehydrate." He showed Hannibal and me how to judge dehydration by pinching a person's skin and checking the rebound.

"Yes Doctor," I replied. "Anything else?"

"Yes," he said. "Keep the house clean as you can, wash their clothes, bedding and especially handkerchiefs. Use very hot water and soap." He paused a moment, looked at me closely and then added: "You and Hannibal need to get some rest if you can."

Hannibal looked at Doc Loving with his steady gaze and asked: "Is this influenza outbreak as bad as 1918?"

Doc Loving returned Hannibal's look and said: "You remember 1918?"

Hannibal nodded. I could see grimness in his expression like I had not seen before. Doc Loving's expression matched Hannibal's.

The Doc packed up his bag, put on his coat and hat and headed toward the front door. As he stepped out, he said: "I suggest that one of you stay in each house." He looked first at me and then at Hannibal and added: "Good luck." Without another word, he turned, walked to his car and then drove off in the direction of the hospital.

Hannibal looked at me and said: "I will stay with Susie, Kitty, Maribel and Kathy during the day; you stay here with Clara, Emily, Sandy and Maria."

"OK," I replied. I placed my hand on Hannibal's arm. "Thank you."

Hannibal smiled and nodded; no other words were needed.

Sunday morning, October 17

This week has been horrible. The girls are all gravely ill. I think Susie and Kitty have pneumonia.

Hannibal has been tireless. He does the washing and drying of clothes, bed sheets, blankets and so on. He goes shopping for groceries. He keeps both houses spotlessly clean. When he is not with the girls next door, he relieves me in my house so I can rest. We prepare meals together. He goes home every evening late and returns early each morning. I have never known a man who cared so much. I think he is driven by something; his eyes show it. Why?

Wednesday evening, October 20

The crisis has passed. All eight girls are on the mend. Susie, Clara and Emily are well enough to help with the chores.

Hannibal and I are exhausted. He left early this afternoon. Before he left, we had coffee in my kitchen.

"I will go home and rest for a while," Hannibal said. "You should do the same." He suppressed a cough and cleared his throat. His face was ashen gray. "Susie, Emily and Clara can take over." He smiled, but his face was strained.

"Yes," I replied. "Thank you, Hannibal; I don't know what else to say."

Hannibal smiled again, drained his cup, stood up from the table and walked to the door. I watched as he quietly closed the door. He didn't whistle as he walked away, and I heard him cough again.

Saturday evening, October 30

Our two households are back to normal. On Wednesday, I met with Scottie. On Thursday I slept all day. On Friday, I felt better, so I re-opened the Victorian. Business is slow, but recovering. The worst of the sickness has passed.

According to the newspaper, the influenza was not as bad as 1918. I'm glad, but whatever the experts call it, I do not want another such experience.

Where is Hannibal? I haven't seen him since he left my house on Wednesday October 20th. I will check on him first thing in the morning.

Sunday evening, November 7

The past week has been another nightmare. I thought I was going to lose Hannibal.

The nightmare started when I walked over to Hannibal's house in the morning on Sunday, October 31st. I knocked on the front door, and there was no answer. The door was unlocked, so I opened it. The house was cold.

"Hannibal?" I said softly as I entered. There was no answer. "Hannibal?"

I walked quietly to the master bedroom. I could see Hannibal in bed, wrapped in several blankets. I could hear his choked, rasping breathing.

"Oh, Hannibal!" I exclaimed.

His response was a muffled groan. A half-empty glass of water rested on the night stand. The floor next to the bed was covered with used tissues and handkerchiefs.

I walked over to Hannibal's bedside and pulled back the covers from his face. I put my hand on his forehead; he was burning with fever. His eyes were closed; he was semi-conscious. He started coughing, a dry, rasping cough. I pinched the skin on his forearm; it remained depressed. "Fever, pneumonia and dehydration," I concluded.

I spent the next hour getting fluids into Hannibal, first water and then hot tea from the kitchen, where I got a fire going in the stove. I cleaned up the mess around the bed.

When water in the kettle on the kitchen stove was hot, I filled a basin with a lukewarm water mix, got some soap, stripped Hannibal and gave him a cool bath while he lay on his bed. I found some clean pajamas in a dresser drawer and got him dressed. I changed the bedsheets and blankets by moving him to one side and then the other.

I finally had him cleaned up and propped up on pillows. His breathing was easier, but he was still semi-conscious.

I then went to the other two stoves in the house cleaned out the ashes and built fires. The house began to warm.

"Time to get Doc Loving," I thought. After a last glance around, I quickly walked out the front door and closed it. The County Hospital was across the street.

I went immediately to the receptionist, explained the situation, and asked for Doc Loving. Fortunately, he was in, making rounds. He sent word that he would meet me at Hannibal's in about an hour. What a good and caring man! I hurried across the street to Hannibal's house.

Good as his word, Doc Loving knocked on Hannibal's door about an hour later. I let him in, and we went into Hannibal's bedroom.

After a thorough examination, Doc Loving swabbed Hannibal's throat with iodine and tenderly covered him up to his chin. He looked at me with a thoughtful expression and said: "I see you have cleaned Hannibal up and provided fresh bed clothes." He smiled briefly and then continued in a soft, re-assuring voice: "Can you stay with him?"

"Yes, of course," I replied. "I will first go home, which is about three blocks away and get more help."

"Fine, fine," responded the Doc. "Hannibal should be alright until you get back. I'll stay for a little while."

"Right," I said. I'll be back in fifteen or twenty minutes." I quickly walked to the living room, put on my coat, and hurried out the front door.

I half-ran to my house, alerted Clara and Emily, grabbed some supplies and half-ran back to Hannibal's house.

I opened the front door. Doc Loving was putting on his coat and hat. "I saw you coming," he said with a smile, and he pointed to the window.

"How much do I owe you, Doctor?" I said breathlessly.

Doc Loving smiled and said: "Oh, just a dollar." He paused a moment, and then added: "Take care of Hannibal."

"Of course," I responded. I fumbled in my purse, found a ten dollar bill, and handed it to Doc Loving.

"That's not necessary," Doc said, and his eyes twinkled.

"Please!" I replied.

Doc Loving took the ten and absently stuffed it his coat pocket.

"Alright," he said. "I'll come back and check on Hannibal in a few days when I visit the hospital across the street." He paused a moment, and then added: "He has pneumonia, and if his coughing or fever gets worse, contact me through the hospital immediately. Do you still have the thermometer?"

"Yes," I responded. "And I will have someone with Hannibal all the time until you say otherwise."

"Good, good," the Doc said, and he smiled absently, touched the brim of his hat, picked up his bag, and walked out the door. He passed Clara and Emily as they hurried up the sidewalk, arms full of stuff. Doc Loving touched his hat again as he passed by the two girls.

And so it was. We three girls set up shop in Frank's empty bedroom, and our vigil began.

On last Wednesday evening November 3rd, Hannibal was asleep. I had been at his bedside all afternoon. We three girls had managed to get the semi-conscious Hannibal to the bathroom a few times during the afternoon.

Clara and Emily had completed the washing, cleaned the house, and kept the fires going in the stoves. They fixed chicken soup with noodles, baked some bread, and they kept Hannibal and me supplied with hot tea, sandwiches, soup and crackers. They made up Frank's bed, made up the living room couch into a bed and generally fussed about. Hannibal was like an older brother that they never had.

My heart felt good; I was proud of my girls.

As the evening progressed, I checked Hannibal's temperature. He still had a fever, but his coughing had subsided. The constant soup, water and tea helped hydrate his body.

Clara and Emily came into the bedroom quietly about eight PM and stood by my chair. We three watched Hannibal's face for a few minutes.

I looked up at Clara and Emily and said: "I'll take the first watch. Will one of you relieve me at midnight?"

"I will," replied Clara.

"And I will take over first thing in the morning," said Emily.

"Good," I replied; please get some rest; it's been a busy day."

The girls left the room, and I was alone with Hannibal. The room was warm, but I could hear the wind outside, a low moaning sound.

Hannibal stirred in his sleep. First, he uttered a low moan, followed by words.

I listened carefully; Hannibal's words indicated another time and place.

"Mother, Mother, can you hear me?" Hannibal's voice was low and plaintive. "Elizabeth and Caroline are in bed like you, and we have two nurses."

There was a pause, and Hannibal stirred restlessly. "Father is here, can you see?" Hannibal's eyes opened, but I could tell his vision perceived a different scene. After a minute or so, his eyes closed.

The moaning of the wind outside increased. I turned and looked out the window. I could see snowflakes. A streetlight gleamed in swirling snow down the street, near the hospital.

I turned back to Hannibal. He stirred again and rose up from his pillows. His eyes opened again, but I could tell he didn't see me.

"Father, Father, they're all gone!" Hannibal's voice was anguished; I had never heard such pain in a voice before. He slowly lay back on his pillows. "Gone," he uttered again.

I reached out and caressed his forehead. It was dry and hot.

"Hannibal, Hannibal," I said softly. "Rest now, just rest."

My words seemed to have an effect. Hannibal coughed a little, and I gave him a sip of water. He began to breathe easier.

Sweat beaded on his forehead. I picked up a clean wash cloth from the nightstand, dampened it from a pitcher of cool water which also rested on the nightstand, and patted Hannibal's forehead and face.

Time passed, and Hannibal slept. Midnight arrived and Clara opened the door, right on time.

"How is he?" Clara whispered.

"Better," I replied. "He dreams and sometimes he talks, but his words are about his family." I paused a moment, and then added: "I think there were deaths."

"Oh no," Clara responded. Her face showed deep concern. "I often wondered about Hannibal's family, but he never spoke of them."

"Yes," I said. "He has kept his past secret from me too." I'm sure my expression said more than my words.

Clara sighed and said: "Get some rest Caroline, I'll stay with Hannibal."

I nodded, rose from the chair, and after a last look at Hannibal, I left the room. Emily was asleep on the couch; so I slept on the bed in Frank's room.

And so it continued. We each took our turn on watch, eight hours each, twenty-four hours a day, for the next three days. The three of us got Hannibal to the bathroom on a regular basis; his body functions were normal now.

The snow came down relentlessly. By the third day, the level ground had over two feet of snow, and there were deep drifts. Everyone stayed inside. Susie came over through the snow and told me that she had closed up the Victorian and everyone was at home. The town came to a standstill.

Doc Loving stopped by twice, walking up through the snow. Clara, Emily and I kept the stoves going, and the house was warm. Hannibal consumed only water, tea and crackers for three days. He drifted in and out of consciousness.

On the morning of the fourth day, I got up in Frank's bedroom. The house was completely quiet. I peeked into Hannibal's bedroom. He was asleep and so was Emily, in her chair. I went to the bathroom and cleaned up.

I then made breakfast for Clara, Emily and me, our eating had been hit and miss since we arrived. I made coffee, orange juice, scrambled eggs, sausage, pancakes and toast. I also re-built and stoked the fires in the three stoves and emptied the ashes.

After everything was ready, I tiptoed to Hannibal's bedroom and opened the door. Emily was still asleep in her chair, but Hannibal was awake.

"Good morning," I said softly.

Hannibal looked up, and Emily stirred.

"I'm awake," stuttered Emily, and she turned and gave me a confused look.

"I can see," I replied and smiled. I then looked closely at Hannibal as I walked across the room to his bedside.

"Good morning," I said again.

The old Hannibal looked back at me with his steady, blue-eyed gaze. He was weak to be sure, but he was awake and alert.

"You look terrible," I said with a smile.

"Hannibal smiled in return, coughed a little and replied: "Thanks."

"Breakfast is ready in the kitchen," I said. I looked at Hannibal closely, his face was thin. "Want some? I made coffee, orange juice, scrambled eggs, sausage, pancakes and toast. I also have tea and crackers."

"Yes, please," Hannibal responded. He paused a moment, and then added: "Just tea and toast for now."

"Breakfast sounds wonderful, Emily chimed in. "I'll fix a tray for you and Hannibal and bring it in." She rose from her seat and walked quickly through the doorway. I could hear her clattering about in the kitchen. Soon I heard both Emily and Clara talking.

After Emily disappeared through the doorway, I sat down in the chair next to Hannibal's bedside. He reached out his hand and I took it in both of my hands. I caressed his hand a little.

"How long?" Hannibal asked.

"Well, the girls and I came over on Sunday, October 31st and now it's Sunday November 14th," I replied. "Doc Loving came over twice."

"How are the other girls?" Hannibal asked.

I thought a moment before replying. It was so like Hannibal to ask about the girls.

"They're fine," I finally said, "thanks to you and Doc Loving." I paused a moment, squeezed his hand and then added: "You helped save them, Hannibal."

Hannibal's eyes grew moist. I could tell that his dreams were still fresh in his memory.

"You talked when you were dreaming," I said. "You mentioned your mother, father, Elizabeth and Caroline."

Hannibal sighed, and he choked a little. He looked out the window at the snow; a few flakes drifted by. I waited, stroking his hand.

After a few minutes, Hannibal said: "About this time in 1918, they all died." He paused, looked back at me, and tears trickled down his cheeks.

I waited. I couldn't speak anyway; there was a lump in my throat. I could tell that Hannibal's illness had weakened his usual reserve; he wanted to talk.

"I had just returned from the war," Hannibal began. "Old Sergeant Alec Feleovich and I had mustered out in November, just after the armistice." He paused, and then continued. "Sergeant Feleovich retired and headed home to Clinton; I went to Pittsburg."

"Pittsburg is your home?" I asked.

"Yes, it was," Hannibal replied. "I was looking forward to seeing my mother, father and sisters Elizabeth and Caroline." He looked at me with his steady gaze, except for the tears. "Caroline was more than your namesake," he added. "She was strong, like you."

I continued to stroke Hannibal's hand.

"Anyway, Mother, Caroline and Elizabeth were all sick with the influenza when I arrived home. Father had the best doctors in the city in attendance, and I hired two nurses, full time." He paused, choked again, and then added: "Elizabeth died first, then Caroline, and then Mother." Hannibal breathed a deep sigh, and said: "Father was last. He had the flu, but I think he died mostly of a broken heart."

Hannibal gave anguished sob, and then another. This lasted for several minutes, sob after sob. Tears streamed down his face.

I stroked Hannibal's hand and waited. Finally, the sobs ceased; it was like a catharsis. I reached over to the nightstand, found a clean handkerchief, and gave it to Hannibal. After a moment, he regained control.

"I took care of the funerals," Hannibal finally said. He then lay back on his pillows and closed his eyes. I continued to hold his hand, and he placed his other hand over mine.

I heard a knock on the door.

"Yes, you can come in," I said. Clara opened the door slowly. Emily stood behind her, with a tray.

"Want some?" Emily said, as she raised the tray up so Hannibal and I could see.

Hannibal opened his eyes and smiled. "Yes, please, he said softly, and coughed a little. "And thank you," he added; he looked first at Clara and Emily and then to me. He squeezed my hand gently.

After breakfast, Hannibal fell asleep. I could tell he was not dreaming again. He breathed quietly; the rasping sound from his lungs was gone. I felt his forehead; the fever was also gone. Emily returned and removed the tray.

I rose quietly, tucked up Hannibal's covers, kissed him on the forehead and left the room. He slept the rest of the day. Clara, Emily and I busied ourselves in the kitchen and elsewhere.

I returned to Hannibal's bedroom at about eight PM with a tray of hot tea and soup.

He was awake, and had obviously been up and around a little. He had washed up, combed his hair and shaved. He had on a clean set of pajamas. It was the old Hannibal, except that his face was thinner, and color had not yet returned to his cheeks.

"Missed you," said Hannibal, and he smiled.

I walked over to his bedside and sat down in the chair. I placed the tray where he could eat, which he did. I sipped my own tea and watched. Finally he finished the soup, lay back against his pillows, and sipped his tea.

I looked at him for a full minute. Finally, I ventured: "Tell me about Pittsburg."

Hannibal watched me over the rim of his cup, just like so many times before.

I waited and fidgeted a little. "Perhaps I'm too presumptuous," I thought to myself.

Finally, Hannibal said: "You have already deduced quite a bit." He paused a moment, and then continued. "Yes, my family is, or was, before their deaths, very wealthy. I am the last of my line."

"I'm so sorry about your family," I said, and I meant every word.

Hannibal nodded. "My father was an associate of Andrew Carnegie and a major stockholder in U.S. Steel, he replied. "I went to Harvard Law School, and I graduated in 1916. I started early, a bit of a child prodigy, I suppose. I was just twenty when the U.S. entered the war."

"You joined the Army?" I asked.

"Yes," he replied. He smiled wryly. "I know you saw my old uniform in the closet."

I fidgeted again, and tried not to blush. "He always knows," I thought to myself.

"Anyway, in France, I served as an intelligence officer," he continued. "Alec was my sergeant. He saved my life at Belleau Wood."

"You said you returned home after the armistice," I ventured. "Are you still with the Army?"

"Only on inactive reserve, that's why I keep the uniform," he replied. "I returned to Pittsburg in late November 1918. After my family died, I placed most of the family money in several trusts." He paused, and he coughed again. This time, phlegm came up, and he used a handkerchief.

"Your lungs are clearing," I said.

Hannibal nodded, and then continued. "I also have several business enterprises, which provide a substantial income." He grinned, and then added: "One is a forensic laboratory in Chicago."

I know my mouth opened wide in surprise. After a few seconds, I realized my expression, and closed my mouth. "You own the lab?" I finally uttered.

Hannibal chuckled a little. "Yes, and we have many contracts, including several with police departments, two with the federal government, and one with a large private detective agency."

He paused, as if reviewing company books in his head, and then continued. "At last count, the lab employs just over fifty people. My managers run the daily operations, but I make most of the strategic decisions."

I'm sure my mouth opened wide again. "Wow," I finally uttered.

Hannibal smiled, and then continued. "I also own a small medical device company and an import-export company that specializes in photographic equipment, including cameras."

My expression caused Hannibal to laugh, which caused him to cough again. After a few moments, he recovered.

I couldn't help myself, so I asked: "How much are you worth? Money-wise, I mean?"

Hannibal laughed again, this time without coughing. "Since you can find out or deduce it eventually, I may as well tell you." His eyes twinkled.

"OK, smarty, how much?" I responded. I blushed at my own impertinence, but waited for an answer anyway.

"Altogether, about one hundred million, not including trusts that finance charities," Hannibal replied.

"But you live so simply," I stated. "Why?"

"Yes, well, you have only seen my home in Clinton," he replied with a smile. He paused, and then added: "I like it here; I am intrigued by the detective work, especially after Alec." His smile disappeared. "Someday we will have justice," he added.

"I don't know what to say," I finally said.

"There is one other thing," responded Hannibal. He smiled again, and reached out his hand and touched my cheek. "I enjoy being with the girls and young Frank. Most importantly, I enjoy being with you."

14

KIDNAPPED

Sunday evening, May 15, 1927

Hannibal and I spend a lot of time together. For example, we go to Valenti's almost every Saturday evening for dinner. We often talk about the future, our likes and dislikes, our mutual fascination with detective work and so on. I'm still not sure where our relationship is going. We are both independent, affluent adults. Money is not an issue; each of us can afford a good standard of living. Hannibal is much further up the scale than me, but I'm certainly not dependent on anyone for my daily bread. Patience, Caroline!

Frank returned to town on Friday. He will be seventeen this summer. Of course, my girls fuss over him whenever they get the chance. Frank loves it; I need to keep a constant eye on that young man. Hannibal just laughs; no doubt he recalls his own misspent youth.

Susie runs day to day operations at the Victorian now. It has become a destination for men and liberated women for miles around. The bar in the main salon has become the focus of social activity; we have a small dance floor, and customers play records on my new Orthophonic Victrola. The "Charleston" is the latest dance craze. My girls spend their time as hostesses rather than with men in the upstairs rooms. I need to re-think my business plan.

Prohibition has fostered a huge underground economy. The local moonshiners produce for the Wabash Valley as well as export to the

Chicago market. Imports to the Valley include Canadian whiskey, scotch and gin. We also get rum from the Caribbean. Speakeasies abound. Highway 41 has become a regular booze highway between the Valley and Chicago. The thirst for alcoholic beverages seems insatiable.

The Capone-controlled gas station between the wagon and railroad bridges on the Parke County side of the Wabash is busier than ever. According to Scottie, convoys of two, three and sometimes four trucks head north toward Chicago twice a month. Smaller loads of Canadian and Caribbean imports come from Chicago on the return trip.

I don't know the Valley distribution point for Canadian whiskey from the Chicago North Side Gang, but I'm pretty sure it comes from Chicago to Indianapolis. A portion then goes along the old National Road from Indianapolis to Terre Haute and then to retail outlets like Scottie's and mine. The National Road is now called U.S. Highway 40.

Lonely stretches of both Highway 40 and 41 are perfect for rival Gang hijackings and gunfights. Rumor has it that several have occurred.

So far, only one gunfight, the one that blinded Johnny Swift, has occurred at Scottie's roadhouse in Lyford. Capone gang and North Side gang members often visit the bar before heading north to Chicago or south to Terre Haute. Maribel, Kitty and Kathy have often heard harsh words. I think it's just a matter of time before another violent confrontation.

Scottie and I have had several discussions about the danger to my girls. Lyford is an unincorporated crossroads town inhabited by coal miners. It is many miles from Rockville, the county seat. It is just too isolated.

Scottie pays attention to my concerns, since I now own a forty percent share in both the North Main speakeasy and the Lyford roadhouse. We get along great; the only two contentious issues are

Scottie's propensity to talk too much and the danger to my girls at the roadhouse.

Scottie is scrupulously honest with me. After salaries for my girls and other expenses, my share of the profit ranges between two and three thousand per month, on the average, with highs during holidays and lows in mid-summer.

Sunday evening, June 5

Edith, Scottie's wife, has taken over accounting for both the North Main Street speakeasy and the Lyford roadhouse. She participates in our Wednesday meetings. She's a sharp gal, with a good eye for financial detail. However, Edith occasionally has an edge to her voice. Her eyes sometimes have a glint that hints at a carefully masked side to her personality. I'm not sure what my perceptions will mean in the future, but I keep my guard up, and I choose my words carefully in our conversations. It is strictly business between us, but I have no reason to complain.

Saturday evening, July 2

I had rotary dial telephones installed at all of my business locations and my two resident houses last week. The new rotary dial phones don't require an operator for local calls, just for long distance. From my home, I can contact my girls at the other house, Scottie's office at the North Main Street speakeasy, the bar at the Lyford roadhouse and the main salon at the Victorian. I can also call long distance to the car dealership in Terre Haute to discuss my investment, car sales, and so forth, and also my broker at the local bank.

Hannibal has had a phone for quite a while. We talk on the phone often, arranging dates and so on. The unspoken understanding between us is that I will always call him for emergencies.

Perhaps I will invest in a telephone company. Phone service is the coming thing. I did a little research, and American Telephone and

Telegraph Company sounds like a good long term bet. I will follow up with my broker at the bank.

The kitchen table at my residence serves as an impromptu office, with a phone, filing cabinet and small writing desk. I need a separate office!

Wednesday evening, July 13

According to Scottie, Anna, Fat Benny's socialite wife, showed up at his North Main Street speakeasy on Saturday night. What a surprise! Maybe she wants to keep a closer eye on her boozing and philandering husband. In any case, she showed up with Benny about eight o'clock in a very modern shear black dress with diamonds a-glitter. She had a gin and tonic, listened to the music and left, with a subdued Fat Benny in tow, after about an hour.

Sunday morning, July 17

My bartender drove me home from the Victorian at about six PM Friday evening. The sun was low on the horizon, and the weather was cool. The breeze came from the west. "Rain later," I thought to myself. "The Victorian is in good hands," my thoughts continued, as I opened the back door to the kitchen. "Susie will manage just fine without me tonight."

I walked into the kitchen and turned on the lights. The stove was warm, so I built up the fire and put on a tea kettle. "Hot tea and maybe a quick sandwich, and then I'll work on accounts," I mused. I sat down at the table and stretched out my legs.

The phone rang. "Now what?" I muttered. I got up and walked over to the phone on the little writing desk by the hallway door.

It was Maribel at the roadhouse. "Oh Caroline," her voice wailed. "Kitty and Kathy have been kidnapped! People have been shot! There's blood everywhere!"

"Calm down, Maribel," I replied, as I tried to keep my own voice under control. "Are you hurt?"

"No," responded Maribel. Her voice was still shaky, but I could tell she was trying to regain her composure. "But four men grabbed Kitty and Kathy, used them as shields, and ran out the door after the shooting."

There was a pause, and I could hear shouting in the background over the phone.

"Maribel?" I asked.

"Yes, I'm here," her voice came back on line. "Kitty and Kathy were not hurt, I think, but they were dragged out the door, and I heard a car take off."

"Listen carefully, Maribel," I said. "Find a safe place, lock yourself in if you can, and stay there." I paused; my mind raced. "I will call Hannibal, and we will be there as soon as we can. Understand?"

There was silence on the phone for a few moments; I imagined that Maribel was thinking. "Maribel?" I finally said.

"Yes, Caroline," Maribel responded. "Hannibal will come?"

"I will call him immediately," I replied. "If he isn't home, I will find someone." I paused again and took a deep breath. "You be safe, Maribel," I said. "Can you do that?"

"Yes, I can," Maribel replied. "I'll go now."

"Goodbye, Maribel," I said, and hung up the phone. I knew Hannibal's number by heart. "Please be home," I muttered as I dialed his number.

Three rings and then a familiar voice answered. "Jones," said Hannibal.

I quickly explained Maribel's call.

"I'll be there in five minutes," said Hannibal. "Frank will be with me." The phone clicked.

I thought quickly. "Rescue mission," I said to myself. "Dress appropriately and take a weapon."

I ran to my bedroom. I emerged just as Hannibal's car clattered to a stop in the driveway. The engine remained running.

I wore loose fitting black slacks, a dark blouse, a short jacket and sensible, laced walking shoes. I also had a loaded snub-nosed revolver that I kept for just such emergencies. "Now is the time," I thought to myself. "My girls have been kidnapped by killers." I hadn't taken it out for years, but I remembered how to use it. I put the revolver in one jacket pocket and a handful of extra shells in the other.

I ran through the kitchen door and out to the car. Hannibal was driving, and Frank leaned out from the backseat window. Both faces were grim.

"Ready?" said Hannibal, as I clambered into the front passenger seat. I glanced to my left at Hannibal, then back to Frank in the rear. "Let's go," I said. My voice sounded harsh; anger was beginning to build. I felt my face flush.

"Twenty minutes and we will be at the roadhouse," said Hannibal, as he backed up the car, turned on to the street, and headed toward the wagon bridge that crossed the river a few blocks away.

"We will probably get there before the Parke County sheriff," said Hannibal, as he turned the car left on Main Street and headed north. "The sheriff is based in Rockville, and assuming someone called him about five minutes before you called me, he will not arrive at the roadhouse for another forty-five to fifty minutes." He paused, looked directly into my eyes, and added: "We'll be on our own."

"Understand," I replied. I touched my revolver in my jacket pocket for reassurance. I thought a moment and then said: "Maribel said that four men took Kitty and Kathy."

"Yes, but more may be with them by now," Frank replied from the back seat. "We need a plan."

Hannibal nodded and said: "If the gangsters with our girls headed north, we might look for fresh car tracks at the left-hand turn-off toward the river bottom lands, just north of Lyford." He paused a moment, and then added: "It's a dirt road, and there are several farm worker camps, barns and other utility buildings along that road as it approaches the levee along the river."

"Why wouldn't they continue north on Highway 41 toward Chicago?" I asked.

"Highway 41 goes toward Rockville," Hannibal replied. "They would know that the Parke County Sheriff will be coming from that direction."

"What about the right turn north of Lyford toward Greencastle?" asked Frank.

I could see that Hannibal was thinking through the possibility. "No," he finally said, "not likely, that road passes a church, a cemetery and several farmhouses. Greencastle also has a small police force, and the sheriff will have certainly notified them by phone of the Lyford shooting."

The car raced to the wagon bridge. As we crossed, I asked: "What if they head south toward Terre Haute?"

"It's possible," replied Hannibal. "However, there are no turn-offs toward the river, and Twelve Points is only about a dozen miles south on Highway 41 from Lyford." He paused, and then added: "Terre Haute has a large police force, and the Vigo County sheriff and the police would have already been notified by the Parke County Sheriff."

"Would the Parke County Sheriff notify Big Bill in Vermillion County?" I asked.

"Probably," Hannibal agreed. "However, the gangsters almost surely would not head toward Clinton. Even if they did, we would have seen them by now, this is the only road from Lyford."

I summarized the logic of our conversation. "The key question then, is whether they headed north or south on Highway 41, with north being the most likely." I paused, and then added: "We will find out when we reach the roadhouse."

"Yes," replied Frank. "I think they will go to ground quickly and hide. The remote buildings in the river bottom lands north and west of Lyford are the most likely destinations."

Our car raced past the gas station between the wagon and railroad bridges, under the railroad overpass, and along the great curve toward Lyford. The sun was low in the sky, and clouds were building behind us to the west.

Hannibal broke the silence in our conversation. "This shooting was a fight between rival gangs. Capone's people and the Chicago North Side Gang are at war over the booze business."

Frank and I both nodded in response.

Hannibal paused and then added: "The other question is: Why the girls? Were they just convenient shields, or do the gangsters think the girls might know something about the opposition?"

My mind raced. "If the girls were just shields, the gangsters will probably kill them and leave," I said, and I know my voice quavered.

"Kitty and Kathy are streetwise," Hannibal said reassuringly. "They might be able to con their kidnappers to stay alive."

"Yes," responded Frank. "Kitty and Kathy both told me that I am the cat's meow, and that shows reasonable intelligence." He paused and grinned. "They'll know what to do."

I laughed a little, I couldn't help it. I knew Frank made his joke to ease the tension and give me hope. "Thank you, Frank," I responded. I laughed again.

Soon the roadhouse came into view. Hannibal pulled into the parking area, stopped the car and pulled out his watch. "Six-thirty," he said; "Frank, see what you can find out inside, I'll do the same outside." He looked at me. "Find Maribel," he added.

"Right," I replied. Frank and I piled out of the car and headed inside. Hannibal walked toward a small group of men standing by parked cars next to ours.

Soon we three returned to the car. Only about five minutes had passed.

"Are you going to stay with Maribel?" asked Hannibal as I approached the passenger side of the car. I gave him a look. "I didn't think so," Hannibal added with a grin.

"North," said Frank.

"I got the same information," responded Hannibal.

We raced north on Highway 41. Five minutes later, we reached the left turn toward the river bottom lands.

"No sign of the sheriff," I said as I looked north along the highway.

Hannibal stopped the car at the turn-off. I got out and looked in the dirt of the road.

"Fresh tire tracks," I shouted over the sound of the car engine, and piled back into the car. Hannibal turned the car left on the dirt road and we bounced along. We moved slower now, the road was rutted and very bumpy.

"What's next?" I asked over the sound of the bouncing car.

"Reach under the seat," Hannibal replied.

I did, and found a 1911 Colt forty-five automatic and Hannibal's old binoculars. I pulled them out and laid them on the seat between us.

"Careful, it's loaded," Hannibal cautioned.

"I have a switch blade knife and a lead-filled sap," Frank volunteered.

"And I have this," I said, as I pulled out my revolver and laid it on the seat next to the Colt.

Hannibal glanced at the revolver as we bounced along. "Smith and Wesson," he said. "Good choice." He grinned at me.

"According to the men in the parking lot, four gangsters have the two girls," stated Hannibal. "There might be more at their hideout."

We bumped along slowly. The fresh tire marks were clear in the road ahead.

"I know this area," said Frank. "The levee is about a mile ahead, near the river. My old camp on the river was just over the levee, straight ahead." He pointed forward for emphasis.

"Good," replied Hannibal. "I know the general layout, but I don't know the exact location of the field worker camps."

"I do," stated Frank with a confident tone. The nearest camp is about a half mile ahead, in a grove of trees." He paused and then added: "A hay barn is on the right, just ahead; we can hide the car there."

"Field workers won't be at the camps," I said. "The crops are laid by, and harvest won't be until fall."

"Agree," replied Hannibal. "When we get to the barn, we can look ahead to the camps." He patted the binoculars on the seat.

"Lights will come on soon, if anyone is there," I responded.

Hannibal pulled the car in behind the barn. We couldn't see the nearest camp from the ground level, so Hannibal motioned that we should climb up into the hayloft. Just before we climbed up, Hannibal picked something up from a shadowy corner. I couldn't see it clearly, I was busy climbing.

We could see the camp clearly through the open hayloft door. We were careful to sit back in the shadows so we couldn't be seen from the camp. Two cars were parked near the main camp building.

Hannibal had his binoculars. We took turns looking through them. The wait wasn't long; the sun gradually set behind the levee. Clouds gathered and blackened the sky.

"Rain, soon," I stated.

"That's good for us," replied Hannibal. "Cover," he added.

A dim light flickered through a window in the main camp building.

"I think we have found our gangsters," stated Frank. "With two cars, there are probably more than four of them."

"Yes," responded Hannibal. "We need to draw them out, one by one."

I could tell that Hannibal was planning his attack. "An experienced military man," I mused to myself. My confidence grew.

The wind picked up a little, and rain began to patter on the tin roof of our barn.

Hannibal leaned back in the hay. I could see he that he was working out details. He also reached down by his side and picked up the item he had found below before we climbed up. He showed it to Frank and me. It was an old axe handle, about three feet long.

Hannibal grinned as he showed us the axe handle. "Nothing like a good piece of hickory," he stated.

Frank nodded. "And I have this," as he pulled out the sap from his rear pocket.

Hannibal looked at Frank and nodded. He then looked at me and stated: "The objective is to rescue Kathy and Kitty. We have to assume that they are still alive."

I gulped a little, and nodded. I pushed the alternatives out of my mind.

"We also want to avoid getting hurt ourselves," Hannibal added. He looked at me with his steady gaze.

"As best that I can remember, there are two doors to the main building, one in front and the other at the back," stated Frank. "We can see the only two windows on either side of the front door."

I gave Frank a questioning look.

Frank understood. "I walked through the place last year when I was still delivering Canadian whiskey." He grinned for emphasis.

"Good," responded Hannibal. "Caroline, can you get to the back door?"

I nodded, and replied: "Yes, I'll use that fencerow and trees for cover." I pointed to the fencerow and trees between the barn and the camp buildings. I could also see several units of farm machinery between the fencerow and the building. "Additional cover," I thought to myself.

Hannibal nodded as he looked toward where I pointed. He then said: "Frank and I will draw attention at the front. Hopefully, you can get to the girls. If you can't, run back to this barn and wait."

"I'll go for the girls; you take care of the opposition," I stated, as I tried to exude a confidence that didn't really exist inside.

"Right," responded Hannibal. "Get in, and then get out with the girls."

"Take this; the gangsters may have tied up the girls," said Frank, as he offered me his switchblade.

"Thanks," I said. I took the knife and shoved it in my jacket pocket. "A knife and a gun," I thought to myself. "I'm as prepared as I can be."

"We'll have to work out details on the fly, since we don't know the exact location or condition of the girls, and we are not sure how many gangsters are in the building," stated Hannibal. "Again, if anything goes wrong, our rendezvous point is this barn, understood?"

Frank and I both stated, almost in unison: "Understood."

"OK, let's go," said Hannibal. "Caroline, I'll give you ten minutes to get to the back door. You will hear a commotion at the front. That will be your signal to go in." He then rose up from the hay and clambered down the ladder from the loft. I followed, and Frank brought up the rear.

The rain picked up, thunder rolled, and lightning flashed as we moved together toward the camp. "Perfect cover," I thought to myself.

We soon separated. Hannibal and Frank moved stealthily through bushes and tall grass toward the front of the main building. I headed toward the fencerow and the back.

As I approached the fencerow, I crouched down and slipped behind the fence and farm equipment. I saw an old singletree next to a horse-drawn wagon, and I picked it up. "Nice club," I thought, "as good as an axe handle."

I approached the back of the building in the rain. Sure enough, it had a back door, and no one was visible outside. In less than two minutes, I slipped up to the door. The door had no latch or lock, simply an old doorknob. I turned it slowly, opened the door and peeked into the shadowy interior.

The room was long, about forty feet. At the back near my door, I could see Kitty and Kathy; they were sitting on two old chairs. Both were bound with cords, hand and foot. A tall figure stood next to them, facing toward the front of the room. I also saw three other men at a table near the front door. A kerosene lamp on the table provided the only light. Another man stood next to one of the windows, peering out into the rainy night.

As I watched, the lookout by the window stepped outside the front door and closed it.

"Five," I muttered to myself. "One outside and four inside." I eased the door shut. "Wait for a commotion," I remembered Hannibal's words. "OK, Caroline, be patient," I thought to myself.

The wait was not long, but it seemed forever.

I heard a car start over the sound of the rain. I then heard a car horn: "Ahooogah!" screeched out into the night.

"Hannibal," I thought. "It has to be you!"

I heard one of the men at the table shout: "Max, what are you doing?" He got up and walked to the front door. The man near the girls also reacted. "What the hell?" I heard him say as he stared toward the front of the room.

Two men got up from the table and stepped out the front door. "Two left inside, I muttered. "Time for action, Caroline."

I opened the back door again. One of the two men still inside peered out the front window. The other remained near the girls. I slipped inside, singletree in hand. Kitty saw me, and nudged Kathy. Both girls stared at me with wide eyes.

Bang! It was a gunshot. Bang! Bang! Two more.

The two men remaining inside drew guns as I moved quickly toward Kitty and Kathy. "Jack, get out there!" shouted the one near the girls. Jack slipped over next to the door, gun ready. The remaining man near the girls stared toward the front door, which was now open.

I slipped up behind the man by the girls. I raised the singletree high over my head as I moved forward. The man must have sensed my approach and started to turn. I didn't hesitate. I swung the singletree down with a bone-crunching blow. The man dropped like a stone.

I let go of my singletree and pulled out my revolver. The man at the front door turned, and his mouth dropped wide open.

Bang! Another gunshot from outside in front. The man by the door turned the other way and looked outside again. His back was toward me.

"Not enough time," I muttered, as I raised my revolver, aimed at the man's head, and fired. Bang! The man screamed and fell through the doorway.

I shoved the gun in one jacket pocket and pulled the switchblade from the other as I approached Kitty and Kathy. I crouched down behind the chairs, pushed the button on the switchblade, and a very sharp-looking blade flicked out. I soon sawed through the cords holding Kitty's wrists.

"Here!" I said to Kitty. I handed her the switchblade and turned toward the front of the room. I pulled out my revolver again. This time I held it with both hands and aimed toward the door.

A face appeared in the doorway. It was Hannibal. "Careful!" He said in a clear voice, and grinned at me.

I let the air escape from my lungs; I had been holding my breath for I didn't know how long. I gave several gasps as I breathed in and out. I lowered my gun. My legs grew weak, and I sat down on the floor. "Wow!" I gasped.

Hannibal approached. "Are you alright?" he asked; his face showed grave concern.

I nodded. "Help me up," I finally uttered. He did, and I stood. I was a little shaky, but my composure gradually returned.

Kitty and Kathy were soon free. Except for angry-looking rope burns, they were not harmed.

"Oh, Caroline!" exclaimed Kitty. Kathy just stared, wonder in her eyes.

After a few moments, Hannibal said: "It's OK, Frank is outside, and the gangsters have been taken care of."

"Dead?' I asked. The gravity of the situation was beginning to dawn in my mind.

"No," replied Hannibal. "But I can see you tried your best." He looked at me with his steady gaze and grinned. "Good job."

The man that I hit with the singletree groaned on the floor. Hannibal reached down, closed a strong hand on the man's collar, and dragged him across the floor to the front door. "Coming out, Frank," he said in a loud voice.

Without further ado, Hannibal held the man's collar in one hand, used the other to grab his belt, and tossed him out the front door. We all heard a thump and another groan.

We three girls joined Hannibal at the front door. We all stared outside. The rain was beginning to subside, only sprinkles now came down. The wind had stopped. We heard the drip-dripping of water from the eaves of the building and the trees.

The man Hannibal had tossed out the door lay directly in front, face down in the mud. His arms and legs moved slowly, and he continued to let out occasional groans.

Frank was there, slightly to one side, sitting on the back of one of the gangsters. The man was face down in the mud. The seat of his pants had a dark stain.

Frank saw my stare. He grinned and said: "You got him in the butt. Good shot!"

"I was aiming for his head," I muttered aloud. Hannibal and Frank chuckled. Kitty and Kathy said "Oh!" almost in unison.

"The other three are over by the cars," stated Hannibal in a matter-of-fact manner. "They will have sore heads, but they're alive."

"The shots?" I asked.

"All theirs," said Hannibal. He paused, and then added: "The gangsters aren't very good shots, no training."

"How?" I asked, and my mouth remained open for a few seconds before I thought to close it.

"Oh, a little applied hickory and a good lead-filled sap," replied Hannibal with a smile. Frank got one, and I got the other two."

Hannibal and I both looked around. Nothing moved in the darkness. The only sounds were the drip-drip of water from the eaves of the building and the trees, punctuated by occasional groans from our former opponents.

After a moment, Hannibal said: "Caroline, can you get the girls back to the barn? Frank and I will finish up here."

"Yes, of course," I replied. "What are you going to do?"

"I'll fill you in later with an after-action report," Hannibal responded, and smiled. "Don't worry, it will be OK."

I nodded and then turned to Kitty and Kathy. "Can you walk?" I asked.

"Yes," they both responded.

"OK, let's go," I replied, and I turned toward the barn in the distance.

After a long, stumbling walk in the dark, we made it to the barn. We were all soaking wet from the rain and its aftermath of wet grass and bushes.

It seemed like forever, but I suppose it was only about thirty minutes. Hannibal and Frank appeared out of the dark. Frank was carrying a large leather briefcase, which he took directly to the car. I watched as he shoved it under the front seat.

Frank noticed my stare and said: "We'll tell you later." He grinned from ear to ear.

"Let's get back to my house, I'll fill you in on the way," said Hannibal with a twinkle in his eyes. "I think you'll like my after-action report."

I was too tired to listen to Hannibal or Frank. The evening's action was overwhelming, both physically and emotionally.

"Just a summary please," I replied. "I don't want gory details."

Hannibal chuckled. "There are no gory details," he responded. "No one died, at least at our hands." He looked at me closely. I could tell he understood. "Later will be fine," he added.

I remained silent for quite a while. I was wet and cold, and I shivered. Hannibal noticed and put his jacket around my shoulders. Frank gave his jacket to Kitty and Kathy, and they huddled together inside the jacket. We three girls piled in the back seat. Hannibal and Frank got in front. Soon we bounced along the dirt road toward Highway 41.

We turned south on the highway. After about ten minutes, we drove up to the roadhouse. We saw the sheriff's car. Hannibal pulled his car over and stopped. He then got out and walked over to the sheriff, who was questioning a group just outside the roadhouse main door. We could see deputies inside through the open door. Maribel saw us from a window, and came out to the car. She got in with Frank, Kitty, Kathy and me.

After a few moments, the sheriff walked over to the car and looked in. He saw Kitty and Kathy in the back seat with Maribel and me. Hannibal walked up along side the sheriff and waited.

"Mr. Jones told me he found you two on the road north of town," said the sheriff. "Are you girls OK?" He stared intently at Kitty and Kathy.

Kitty and Kathy exchanged looks. I nudged Kitty in the ribs.

"Yes," responded Kitty. "It was just like Mr. Jones said." She paused a moment, gave the sheriff a pitiful look, sniffled a little and added: "Can we go home now?"

The sheriff melted a little and replied: "Yes, yes, of course." He looked back at Hannibal. "Will you take them home?"

"Yes, sheriff, be glad to," responded Hannibal in a quiet confident voice.

That was enough for the sheriff. He looked again at Kitty, Kathy, Maribel and me and said: "Take care, ladies." He touched his hat, turned and walked back to the other witnesses. I guessed what he was thinking. The kidnapped girls were safe and he had a murder inside to investigate.

I breathed a deep sigh of relief. "Thank goodness for Hannibal," I thought to myself.

Hannibal got in the car. Soon we were headed back toward Clinton and Hannibal's house, with a stop at my house on the way. We girls knew we could get warm baths and dry clothes. Afterwards, I would get a complete "after action report."

15

AFTER ACTION REPORT

Late Monday evening, July 18, 1927

What a day! As promised, Maribel, Kitty, Kathy and I got an after-action report from Hannibal and Frank. Their solution to the fight at the gangster's hideout was ingenious; more on that later. My primary concern is the safety of my girls.

So far, the girls at my Victorian and Scottie's North Main Street speakeasy are safe enough. Their roles are changing; they are becoming hostesses rather than "ladies of the evening."

Susie, Clara, and Emily left for work at the Victorian about noon today. Susie manages quite well. In addition to the two girls, she has the bartender, a cook and two housekeepers. She also manages several contractors for landscaping and maintenance.

Sandy and Maria work at Scottie's place on North Main from two until ten PM. Much like business at the Victorian, the girls at Scottie's place serve as hostesses to a mixed clientele of sophisticated men and liberated women. Good!

The problem is the Lyford roadhouse. Thanks to Hannibal and Frank, Kitty and Kathy were extremely lucky. Understandably, Maribel is a nervous wreck.

Late this afternoon, we got Hannibal's report. After a phone call to arrange a meeting, Maribel, Kitty, Kathy and I walked over to Hannibal's house about four PM. Hannibal and Frank were waiting. They had tea and hors d'oeuvres ready; they served them to us on fine china and silver trays. I could smell a roast cooking. A cook bustled about in the kitchen; we could see her through the doorway. What a change from the old days!

After we settled in with tea and so on, Hannibal began with details on the roadhouse shooting. Clearly, he had done his homework, and he presented his narrative in an objective, almost military manner.

"The fight at the roadhouse was between several Capone men and five members of the North Side gang," he began. "One North Side gangster was killed. Sam, our moonlighting local cop, was also killed; he was caught in the crossfire." He paused to let us absorb this news.

Kathy nodded; Hannibal's narrative was consistent with her recollections. "Sam shot the North Side guy," she said.

"Poor, Sam," I responded. "He was in over his head. Still, he tried."

Hannibal nodded and continued: "The four remaining North Side gangsters grabbed Kitty and Kathy, used them as shields and backed out the front door."

"Yes," responded Kitty. "Kathy and I had scrambled from tables where we were sitting with customers." Her face had a frightened look as she recalled events of that terrible night. "We were together in a corner near the front, and they grabbed us."

"I was upstairs," added Maribel. "I heard the shooting and ran to the top of the stairs; I could see everything."

Hannibal continued. "After the gangsters shoved Kitty and Kathy in a car outside, they roared off north toward their hideout in the bottom lands where we found them." One other gangster was waiting at the hideout with a second car."

"They pushed us to the floor in the back of the car," said Kathy. "We couldn't see."

I looked at the two girls and a lump formed in my throat. "How horrible!" My resolve hardened. "The girls will not go back to that roadhouse," I thought to myself.

"After we got to the hideout, two of the men tied us to chairs," said Kitty. Her hands were wringing as she sat in her chair. Fortunately, her tea was on a nearby end table.

I nodded; the image of the two tied, frightened girls at the hideout was seared in my memory. I reached over from my seat and patted Kitty's hands. After a moment, she calmed down.

Hannibal looked at me with his steady gaze. "You know the story from that point until you, Kitty and Kathy ran to the barn in the dark," he said.

"What happened after we left?" I asked the obvious question.

"Now the story gets interesting," piped up Frank, who had been sitting quietly in an easy chair, munching on a little biscuit sandwich. He had already consumed several.

The three girls and I looked at Frank in expectation. Hannibal smiled and nodded to Frank.

"We had four gangsters with sore heads and one with a bullet in his butt," Frank began with a grin. We tied them up with the cords you had left by the chairs," and he looked at me. "We were not gentle," he added.

I squirmed a little with Frank's reference to my marksmanship, but Kitty and Kathy both nodded. I could tell from their expressions that they took some satisfaction in Frank's words. "A little payback," I thought to myself.

"After the gangsters were secure back in the building, we searched the place," Frank continued. He then got up and walked to a nearby closet, opened it, and took out the briefcase that I had seen in Frank's hand when he returned to the barn that night. He brought the briefcase over and set it on the coffee table where all could see, and opened it.

Kitty, Kathy, Maribel and I all gasped. "Oh!" was our universal reaction. Frank grinned from ear to ear. Hannibal also had a smile on his face, and he folded his arms. The briefcase was full of money.

After a moment, I recovered. "How much?" I asked. After all, I am a practical woman.

Hannibal chuckled. He had expected no less from me, I'm sure. "We counted fifty thousand," he stated matter-of-factly. "All in one hundred-dollar bills."

The girls and I were stunned. Kitty's hands flew up to her face. Kathy exclaimed: "Oh my!" My mind raced.

Finally, I stated: "Since you didn't kill the gangsters, they know you have their money."

"Well, not exactly," replied Frank, and he paused for effect. "They think we are Capone men." He looked at me with a smile and added: "and ladies."

"That's right," added Hannibal. "After we got them into the main building and tied up, we had a long, rather one-sided conversation."

"A couple of the gangsters talked, and they revealed a great deal about their war with the Capone gang," said Frank. "The five men were all North Side Gang members, and four had just robbed a Capone convoy north on Highway 41."

"The four North Side gangsters stopped at the roadhouse earlier that afternoon," said Hannibal. "Apparently, they met a fellow gang member who planned to escort them to the hideout where they could lay low for a while."

"Unfortunately for them, Capone men followed them in, and the shootout happened," added Frank. "One of North Side gangsters was killed, along with Sam."

"The remaining three North Side gangsters and their local fellow gang member grabbed Kitty and Kathy and escaped," said Hannibal. He turned to Kitty and Kathy, and added: "You were just shields," he said. "They didn't think of you as being part of the Capone gang."

My mind raced. "Why didn't they kill Kitty and Kathy after they had escaped from the roadhouse?" I asked.

Kitty piped up. "I think it's because we convinced them that we knew about the Capone operations in the Valley," she said in a quiet voice. Her hands were no longer shaking.

Hannibal, Frank and I looked at the two girls in expectation.

"Yes," added Kathy. "One of the men, his name was Max, wanted to shoot us and be done with it just as soon as we got to the hideout."

"We were scared to death," said Kitty. "But I told Jack, who seemed to be in charge, that we had heard things while we worked at the roadhouse."

"Kitty said we knew where the roadhouse got their whiskey and gin," added Kathy. "Jack seemed interested."

"They were in the process of discussing us when you showed up," added Kathy. "First there was the noise out front, and then we saw you, Caroline, when you opened the back door."

"They expected Capone's men to show up," said Kitty. "The guy who maintained the hideout, his name was Smitty, I think, kept asking Max to keep close watch out front toward the road."

"Perfect for us," responded Hannibal. "After the rescue, it was relatively easy to convince them that we were Capone's people."

"I see," I responded. "The North Side gangsters had just robbed a Capone convoy; they got away with the briefcase full of money, and they were being chased by Capone's men."

"That's about it," replied Hannibal. "We told the gangsters at the hideout that they were left alive to carry a message." He paused for effect, and then added: "The message was: Tell your boss that the Valley belongs to Capone, and to stay out."

Frank added: "The North Side Gang thinks Capone's men recovered the money, and Capone's people think that the North Side robbers got away with it."

"Wow!" I exclaimed. I was joined in expressions of amazement from Kitty and Kathy.

After a few moments, Kitty asked the question that was on everyone's mind: "What do we do with the money?"

Hannibal laughed. "I have some ideas, but Caroline and I need to discuss it," he said. "Don't worry, I think everyone will be pleased."

Hannibal's response to Kitty was perfect. I added: "Let's enjoy dinner tonight, and Hannibal and I will talk later."

Nods and expressions of agreement came from Frank, Maribel, Kitty and Kathy. And so it was; the rest of the evening was spent consuming good food, a glass or two of wine, and pleasant conversation.

Sunday morning, July 24

Hannibal and I had a wonderful date last night. We had dinner at Valenti's. Tony and Louisa run it now, Mom and Pop Valenti are happy in their retirement. After dinner and a second glass of "grape juice," we discussed the money.

"Fifty thousand," I mused. "What shall we do with it?"

"First, we need to clean it," replied Hannibal. "We can't just deposit fifty thousand in one hundred-dollar bills in a bank." He paused a moment and then added: "Bankers and their friends, legitimate and otherwise, might get suspicious."

"I agree," I said. I understood the problem; much of my money had to be "cleaned" before it went into investments, checking accounts and cash spending money. "I've heard a new term for cleaning money; it's called "laundering." I laughed a little.

"Sounds good," replied Hannibal. "Anyway, if we break it up into increments of five thousand and put into various legitimate business accounts, yours and mine, the money will come out appropriately laundered."

"What's next?" I asked.

"Well, neither you nor I need the money," replied Hannibal. "I can think of some young people that could use a nest egg."

"Frank, Maribel, Kitty and Kathy," I responded.

"Exactly," replied Hannibal. "How much are you thinking for each?"

"Well, I don't want the three girls going back to the roadhouse, and I would like to see them out of their current occupation for good,"

I answered. I paused a moment, and gave Hannibal a questioning look. "How about ten thousand apiece for the girls? I think Frank has some ideas about his future, and twenty thousand would be a good start."

"Agreed," said Hannibal. "I was thinking the same thing." In turn, he gave me a questioning look. "Should we make sure the money is spent wisely?"

"Absolutely," I stated. "I will talk to the girls and guide them. Can you talk with Frank?"

"Yes," Hannibal responded. "He has talked about the farm that his elderly Uncle Jim and Aunt Mary own south of Terre Haute." He paused, and then added: "I think the farm is mortgaged and a young person is needed to make it profitable again."

"Will twenty thousand do it?" I asked.

"I think so," replied Hannibal. "According to Frank, the farm has over 320 acres. Over half of it is under cultivation." He paused a moment, and then added: Frank has also saved a substantial amount on his own."

"Frank the farmer," I laughed. "Quite a change!"

Hannibal chuckled. "Yes," he replied. "But I can tell from Frank's talk that the farm has special meaning to his family, and I think that's what he wants to do." He paused, and then added: "I can work with Frank's father on the money. I can make a good case that Frank earned the money working for me." He laughed a little. "In a very real sense, that is true."

"OK with me," I responded. "I will talk to my girls."

And so, it was settled. I will talk with the girls soon. In the meantime, let the money laundering begin!

Sunday morning, August 14

Frank left for Indianapolis yesterday. I shall miss him terribly. So will the girls and Hannibal. With the money he had saved and his share of the Capone loot, Frank will have twenty-five thousand dollars. Not bad for a seventeen-year old who wanted adventures on the river.

I think Frank will not be back next year. Our fellowship will continue with occasional visits, but we all know that he must move on. Oh, well.

I had long talks with Maribel, Kitty and Kathy. I had many questions about their plans and aspirations before committing the money that Hannibal and I had discussed.

Last Monday I talked with Maribel. At twenty-five, she is the oldest of the three. On Monday evening, we sat in the kitchen together, sipping tea and eating fresh-baked cookies, which we both knew that we shouldn't do. We laughed a little as we discussed our little sin. However, we continued to munch away.

Finally, after we were thoroughly relaxed and semi-full of cookies, I asked: "Maribel, do you ever think about what you want to be when you get older?" I paused a moment and then added: "I mean when you are really ancient, like thirty or thirty-five?"

Maribel laughed and then replied: "Oh, I don't know, I often think about a husband, children and a home, but that seems unlikely, given my profession." Her smile turned a little wistful.

I responded with a question. "What if your profession changed, and you moved in different social circles?"

Maribel's smile broadened a little. "Well, I suppose I would meet different people if I became a secretary for some large company." She paused and then added: "But I don't have the education for that." Her smile turned wistful again. "I have to be realistic."

"I think Hannibal knows about secretarial schools back East," I responded. "If you had the money, would you go?"

"Yes of course," Maribel replied. "But I don't think I am prepared for such a thing, I didn't even complete high school."

"Neither did I," I said with a laugh. "Tutors are available. You can finish high school, and I expect that Hannibal can get you into a good secretarial school." I paused to let my words sink in, and then I added: "Money can be arranged."

"Oh!" responded Maribel. Her hands flew up to her face. She bumped her teacup in the process.

I laughed as we wiped up the spill. "Hannibal and I can put up ten thousand from the Capone loot for your living expenses, tutors and secretarial school." I paused to let Maribel consider my offer, and then said: "You wouldn't have to work; you could concentrate on school."

"That would be wonderful!" exclaimed Maribel. "Afterwards, I could get a job as a secretary!" She paused a moment, and then asked: "When can I start?"

"I'll talk to Hannibal, but I think you could start this fall," I said with a smile. I thought a moment, and added: "Maybe that husband, children and a home will follow."

Our conversation ended with hugs. "These young people can be so emotional," I thought to myself. I took a final sip of tea to clear the lump in my throat.

On Tuesday, I talked with Kitty, the youngest. The conversation was very similar to my conversation with Maribel, except that Kitty wants to be an elementary school teacher. Apparently, her first-grade teacher made a strong impression. So be it; Hannibal and I will make it happen.

Wednesday afternoon was Kathy's turn. She wants to go to California; she has seen moving picture shows in the local theater.

"So glamorous!" she exclaimed.

"OK Kathy," I said. "We can give you ten thousand for a new start in California. However, we expect letters telling us about your adventures."

Kathy laughed and clapped her hands. "That's wonderful! Of course, I will write!"

"Kathy is a very pretty girl," I thought to myself. "Who knows, she might make it in the movies." I reflected a moment on the starry-eyed dreams I had many years before. "So be it," I concluded.

So, Hannibal and I have our work to do. We have a plan, and we know how to get it done.

Now on to the next problem. What are we going to do about Scottie?

16

SCOTTIE'S WEB

Sunday morning, September 4, 1927

My girls are progressing nicely, and I am proud of every one of them. Scottie remains a problem, but more on that later.

Maribel, Kitty and Kathy have started on their chosen paths. Thanks to Hannibal, Maribel has moved to Pittsburg. She has started secretarial school. Kitty still lives with me, but she is studying with tutors to get her high school diploma. When she is ready, she will apply for the teacher's education program at Indiana University in Bloomington. Kathy said goodbye to everyone at the train station on Saturday; she's off to California and golden opportunities.

Susie manages the Victorian, and Clara and Emily are full-time hostesses in the main salon. Maria has shown an unexpected talent; she has an excellent singing voice. Scottie lets her sing three nights a week, and she is very popular with the customers. Sandy is Scottie's front desk hostess; she greets customers and guides them to tables. Maria assists her when she isn't singing.

So many changes! I have also had to adapt; my investments are paying off nicely, thank you. I watch the stock market now, with Hannibal's help. I take his advice rather than the advice of my stock broker at the bank; that nut is just too speculative for my tastes. I have him do research and make the transactions, but Hannibal and I make the decisions.

Hannibal has an eye for growth companies. He has guided me away from overblown speculative stocks. He said several times that many companies and stocks, especially banks and financials, are overpriced and due for a fall. We shall see.

My investments provide a tidy income. In addition to the Victorian and my forty percent partnership with Scottie, I have substantial investments in the car dealership in Terre Haute, a trucking company in Indianapolis and some commercial property on Lake Shore Drive in Chicago. I own common and preferred stocks in large companies with solid dividends: steel, telephones, electrical equipment, automobile manufacturing and consumer food products. I also have a stash of U.S. treasury bonds. My personal income is now over one-hundred thousand per year, after taxes. Not bad for a poor girl from the wrong side of the tracks!

I also keep two safe deposit boxes at the local bank. One has my personal papers and a ready stash of cash. The other has all of the evidence, photos and analysis documents for our little "River Rat Detective Agency." Hannibal and I hope justice will be done someday with regard to Alec and Ogle. Also, our little collection of photos provides good insurance against our potential adversaries in local politics and in the booze business. What a tangled web we weave!

Now to the problem of Scottie: he has enemies and he doesn't know when to shut up. His wife Edith is the brains behind Scottie's solid business achievements, and even she has expressed concern over Scottie's free-wheeling ways. What are we going to do? I will talk to Hannibal.

Sunday evening, October 30

Over the past few weeks, Hannibal and I had long discussions about Scottie. We started our discussion over dinner at Valenti's on Saturday evening, September 10th. As we sipped our second glass of "grape juice," I began the conversation.

"Scottie has made enemies over his purchases of Canadian whiskey and gin," I began. "Even his wife Edith is concerned."

Hannibal nodded and replied: "Johnny said the same, and so did Jim the bartender."

"Scottie buys his products from both Capone's people and the North Side Gang," I responded. "I'm sure both gangs know what Scottie is doing, and both have threatened him."

"I know about Louie and Carlo," replied Hannibal. "Tell me about the North Side Gang."

"Well," I said, "During our last Wednesday meeting, Scottie was still very angry; apparently Max and Jack, two of the North Side gangsters that we encountered at their hideout in July, threatened Scottie about his purchases from Capone's people."

"When?" asked Hannibal.

"According to Scottie, he was threatened several times, the last time just before the kidnapping of Kitty and Kathy," I replied. "The war between gangs continues, according to the newspapers and gossip."

Hannibal was silent for quite a while. Finally, he said "Does anyone besides Scottie, Edith and your trusted employees know about your partnership with Scottie?"

"I don't think so," I replied. "At least our relationship isn't common knowledge. Scottie has been quiet on that topic so far." I thought a moment, and added: "Scottie gets angry when he's threatened, and he threatens back; I think that's all."

"Louie, Carlo, Max and Jack are poor choices for threats, especially when Scottie can't back them up," replied Hannibal.

I nodded in response. "Sam, Scottie's hired guard, is dead, and I doubt whether Big Bill will stand up to any of them."

Hannibal leaned back and sipped his grape juice. He then asked: "Did Scottie give you any trouble about losing Maribel, Kitty and Kathy from his Lyford roadhouse?"

"No," I replied. "Actually, he was quite good about it." I thought a moment and added: "The roadhouse makes a lot more money selling booze than from my girls anyway."

I sipped my grape juice and then continued: "Hard-drinking coal miners make up most of the clientele. They stop by after work and on weekends. After a few drinks, most just want to go home to their families."

I paused, and then added: "Obviously, the roadhouse also gets gang-related travelers from the Highway 41 booze route."

Hannibal gazed off to a corner of the restaurant for a while. I waited and watched his face.

After a minute or so, Hannibal turned back to me and said: "For now, I suggest that you caution Scottie about his idle threats at your next meeting."

"I will," I replied. "I think Edith will help us in that regard."

Hannibal nodded, then smiled. "Enough business," he said. "Now let's talk abut us." He reached over and we held hands.

Hannibal and I looked at each other for a long time. The table was between us, but our minds seemed to touch.

Finally, I said: "I don't know where to begin."

Hannibal nodded, as if to encourage me to continue.

I responded to his look with: "I have no family ties. My parents are dead and my only sister disappeared long ago."

"Yes," replied Hannibal. His eyes had a far-away look for a brief moment. He then returned to the present and smiled. I could tell that he meant: "You know my family history."

"Of course, we both care about my girls, past and present," I said. "I think we both want them to succeed."

"Yes," responded Hannibal. "I think of them as younger sisters."

"Me too," I replied. "They are the nearest to family that we both have." I paused a moment, and then added: "I think we have the resources to provide them with meaningful opportunities."

Hannibal smiled and nodded. He then changed the subject: "Now what about us?"

I smiled in return. "I am thirty-two years old, financially independent and ready for adventure!" I laughed openly, sincerely and with warmth. "How about you?"

Hannibal responded with a chuckle. He looked long into my eyes and said: "I'm your senior by a year, and I will join you in whatever lies ahead."

I returned Hannibal's steady gaze. Hannibal leaned back in his chair as if to give me space.

After a moment, I let go of his hand in a tender, smooth way, reached over the table, picked up our two full wine glasses and handed one to Hannibal. He understood.

"To our adventures together," he said. He leaned toward me and raised his glass.

"Together," I replied, and we clinked our glasses. We then drained them simultaneously.

And our discussion about our future ended. No formal declarations, but commitment nevertheless. We both, I think, were satisfied.

Wednesday evening, November 2

Scottie, Edith and I had our usual meeting at the speakeasy this morning. It went well, I think. After going over the accounts to everyone's satisfaction, we had a conversation about threats.

I began the conversation by leaning back in my easy chair and looking directly at Scottie for a long moment. He squirmed a little; I think he knew what was coming.

"Have you resolved the dual supply problem with regard to the deliveries of Canadian booze?" I asked.

"Well," replied Scottie; "I still buy from the Capone people and the North Side Gang, if that's what you mean." His tone was slightly defensive.

I nodded and then said: "I understand that you have been threatened by both gangs."

Scottie flushed; I could tell that the reminder of past threats made him angry. He then said: "Those weasels!"

I sighed and then responded: "That's the problem, Scottie." I paused for effect, and then continued: "I know you have made threats in return."

Edith entered the conversation with: "Listen to Caroline, Scottie." She looked at Scottie, then me and back to Scottie. "You can't threaten those people; they might kill you."

I looked at Edith. I could tell we were on the same page. I then said: "Edith is right, Scottie." I paused to let our combined words sink in and then added: "There is a war going on, and we are small potatoes. They would kill you without a second thought."

Scottie responded very defensively; but I think he already knew what my response would be. "Big Bill provides protection. There's also the mayor. I pay them both." Scottie looked first at me, then to Edith and then back to me.

I looked intently at Scottie and said: "Bill is a bully and a coward." I paused and then added: "especially after Sam was killed." I paused again and then said: "Fat Benny is a blowhard politician."

"Caroline is right on both counts," added Edith. "Listen to Caroline, and stop making threats; you won't get meaningful help from Bill or Benny. All you can expect is that they will leave you and our business alone."

"Also, you need to solve the problem of dual supplies of Canadian booze," I said.

Edith nodded.

I then asked: "Have you considered buying Canadian whiskey and gin for this speakeasy and my supply for the Victorian from only Capone's people and buying the supply for the roadhouse only from the North Side Gang?"

Scottie looked at me intently, then leaned back in his chair. After a few moments of silence, he said: "I could have Joe, the bartender at the roadhouse, be the contact for the North Side Gang." He pursed his hands. "I would be out of that loop." He looked at me, and his eyes twinkled. "What do you think?"

"Good idea," I responded. "Having a buffer couldn't hurt." I reflected a moment to myself, and then added: "You could tell Louie and Carlo that you no longer handle purchases for the roadhouse, and that would be true."

Edith caught on immediately: "Joe doesn't need to know about the source of booze for this establishment." She looked at me and added: "Or for the Victorian."

"Also, for the long term, you might consider selling the roadhouse and using the proceeds to invest elseware," I said.

"Like you, Caroline?" asked Edith.

"Yes," I responded in a matter-of-fact tone. "Diversification is always a good idea."

Edith got the point, and her fishing expedition stopped.

"OK, OK," said Scottie. "I'll talk to Joe the bartender, he might be interested in buying the place." He then looked at me and then Edith, and then back to me. He grinned. "Am I off the hotseat now?"

I laughed, nodded in agreement and changed the subject. "Now let's talk about Maria and her singing career."

Scottie and Edith both smiled. The meeting continued in pleasant conversation.

Sunday evening, December 4

The holiday season is in full swing. Over dinner at Valenti's, Hannibal asked me if I would like to take a two-week vacation with him. How exciting!

Apparently, he knows a plush little place in the Florida Keys. It would take three days each way by train, and we would have eight days at his hideaway: sun, a beach and palm trees!

Of course, I said yes. I have never been farther from home than Chicago. What a wonderful Christmas present!

Susie and Scottie promised to manage local business. Susie will be fine, and Scottie seems to be out of trouble for now. Joe the bartender at the roadhouse is trying to raise the money to buy the place.

During our meeting last Wednesday, Scottie mentioned in passing that Fat Benny and his wife Anna are now regular customers every Friday evening. Carlo and Louie also show up on Fridays, have a free drink, meet with Scottie and then leave. Big Bill, full of bluster, also shows up. Scottie said that Anna doesn't like Bill, and it shows. "She looks down her nose at him and doesn't say a word," was the way Scottie put it. Anna may be a snooty society woman, but I don't like Bill either. We have something in common after all.

Sunday evening, January 15, 1928

Hannibal and I just returned from the new Casa Astoria Resort in Key West. The train ride down was first class, the resort was exclusive, very private and absolutely beautiful. We hated to leave, but even the train ride back made sweet memories, like a fine Moscato d'Asti with fresh peaches after a light but sumptuous dinner.

Hannibal was a perfect, attentive gentleman. Our walks in the moonlight and special moments together will reside in my memories forever. For the first time in my life, I love a man. I am all-a-twitter, just like a school girl. Where do we go from here? I don't know, but something in my heart tells me our future will be wonderful.

Sunday evening, January 22

Maria asked if Hannibal and I would attend her performance at Scottie's speakeasy next Friday evening. Of course, we said yes.

According to Scottie, Maria has developed into an accomplished performer; she specializes in torch songs. Scottie has expanded the band to include a piano, clarinet, saxophone, violin, base and drums.

Maria is the star performer. Hannibal and I are looking forward to attending, even though other guests may not be to our tastes. We will be on our guard.

Wednesday evening, January 25

Scottie announced at our meeting today that Joe the bartender has purchased the Lyford roadhouse. The sale price was thirty thousand. Scottie got half in cash and agreed to a promissory note for the remainder, at six percent interest. Scottie even paid me twelve thousand, my forty percent share, in cash. Scottie is such an honest man. Great solution!

Friday midnight, January 27

Scottie was murdered tonight. I am writing this down while it is fresh in my memory. I swear I will find the murderer and bring that person to justice.

How do I know all this? I was there with Hannibal, in the main salon, listening to Maria sing, from about seven until ten PM, when the body was discovered.

At about ten, we all heard a heart-rending scream. The music stopped, followed by exclamations of surprise from several customers.

The scream came from the hallway that passed by Scottie's office. Hannibal and I jumped up from our table and ran toward the sound. Others followed.

We found Edith standing by the open office door, key in hand. I looked in. Scottie was alone, on the floor, dead.

A rush of people from the salon crowded into the hallway. Hannibal, Edith and I were pushed into the office. People crowded in behind us. Someone, Jim the bartender I think, called the police. I quickly looked around the room and at Scottie.

The back of Scottie's skull was crushed. There was a pool of blood on the floor under his face and head. I also saw a heavy multi-faceted crystal liquor decanter on the floor next to his body. It was empty. I had seen it before; Scotty used it for decoration on top of his liquor cabinet.

Scottie lay face down on the floor next to a small table near the liquor cabinet. Two glasses were on the table. A bottle of Scotch lay on the floor next to Scottie's right hand. Clearly, he had turned, stepped away from the cabinet and was about to pour two drinks when he was hit from behind with the decanter. Scottie knew his murderer.

My attention returned to the people crowding into the room. Big Bill, in a loud voice, ordered people to keep away from the body and the immediate area next to the desk, liquor cabinet and table. "Good, Bill," I thought to myself. "That's the right thing to do." I reflected a moment on the situation. "However, I can't examine the evidence near Scottie. What will the police do?"

We all cooperated with Bill, but I scanned the crowd as we stepped back. Among many others, I noted that the crowd included Benny, his wife Anna, Carlo and Louie.

According to the clock on the office wall, the police arrived at about ten minutes after ten. Everyone was ushered out of Scottie's office and the hallway into the main salon. Big Bill and Fat Benny both conferred with the police. The Chief was there, and so was a young sergeant.

Hannibal and I escorted Edith out of the office to our table. Edith was crying, but otherwise remarkably calm.

The police sergeant took the names of everyone in the place. Since there were no immediate suspects, everyone was allowed to leave. However, we were told to be available for questioning later. The place was closed. Since the speakeasy was an illegal operation, what will the police do about shutting it down permanently? I don't know.

Hannibal arranged for Jim to take Edith home. "Don't worry," said Jim. "I'll make sure someone stays with Edith tonight." Jim is such a nice guy.

Before Hannibal and I left, Blind Johnny motioned for me to come over to his table in the corner of the room near the entrance to the hallway. I walked over and bent down near Johnny's face.

"Yes, Johnny?" I asked.

"We need to talk," whispered Johnny: "later, when we are alone."

Based on Johnny's acute hearing abilities, I knew he had evidence to share. "See you tomorrow," I whispered, and moved quickly away. As I returned to Hannibal as he stood near our table, I looked around the room. No one was paying attention to me.

Relieved, I whispered to Hannibal. "Let's go."

Hannibal nodded, and he got permission to leave from the police sergeant. We left the building. The sergeant seemed like a nice young man, and Hannibal talked with him for a few minutes before we left.

Hannibal dropped me off at home. I can barely concentrate to write these notes; I am emotionally and physically exhausted. It's after one AM. I will write more after some sleep. "Oh, Scottie," I reflected in anguish. "Who did this to you?"

17

MURDER AT THE SPEAKEASY

Saturday morning, January 28, 1928

So, what do I know? Scottie was killed between eight and ten PM last night. I know this because I saw Scottie in his office at about eight. Edith screamed at about ten.

As I left Scottie's office at about eight, Scottie walked me to the door and said: "I'm going to lock the door, I don't want people walking in. I have lots of paperwork."

"OK Scottie," I replied. "Goodnight."

"Goodnight Caroline," Scottie responded with a smile and a final comment: "Enjoy Maria's singing." I heard the lock click after Scottie shut the door.

After leaving Scottie's office, I rejoined Hannibal at our table in the main salon. As I sat down, I looked around the room.

Fat Benny and Anna were at a nearby table. They were pretending that they didn't see me.

Big Bill, Louie and Carlo were at another table near the bar. Big Bill was loud and obnoxious, as usual. Louie responded to Bill in kind. Carlo was quiet and looked sinister. For the most part, he stared at a corner of the ceiling, as if he was thinking about something else besides the chatter of his two companions.

I also saw the speakeasy staff and other customers. Maria was on stage, and the band was in its usual location between the stage and the bar. Sandy stood at the small podium near the front door, ready to greet new arrivals. Blind Johnny sat at his table in the corner near the hallway entrance, and Jim was tending bar. There were about twenty customers in the room whose names I didn't know.

Someone got to Scottie in a locked room. Given that Scottie had locked his door from the inside, he had to have let his murderer in or the murderer had a key. The only way to lock or unlock the door from the outside is with a key.

Edith had a key in her hand when I saw her at Scottie's office door. Apparently, she had unlocked the door, saw the body and screamed. Are there other keys?

If Edith did not kill Scottie, how did the murderer get out of the room and re-lock the door? So many questions! I desperately need to talk to Hannibal and to Johnny.

I must stop writing for now, the phone is ringing.

Sunday afternoon, January 29

Hannibal was on the phone when it rang Saturday morning.

He began by asking: "How are you doing, Caroline?"

"He always thinks about others, including me," I thought before answering. "OK I guess."

"Shall we get together and talk?" Hannibal responded. "I think we should also see Johnny as soon as we can; I saw you two whispering before we left the speakeasy on Friday night."

"How does he do this?" I thought to myself. "He always knows." To Hannibal, I said. "Can we get together at my place this afternoon?"

"Right," replied Hannibal. "I'll pick up Johnny on the way. See you about one o'clock?"

"Sounds good," I replied. After goodbyes, I hung up my phone. I looked at my clock. I had a couple of hours before I expected Hannibal. I decided to clean up the place and take a bath.

Sure enough, Hannibal drove up to my house at five minutes until one. Johnny was in the seat beside him. My bath had refreshed both body and soul, and the coffee was on the stove.

I watched from my kitchen window as Hannibal and Johnny got out of the car and walked to my kitchen door. Johnny had a long white cane, which he used to find his way around the car, along the walkway, and to the door. Hannibal let Johnny walk on his own, but he observed Johnny carefully.

"Johnny has gained confidence," I mused to myself. "Nice touch, Hannibal," my thoughts continued. "You let Johnny manage on his own."

I opened the door as the pair reached the steps. "Come on in," I said.

My girls were all off on errands, and Hannibal, Johnny and I were alone. Soon we were at the kitchen table with coffee in hand.

Hannibal sipped his coffee and looked at Johnny with his steady gaze. "Tell Caroline what you told me," he finally said.

Johnny turned toward me. I could tell he sensed my presence and location, even without eyes.

"As you know, I sense and can remember footsteps," responded Johnny. "My table at the speakeasy is next to the entrance to the hallway that passes Scottie's office."

He paused a moment, and then stated: "In a normal stride, it takes six steps from the hallway entrance down the hallway to Scottie's office door, which is on the left." He paused again and then continued: "It takes four more steps to the door to the back of the bar, which is on the right, and another four to the entrance to the ladies' restroom, also on the right." He paused again as he pulled observations from memory. "Four more steps take you to the men's' restroom on the right. The back door to the building is straight ahead, four more steps past the men's restroom."

I took a deep breath as I thought about the implications of Johnny's description. After a moment, I said: "Did you keep track of footsteps down the hallway the night of Scottie's murder?"

"Yes," replied Johnny in a confident tone. "I remember your footsteps to and from Scottie's office and all the footsteps afterwards until Edith's scream."

Hannibal nodded, looked at me and said: "You visited Scottie in his office at about eight PM."

"Yes," I replied. "We talked for a few minutes and then I left. Scottie locked the door."

Johnny smiled and then said: "You walked six steps from the hallway entrance to Scottie's door. You knocked. Scottie opened the door. You two exchanged greetings. You both then went into the office and closed the door. A few minutes later, the door opened. I heard Scottie say: "I'm going to lock the door, I don't want people walking in. I have lots of paperwork."

Johnny paused, recalling events. "You and Scottie both said Goodnight, and then you walked six steps back to the turn into the salon. You passed the turn, walked back to your table and sat down."

"Wow!" I exclaimed. "You have remarkable recall, Johnny."

"Thank you," replied Johnny with a smile. "Only seven sets of footsteps walked down that hallway between your visit in Scottie's office and Edith's scream."

"Do you know who made the footsteps?" I asked.

"Not sure," replied Johnny. "But two were women in high heels and four were men. One of the women went twice." He paused a moment, and then added: "Edith was the one who went twice, because at the end of the second trip, she screamed, and I know her voice. The footsteps just before the scream were the same as one of the earlier sets."

"Did Edith stop at Scottie's office on both trips?" I asked.

"Yes," replied Johnny. "On her first trip at about eight-thirty, she stopped after six steps. There was a pause of about a minute. Afterwards, her footsteps continued down the hall to the ladies' restroom. After another several minutes, her footsteps returned to the salon." He paused, and then added: "On the second trip at about ten, she took six steps, paused, and then screamed."

"Could you hear a key turn the lock?" asked Hannibal.

"No," replied Johnny. "Footsteps are a distinct sound, and my hearing and other senses pick them up quite well. I can't always distinguish keys turning locks from background noise. If the sound is loud enough, I can sense closing doors, but the band was playing and the drummer, well, you know what I mean."

"Other senses?" I asked.

"I feel the rhythmic vibrations of footsteps through my feet on the floor and my hands when I touch the table," responded Johnny. "I don't know how to describe it."

"Different frequencies for different sounds," said Hannibal. "You can sense some frequencies with heightened abilities, but not others. Also, as you said, the drummer muffled the possible sound of a door and a turning lock."

"Yes," replied Johnny. "I don't know if Edith opened the door or just stopped outside."

I thought a moment and then asked: "How can we match footsteps to names?"

Hannibal responded: "We need to get each suspect to walk by Johnny in the speakeasy." He paused and then continued: "We will know each person who walks by, and Johnny can tell us if those footsteps match a set in the hallway on the night Scottie was murdered."

"Yes," responded Johnny, "that will work. Even if they wear different shoes, I remember the sounds by stride, timing, weight impact and other nuances that are hard to explain, but real." He grinned and added: "Real, at least, to me."

Silence reigned for several minutes. We all sipped our coffee.

Finally, I said: "Our suspects must not know they are being tested for the sound of their footsteps."

Hannibal and Johnny both nodded. Hannibal then said: "We also need a control group."

Johnny and I looked puzzled. "What does that mean?" Johnny finally ventured.

"Part of the scientific method," replied Hannibal in a matter-of-fact way. "We need non-suspects to walk down the hallway before and/or after each of our suspects. Johnny won't know who any of the walkers are, and he will choose the ones that create footsteps that match the footsteps in the hallway, if any, on the night Scottie was killed."

"I see," I replied. "Johnny will identify the footsteps and we will know the names."

"Right," responded Hannibal.

"I understand my job," said Johnny. "But how do we set this up without our suspects knowing?"

"That will take some thought," admitted Hannibal. "Still, I think it can be done."

"But the police closed the speakeasy," I said. "How can we run our tests there?"

Johnny grinned and said: "The speakeasy will re-open a week from this Friday."

I know my mouth dropped open. "How?" I finally uttered.

"I don't know for sure," Johnny replied. "But I do know that the news of Scottie's murder has been downplayed by the police due to continuing investigations, whatever that means." He turned to me and added: "Edith told me to report to work a week from Friday, February 10th. Jim will report this Wednesday."

Hannibal leaned back in his chair, looked first at Johnny and then at me and said: "I think Edith will want Maria and Sandy to return to work."

It was my turn to summarize. "Interesting," I said. "Scottie's funeral is this Wednesday; the police haven't followed up, and Edith doesn't appear to be particularly grief-stricken." I paused a moment and then added: "I wonder if Edith will want to meet on Wednesday after Scottie's funeral?"

"You probably will get word from Edith soon," said Hannibal. "Let's see what happens at the meeting. In the meantime, I will make some inquiries."

Hannibal didn't elaborate, and I chose not to ask. Nevertheless, we had a plan. The problem now was: how do we implement it? We need more information.

Wednesday evening, February 1

What a day! Scottie's funeral was in the morning, and Edith and I met at the speakeasy this afternoon.

The funeral was a sad affair. Many people attended; Scottie was well-liked. His obituary in the local paper expounded upon his community service, his grieving widow and so on. No mention was made about the manner of his death. However, local gossip provided lurid and often inaccurate details. Edith cried during the service, but I couldn't tell if it was real or contrived.

At Edith's request, we met at the speakeasy in the afternoon, after the service. I walked through the front door at about one-thirty. No police were there, but Jim was behind the bar stocking shelves.

Jim tried to smile as I walked in.

"Hello Jim," I said.

"Hello, Caroline," Jim replied. His eyes were moist; he and Scottie had been friends. "Edith is in the office." He gestured with a look to his right, toward the hallway.

"No police?" I asked.

"Not since yesterday," Jim stated matter-of-factly.

"I see," I replied. I started to walk around the partition into the hallway, but stopped. "By the way, Jim, who has keys to Scottie's office?"

Jim looked at me for a moment and then replied: "Let's see, I have a key, so did Scottie and Edith." He paused, thinking: "That's all," he finished.

I looked at Jim closely. There was no sign of guile, no obvious intent to deceive. "I believe him," I thought to myself. I then continued into the hallway.

The office door was open. I looked in. The office was the same as before the murder. It had been completely cleaned. As far as I could tell, there were only two differences: Edith was sitting behind Scottie's desk, and the heavy decanter was not in its old place on the liquor cabinet.

"Come in, Caroline," said Edith. "We have a lot to talk about." Her voice was clear, and there wasn't a hint of grief, not even a tear.

I walked through the doorway and sat in my usual easy chair. I waited for Edith to begin.

"You may as well hear it from me," Edith began. "I'm sure you would find out anyway," she added, with a wry smile. She paused a moment and then said: "Scottie had a rather large life insurance policy. Also, his will left everything to me."

I know I took a deep breath. I looked straight into Edith's eyes. She stared right back.

Finally, I said: "I'm sure that's what Scottie wanted."

Edith raised her eyebrows slightly. After a moment, she replied: "Yes, well, I want to use some of the money to buy your forty percent share." She paused again, and then added; "Think about a price." Edith's eyes had a steely glint.

I saw the hidden meanings. It was time to bail out. After a few moments, I said: "Of course. I think the business is worth about one hundred thousand."

Edith gave a slight nod, and then caught herself. I think she was prepared for a larger number. I watched her carefully.

I then said: "In addition to my forty thousand, Sandy and Maria come with me."

Edith stared back at me. I didn't lower my gaze. Finally, she said: "It's a deal." She rose from her seat. "I will send you a cashier's check by Friday." She extended her hand and smiled in a cold way.

I rose from my seat, smiled, shook hands, turned and walked out. I closed the door behind me as I left. "This complicates things as far as our testing of footsteps," I mused as I walked to the parking lot. "Still, I think we can do it."

Hannibal was waiting in his car.

Thursday evening, February 2

Hannibal and I discussed my meeting with Edith on the drive home yesterday.

"You did the right thing with regard to Sandy and Maria," he said after I finished my story. "Shall we talk about their futures over dinner at Valenti's on Friday night?" He paused, looked over at me and smiled. "I don't think going to the speakeasy would be a good date."

I gave Hannibal a dig in the ribs. "OK Smarty," I replied. "What about Sandy and Maria?"

Hannibal was quiet for a moment. Finally, he said: "Perhaps Sandy can work for Tony and Louisa as a greeter and scheduler of reservations. I know Tony and Louisa plan to expand the restaurant."

I instantly liked the idea. "I will call Louisa when I get home; they have a telephone now."

Hannibal nodded and said: "We also have to think about Maria." He paused a moment and then added: "Have you seen the new motion picture titled: "The Jazz Singer?" I understand it's all the rage."

It took a minute, but I finally caught the drift. "California!" I exclaimed. That new talking motion picture was made in California! My mind raced. "Kathy's last letter described a little town called Hollywood. I think she works there now, at a place called a motion picture studio."

Hannibal nodded and smiled again. "With talking motion pictures, maybe they will need singers."

"What a wonderful idea!" I replied. "I'll talk to Maria first, and then, if she agrees, I'll send a letter to Kathy."

"We can work out a plan to test for footsteps later," Hannibal replied. "People come first."

I reached over and kissed Hannibal on the cheek. "Thank you. I'll even buy dinner Friday night."

Hannibal laughed and said: "It's a date!"

18

WHO DUNNIT?

Saturday morning, February 4, 1928

Hannibal and I had dinner at Valenti's Friday night. I had already completed my homework with regard to Sandy. Tony, Louisa and Sandy all readily agreed; Sandy would start to work at the restaurant on Monday. Tony and Louisa even joined Hannibal and me in a grape juice toast.

Maria was excited about the prospects of joining Kathy in California. I sent Kathy a Western Union telegram, it's the modern way. Kathy replied by telegram; she was so looking forward to seeing Maria. I followed up with a letter that had all the details, and I'm waiting for a reply.

I also told Hannibal that I had received Edith's cashier's check on Friday. I had cashed it immediately and put the forty thousand in my safety deposit box. "Money for a rainy day," I had told myself.

Hannibal and I also discussed our footstep test problem. I proposed a solution: beer and peanuts.

"Friday night, February 10th, is the grand re-opening of the speakeasy," I began. "What if Jim served half-priced beer and free peanuts on each table?"

Hannibal looked at me for a long moment. Finally, the light came on, and he grinned. "Salt and liquid," he replied; "lots of trips to the restroom."

"Right," I said. "Now we need someone to take names."

Hannibal thought a moment and then said: "Someone could sit with Johnny."

"Yes," I responded. "Susie is perfect. She knows all the suspects, and she has never been to the speakeasy."

"Edith doesn't know Susie," Hannibal mused. "Still, Bill and Benny might remember."

I replied: "Susie is good at dressing the part; remember the funeral parlor seven years ago?"

Hannibal laughed. "I agree, Susie is perfect." He was silent for a moment, and then added: "I will work out details with Jim and Johnny; you can brief Susie."

It was my turn to laugh. "Susie will love it," I replied.

Saturday evening, February 11

Our plan worked. Beer and peanuts did the trick, and lots of customers went down the hallway to the restrooms, including Big Bill, Fat Benny, Anna, Carlo and Louie. Hannibal also had his control group; trips down the hallway by the suspects were interspersed with trips by many other customers.

Johnny picked out the footsteps of all five suspects. They matched the footsteps of the five persons who, in addition to Edith, made the trip down the hallway the night Scottie was murdered. Susie sat inconspicuously with Johnny and recorded names.

I got Susie's report this morning. After a quick read, I called Hannibal.

"I'll be right over," said Hannibal over the phone.

Susie and I waited in my kitchen. The coffee was ready when Hannibal drove up.

After we were all seated at the table, I began the conversation. "OK Susie, tell Hannibal what you told me."

Susie nodded and said: "All five suspects walked down the hallway between about eight-forty-five and about nine forty-five, between

Edith's two trips." Susie looked at me and then at Hannibal. "Johnny picked out the footsteps of each suspect during our tests on Friday night."

"Have you matched the names to footsteps and did Johnny remember the footstep counts the night of the murder?" Hannibal asked.

"Yes," replied Susie. "We can eliminate all of the suspects, except Edith and one other." She looked at her notes and then continued: "Big Bill was first at about eight forty-five. He walked eighteen steps to the men's restroom. He stayed about five minutes and then walked eighteen on the return. He didn't make any stops."

"Who was next?" I asked.

"Louie," responded Susie. "He entered the hallway at about nine o'clock. He made twenty-two footsteps to the back door. Johnny heard the door open, it has one of those dead-bolt door latches, and it was loud. Louie went outside, came back in a few minutes later and returned twenty-two steps back through the hallway."

"No stops?" Hannibal asked.

"None," replied Susie. "Anna was next. She walked down the hallway at about nine-ten." Susie looked at me and then at Hannibal. "Anna went ten steps to the door that enters behind the bar. She paused for about a minute and then continued to the ladies' restroom. There were no stops on the return."

"She apparently looked at the area behind the bar," I said. "Maybe she was just nosy."

"Maybe," mused Hannibal; "interesting though."

Susie continued. "Fat Benny was next at about nine-thirty." She giggled. "Johnny said the footsteps sounded like an elephant."

I couldn't help but smile. "Where did he go?" I asked.

"He went to the men's restroom and returned," replied Susie. "He didn't stop either way. He spent about ten minutes in the restroom."

"Elephants have to go too," I responded with a slightly suppressed giggle.

Even Hannibal gave out a chuckle. He then asked: "What about Carlo?"

Susie nodded and replied: "He was the last before Edith's final trip." Susie paused and looked to Hannibal and back to me. "At about nine forty-five, Carlo walked six steps and stopped. Johnny did not hear a return."

Hannibal leaned back in his chair and sipped his coffee slowly. Susie and I watched and waited.

After a full minute, Hannibal said: "Interesting timing: Edith's first trip to Scottie's door was at eight-thirty, and Carlo walked to the door at nine forty-five. Edith returned to the door at about ten, opened the door with her key and screamed."

"Yes," I responded. "Edith and Carlo both had motive and opportunity. Also, they might have worked together."

"But no proof," said Susie. "We don't know if Carlo actually went into Scottie's office and killed him."

Hannibal put his coffee cup down on the table and said: "May I please have another cup of coffee?"

I looked at Hannibal intently. "There you go again!" I said in an exasperated tone. "You know something!"

Hannibal smiled and said: "I said two weeks ago that I would make some inquiries. I did." He paused and then said: "I will call you in a day or so."

I fidgeted in my chair in frustration. Susie giggled as she watched me. Finally, I blurted out: "No, you may not have more coffee!"

Both Hannibal and Susie laughed.

"OK," said Hannibal. He got up, bent over and kissed me lightly on the cheek. Without another word, he turned and walked out the door.

Susie continued laughing.

"Oh shut up, Susie!" I exclaimed. The laughter continued.

Wednesday evening, February 15

Hannibal called this morning. He said that I should expect a call from the police. What does he know? How frustrating!

Sure enough, I got a phone call about an hour later. "Miss Case?" The voice on the phone asked.

"Yes?" I answered tentatively.

"I'm Officer Reed from the police department," said the voice. "Would you please come to the establishment where Scottie McDonald was murdered on the night of January 27th? The police department is convening a meeting there tomorrow morning at nine o'clock." Mr. Hannibal Jones said that your participation would be very important."

"Yes, of course," I replied.

Officer Reed then said: "Thank you," and hung up the phone.

What is Hannibal up to?" I muttered to myself.

I immediately called Hannibal. Before I could say a word, Hannibal said: "Yes, Caroline?"

My mind raced. "How did he know it was me?" I thought to myself. To Hannibal, I asked: "What's going on?"

"I'll pick you up tomorrow at eight-thirty," Hannibal replied. I could also hear a slight chuckle. "I'll bring Johnny," Hannibal continued. "Can you bring Susie?"

"Yes," of course," I responded. Before I could say another word, Hannibal said: "Thank you," and hung up the phone. That rascal!

Thursday afternoon, February 16

I'm writing all this down before I forget the details. What a morning!

As promised, Hannibal drove up to my house at eight-thirty sharp. Susie and I were watching out the kitchen window. The thermometer hanging outside my window read twenty degrees F. Susie and I had on hats, heavy coats and gloves, and we were ready to go.

We went out the door as soon as the car stopped. I could see Johnny in the back seat, all bundled up. Susie got in the back with Johnny, and I got in next to Hannibal. I looked over and noticed that he was wearing heavy slacks, warm leather gloves, boots, a hat and a cashmere scarf. His leather jacket bulged slightly at the right pocket.

Before I could ask the obvious question, Hannibal said: "I will explain on the way." And he did. By the time we arrived at the speakeasy, I was fully prepared, or so I thought.

We parked in the lot at the back. There were several other cars. I recognized the mayor's car, the one driven by Louie that I had seen at the gas station and Bill's car with the sheriff's emblem. There were several others. "Interesting," I thought to myself. "We have a good audience."

We all got out and walked around the building toward the front door. Hannibal took out his watch as we approached the door. His watch read: eight fifty-five. "Perfect," I thought to myself.

Hannibal opened the door, and we walked in. The young police sergeant that I met on the night of the murder was standing just inside. A number of people were sitting at tables. I saw Benny, Anna, Bill, Carlo and Louie. Edith and Jim were standing near the bar. Two uniformed policemen stood at the front and the back of the salon, near the exits.

"Introductions are in order, I believe," said Hannibal. "Caroline, Susie and Johnny, this is Police Sergeant Enzio Valenti." He paused a moment and added: "Sergeant Valenti, I believe you know the full names of everyone."

My mouth dropped open. After a second or two, I closed it and stammered: "Nice to meet you Sergeant."

"Nice to meet you, Miss Case," replied Sergeant Valenti. "My Aunt and Uncle told me that you and Mr. Jones were regulars at their restaurant." He smiled warmly. He turned to Susie and Johnny and greeted each politely.

I gave Hannibal a dirty look. He hadn't told me the sergeant's name while we were in the car. Hannibal just smiled. Again, that rascal!

While this exchange of looks was going on, Sergeant Valenti stepped back and said to us all: "Please, have a seat and make yourselves comfortable."

We took off our coats, hats and so on. We walked over and sat at two empty tables near the stage. We laid our stuff on nearby empty chairs. I noticed that Hannibal draped his coat on a chair next to his right hand. I sat on his left. Johnny and Susie sat at the table between us and the wall, which was Johnny's usual table.

Sergeant Valenti walked to the little stage by the back partition. He turned and addressed the group.

"We are here to discuss the murder of James McDonald, known to everyone here as Scottie." Sergeant Valenti paused for effect, and his gaze swept around the room. Several people fidgeted, including Edith and Carlo.

Sergeant Valenti continued: "Major Jones and Miss Case have gathered important evidence and provided an official report to me. I've read the report. Major Jones, would you please begin?"

There were several expressions of surprise at Valenti's mention of a title for Hannibal. Even Johnny looked surprised. Sergeant Valenti stepped down from the stage, walked to the front door and waited.

Hannibal stepped up to the stage and turned to the audience. His gaze swept the room, and he began speaking in a practiced, military fashion. "Miss Case came up with a concept to determine motive and opportunity with regard to Mr. McDonald's murder. The credit for gathering the evidence goes to Mr. John Swift and Miss Susie Adams."

Susie and Johnny both smiled. They were pleased that Hannibal had referred to them in a formal and complementary way; that didn't happen often.

Hannibal had told us in the car that "the cat would be out of the bag" with regard to our detective work. I was prepared. So were Johnny and Susie. We all realized that our lives would be different from now on. Except for the police, everyone else in the room had expressions of surprise on their faces.

Hannibal looked at me. I smiled back. My little temper tantrum was over.

Hannibal continued. "Our report identifies everyone who stopped at or passed by Mr. McDonald's office door between eight-thirty and ten o'clock on the night of January 27, 1928."

In a clipped, formal and confident tone, Hannibal laid out the activities and times for Edith, Big Bill, Louie, Anna, Fat Benny and Carlo, in that order. He referred to each by their titles and full names; he was not in the least disrespectful. Hannibal's professionalism showed, and it had the desired effect.

"However," Hannibal continued, "the door was locked until Mrs. McDonald opened it at about ten o'clock, according Mrs. McDonald's statement to the police. I saw the key in her hand myself that night as she stood by the door. Clearly, she didn't have time to go in, kill her husband while he poured two drinks, and step back out the door during her stop at the door at ten. So, who was the killer, and how did that person get out of the room and re-lock the door?'

Carlo and Louie were especially surprised that Hannibal knew their last names. "Hannibal has done his homework," I thought to myself.

When Hannibal stopped talking, heads turned toward Edith and Carlo. Edith's composure melted. She put her hand to her face and stepped backwards, bumping into the bar. Carlo's face contorted into a savage look, like a cornered animal. The two policemen at the doorways tensed and watched closely. The room grew deadly quiet.

Hannibal broke the silence. "From the information that I have presented, we only know that Edith McDonald and Carlo Nitti stopped at the door to James McDonald's office. However, Mrs. McDonald did not have time to go in and murder Mr. McDonald at eight-thirty and return to the main salon about a minute later; neither did she have time to murder her husband at ten. On the other hand, I have not presented evidence that Mr. Nitti actually went in."

Both Edith and Carlo relaxed a little.

"We have additional evidence," stated Hannibal in a quiet, confident tone. "Sergeant Valenti, would you please step forward?"

Sergeant Valenti had been standing by the front door. He picked up a cardboard box that had been resting inconspicuously on a nearby chair. He strode up to my table near the stage, pulled a set of white rubber surgical gloves from his pocket, put them on and reached into the box.

Carefully, he raised a twinkling object from the box. It was the crystal decanter from Scottie's office. "The murder weapon," he stated matter-of-factly.

Hannibal then said: "Sergeant Valenti collected this decanter at the scene of the crime." He paused for effect, and then continued: "Using proper police procedure, he packaged it and sent it to a certified laboratory in Chicago, along with other evidence. He got it back yesterday, along with a full report."

"I bet I know which laboratory," I thought to myself with an inward smile.

Sergeant Valenti picked up the narrative. "The report identified the victim's blood type on the murder weapon." He paused and looked around. "It also identified fingerprints." The policemen near the doors tensed again, the narrative was nearing a climax.

Sergeant Valenti continued: "We have access to a data base of fingerprints gathered earlier." He glanced briefly at me. He turned to the audience and added: "We have identified the person who wielded the decanter and hit Mr. McDonald on the back of the head." He looked directly at Carlo.

"How could it be me?" Carlo snarled as he looked at Sergeant Valenti and then Hannibal. "You said yourself that the door was locked when the lady arrived at ten!" He looked over at Edith.

"The answer is simple actually," replied Hannibal. "You did not leave the room after the murder. Instead, you stepped into Mr. McDonald's private restroom and waited. When everyone crowded into the room at ten o'clock, you stepped out and blended into the crowd, unnoticed."

Carlo's face fell, and he tensed.

Hannibal continued: "Sergeant Valenti also found your fingerprints on the restroom doorknobs, both inside and outside. He did not find your prints on the inside doorknob of the office door, so Mr. McDonald must have locked it after you entered. We found Mr. McDonald's fingerprints on the inside doorknob."

There was a blur of action. Carlo jumped up and ran toward the policeman at the front door. This policeman was in the process of drawing his service revolver, and Carlo grabbed it. After a brief struggle, Carlo had the gun, turned and was about to fire when two shots deafened everyone in the room. Carlo fell backwards. He was dead before he hit the floor. It was over.

Sergeant Valenti and the other policeman had both drawn their weapons and had fired. Both hit the target, which was Carlos' chest.

Hannibal had his Colt in hand. He had silently moved to the chair where he had placed his coat while Sergeant Valenti was finishing his last sentence. He had not fired, but he was pointing his gun at Louie, who was standing, about to support his boss.

Louie saw Hannibal and the deadly gaze in his eyes. He thought about the consequences of his intended action, slowly sat down in his chair and placed his open hands on the table.

It probably dawned in Louie's mind that his boss was dead, and there would be questions. Eventually, he would realize that his participation in the deaths of Alec and Ogle would come to light. His future prospects were not good.

Edith knew that she remained under suspicion. She had motive and could have colluded with Carlo with regard to her husband's death. Given Sergeant Valenti's action, the future of the speakeasy was in doubt. After all, her operation was illegal.

Big Bill, the coward, had dropped to the floor when the shooting started. It was clear that Sergeant Valenti had not brought the Sheriff in on the game; Bill was as surprised by events as others in the room. How much did he really know about the Capone people and their local contacts? Could he deliver on protection from local authorities? Good questions.

Fat Benny had also cowered when the action started. At least some members of his own police force had not kept him informed. Like Bill, his bribery-extortion days were probably over.

Johnny's job at the speakeasy was over. Edith would view Johnny with suspicion; he had nearly implicated her in the death of her husband. I will discuss Johnny's future with Hannibal.

Edith's suspicion would eventually fall on Jim as well. He had clearly cooperated in gathering evidence. Jim would also probably need employment elsewhere.

Anna's reaction was very interesting. She was surprised by the detective work of our little group, but she did not cower like Bill or her blustering husband. She remained seated and silent; she seemed to be evaluating events in a cool, calculating manner. Anna is a woman to watch closely, Caroline!

Sergeant Valenti appears to be an honest cop. At least, he had demonstrated that he drew the line at murder. He had done the right thing with regard to Scottie. What was his attitude toward speakeasies and the booze business? What did his superiors know and what would they do? What was Valenti's relationship with Hannibal? I will find out.

19

CRESCENDO OF VIOLENCE

Sunday evening, April 15, 1928

The gang violence has reached an almost unbelievable level. The newspapers are full of stories. Capone rules in Chicago, and according to rumor, he has a personal income of over six million per year from his illegal operations.

Capone also controls Chicago politics. After four years away from City Hall, Big Bill Thompson ran for mayor last year. He campaigned for a wide-open town, hinting strongly that he would re-open all of the speakeasies closed by the previous Dever administration. Thompson beat Dever by a margin of fifty-two percent to Dever's forty-three percent, with John Robertson getting five percent. According to the newspapers, Capone contributed two hundred fifty thousand dollars to Thompson's campaign and hung a portrait of Thompson in his office.

Capone's influence in politics includes Cook County and the entire state of Illinois. The current primary election is filled with intimidation, shootings and bombings. The newspapers call it the Pineapple Primary. The word "pineapple" is a slang term for a hand grenade. According to the newspapers, at least sixty-two bombings have taken place in Chicago over the past six months.

The violence extends deep into the Wabash Valley. In addition to Scottie, "Handsome Jack" Morrison, George Aiduks, Dutch Rebec,

Blackie Wright and Elmer Slover have been gunned down. All were rumored to have been associated with Valley illegal booze.

It's a standing joke among locals that the most popular roadhouses north of Terre Haute are not far from town, but too far for the County Sheriff to see them. Highway 41 has a constant flow of booze in both directions. What a wild and wooly situation!

Rumor has it that the going rate for speakeasy payments to local cops for "anti-raid insurance" is now two-hundred dollars per week. "That's about right," I thought to myself. "Fat Benny had reached that amount before Scottie was killed." However, neither Bill nor Benny have made any attempt to collect since Carlo was killed. "Good," I concluded.

Sunday evening, April 22

More violence: however, this death brought mixed emotions. According to the local newspaper, Sheriff Big Bill Johannsson was killed last Monday when his Cadillac roadster catapulted over an embankment on Centenary Road northwest of Clinton. Also, according to the newspapers, the Clinton police are looking for a Mr. Louie Abogado, who has disappeared. Was Bill's death an accident? Unlikely. Who was behind this?

My dealings with Edith are now strictly through Jim the bartender. Like Scottie, Edith supplies the Victorian with good Canadian whiskey and gin. I don't think this will last. According to Jim, Edith still pays Fat Benny, but I'm not sure. I do know that her speakeasy has lost much of its former clientele. Business at the Victorian has picked up, but I think it's time to sell out. I will talk to Hannibal and Susie.

Sunday evening, April 29

I talked to Hannibal and Susie on Friday. They both agree, it is time to sell. The business is just too dangerous. Besides, good times can't last forever; and it's time to take some winnings off the table.

I also talked to Clara and Emily yesterday at my kitchen table. After I explained the situation, Emily said: "We trust you, Caroline." She reached over and put her hand on mine. "Do what you think is right." Clara nodded in agreement. I got a lump in my throat as I looked into their faces. I just nodded in response. In my thoughts, I vowed: "I will take care of you both."

Monday evening, April 30

I put feelers out through my various contacts today. The Victorian business is for sale. However, the personnel will have a choice as to whether or not they want to stay. Let's see what happens.

Sunday evening, May 6

The response has been overwhelming. The Gosnell group, Lawton & Jenkins, Barker & Dycus and Ed Wyatt have all called me. Even Edith let Jim know that she would be interested. Wow!

Wednesday evening May 9

I sold the Victorian, lock, stock and barrel, for two hundred fifty thousand cash, which was delivered today in a briefcase. I put the money in my safe deposit box at the bank. Hannibal will know what to do with it. That was quick!

Clara and Emily decided to stay with me. Others have asked the new owner if they could stay at the Victorian. I gave everyone who wanted to stay a glowing recommendation.

I will celebrate Friday night with Hannibal, Susie, Clara and Emily. All of my other girls are gone now, off to new horizons.

Saturday morning, May 12

Hannibal had everyone over to his house for steaks on his new-fangled grill. In addition to steaks, baked potatoes, fresh green beans and carrots, we had some good "grape juice" supplied by the Valenti Restaurant. I don't know where Hannibal got the fresh vegetables, but they weren't local. We had homemade vanilla ice cream for dessert.

Hannibal also had two surprise guests. Jim Hansen, Edith's former bartender, and Johnny Swift were there. They were invited by Hannibal, of course. We all had a wonderful evening.

Sunday morning, May 13

Hannibal called a few minutes ago. He asked me to come over for lunch. Of course, I said yes. The day promised to be beautiful, so I told him that I would walk to his house.

Hannibal said: "Are you sure you want to walk?" He paused on the phone and then said: "I would like to pick you up."

"No," I replied. "The day is beautiful, and the walk will be good exercise."

"OK," responded Hannibal. "See you soon." He then hung up the phone.

"Time to stop writing, Caroline," I said to myself. I'll wear something nice for Hannibal. "Wonder what he has in mind?"

Monday morning, May 14

What a Sunday! It began on a pleasant note. I had put down my writing, got dressed in nice slacks, a print blouse, silk neck scarf, light jacket and stylish walking shoes. I also wore a hat and gloves in the latest fashion.

I stopped by the mirror in my hallway before going out the kitchen door. "I look pretty good, if I do say so myself," I thought. I laughed, turned and walked out the door.

Hannibal's house was only three blocks away. As I approached the street in front of my house, I glanced north along my street. I saw a black car parked along the street about a block away. "I haven't seen that car before," I mused to myself.

I turned south and headed toward Hannibal's house, two blocks south and one east. As I walked, I heard the car start. I glanced back over my shoulder. The car was moving slowly down the street toward me. The hair on the back of my neck started to prickle. I picked up my pace. The car continued to follow, slowly getting closer.

"Oh my God," I thought. I was halfway to Hannibal's house. "Go forward, Caroline," I muttered. I was really scared.

I crossed a side street. The car was getting closer. Suddenly I heard another car approaching from the street that I had just crossed. I turned in panic toward the sound!

It was Hannibal. He turned his car and pulled close to the curb next to me. He then reached across the seat and opened the passenger side door. "Get in!" he said in a clear and commanding voice.

I didn't need a second invitation. I ran to the car, jumped in and shut the door. Hannibal gunned the engine and the car took off toward his house.

I turned to Hannibal, who was glancing in the rearview mirror. "Look," he said, as we picked up speed.

I turned and looked out the back window. The car was still following, half a block back and gaining.

"Oh!" I exclaimed.

Suddenly a different car roared out from a side street just behind us. I saw white words and an emblem on the door just as it turned toward the following car.

"The police!" I shouted over the sound of our engine.

"Good!" Hannibal replied.

The police car headed directly toward the following car, which was now only about one hundred yards back.

Suddenly, the following car swerved into a side alley and sped away. The police car followed, at high speed. I could hear both cars as they roared off, over the sound of our own engine.

Hannibal slowed our car. I turned and looked forward. We were pulling into Hannibal's driveway.

A few minutes later, Hannibal and I were inside, in the kitchen. Hannibal took his Colt out of his pocket and laid it on the table.

"Oh Hannibal," I said. "What just happened?"

Hannibal gave me a long look and then answered. "You were about to be abducted and killed."

My mind was racing. Finally, I said: "But you were there."

Hannibal nodded and replied: "Sergeant Valenti and I have been taking turns watching your house when you were home." Hannibal observed me for a moment. "When you said you were going to walk during our phone conversation, I called Sergeant Valenti." He paused again, and added: "We both headed toward your house immediately."

I thought a moment and then asked: "When did that start?"

"The day after Big Bill was killed, Hannibal replied. "We both know his death was not an accident."

I walked over to Hannibal and put my arms around him. He hugged me back. "I'm very glad you did," I said.

Suddenly there was the sound of a car in the driveway. Hannibal released me, picked up his Colt and walked over to the window. I raised my hands to my face.

"Who?" I said.

"Sergeant Valenti," Hannibal replied. He turned, put his gun back on the table and walked to the door.

In a minute or so, Hannibal let Sergeant Valenti in.

"Lost them," said Valenti, as he stepped inside. "But two men were in the car."

"Probably replacements for Carlo and Louie," Hannibal replied.

Sergeant Valenti nodded, turned to me and asked: "Are you alright?"

I took a couple of deep breaths and tried to smile. I'm sure the smile looked forced. "Yes," I finally replied: "Thanks to you and Hannibal."

Hannibal smiled, looked at me with his steady gaze and said: "Would you please make some coffee?"

I laughed, I couldn't help myself. I know Hannibal had just given me a familiar task to relieve my tension.

"Yes, of course!" I replied. Soon I was busy at the stove. Hannibal got three cups out of a cabinet and set them on the table. While he was doing this, he glanced at Sergeant Valenti and said: "There's some biscotti in the pantry over there."

Soon Sergeant Valenti had the biscotti on a plate on the table. We all sat down and listened to the perking coffee. It was a soothing sound.

Finally, I asked: "Sergeant Valenti, are you at risk for helping us?"

"Well," Valenti replied. "I am not in the good graces of my police chief right now." He grinned and added: "I have to be careful."

Hannibal nodded and said: "Sergeant Valenti and I have found a solution." He smiled, looked at Sergeant Valenti and then back to me. "I have offered him a position as Chief Field Investigator for my forensics laboratory in Chicago. He would be in charge of investigating and preserving evidence at crime scenes."

I opened my mouth in surprise and then uttered: "Oh my!" After a moment I regained my composure, turned to Sergeant Valenti and said: "Are you going to accept?"

"I already have," Valenti replied. "Hannibal offered me a nice salary, I'm single, and my work in Chicago will undoubtedly be exciting." He paused, grinned and added: "Please call me Eddie; my friends do." His smile broadened, and he continued: "Besides, my police sergeant title won't apply after this Friday, when I resign from the force."

"OK, Eddie," I responded. "You made a good choice; this town isn't safe for honest cops."

Hannibal and Eddie both laughed. Hannibal responded with: "Eddie's worth every penny."

The coffee had finished perking. I got up and poured three cups. All three of us drank our coffee black, but we nibbled and dipped our biscotti.

After a few minutes, I had calmed down. Eddie turned to me and said: "Now let's talk about you. You had a close call today."

"Right," responded Hannibal. "You have enemies, Caroline, in spite of the fact that you have divested yourself from your illegal enterprises."

"You have the attention of the Capone gang and our illustrious mayor," said Eddie. "You know too much."

Hannibal nodded and said: "The mayor also knows that you have incriminating photos."

My mind began to whirl again. After a moment, I collected my thoughts and responded: "Perhaps I should leave the Valley." I thought another moment and then added: "I have lived here all of my life." A lump formed in my throat.

"Yes," replied Hannibal. His eyes showed sympathy. "But how does Chicago sound?" He smiled and added: "With me?"

I was silent for a long while. Finally, I said: "You know I want to be with you, Hannibal." I got up, walked around the table, leaned over and kissed him on the cheek. I straightened, looked into Hannibal's eyes and added: "But we have unfinished business here."

Like Hannibal, Eddie's look of sympathy changed to a smile. He looked to Hannibal.

"Yes, well, I have thought about that," said Hannibal. He looked at me with twinkling eyes and added: "Jim Hansen, Edith's former bartender, and Johnny Swift have agreed to be our local eyes and very well-tuned ears."

"Oh!" I responded. "How?"

"Jim has applied for and got a job as a bookkeeper at Mayor Benny Nuardi's car dealership. It's a good job and a great position for gathering information," replied Hannibal. "Of course, he will also be on my payroll."

Hannibal smiled as he anticipated my next question. "Reporting illegal activities, especially payoffs, laundered money and planned murders, is not disloyal, so I don't think Jim has any moral conflicts." He paused and added: "Such activities are on a different level, compared to just selling folks cars and illegal booze."

I nodded and then asked: "What about Johnny?"

"Johnny will let it be known that he has just got a substantial inheritance," replied Hannibal. "He won't have to work. Of course, he will really be on my payroll."

Hannibal continued: "Johnny's job will be to visit speakeasies and keep his well-tuned ears and recall abilities busy." Hannibal paused and then added: "Jim will send regular reports to us that include Johnny's findings as well as his own."

I was silent for quite a while. Hannibal and Eddie waited patiently.

Finally, I said: "I still have Susie, Emily and Clara." I paused again, thinking. "If Susie is willing, she would make an excellent personal assistant for me."

Hannibal nodded and said: "Good choice." He looked at me with his steady gaze and asked: "Would Emily and Clara consider going to school?" Hannibal paused and then added: "I will fund their education and provide job opportunities afterwards." He grinned and continued: "I'm sure I will get a good return on my investment."

My heart almost melted. "Hannibal, you are the nicest man in the world." I leaned over and kissed him again. "I will ask, but I am almost certain they will agree." I know my eyes were shining.

"You still haven't answered whether or not you will go to Chicago," said Eddie, with a broad smile.

"Of course, I will, Smarty," I responded. A tear rolled down my cheek. I brushed it away. I'm sure my face had a radiant smile.

"Oh good," responded Eddie. "The River Rat Detective Agency will set up shop in Chicago." He laughed out loud.

I hugged Hannibal and we joined Eddie in heartfelt laughter. New adventures are waiting!

20

FROM DIZZY HEIGHTS

Sunday morning, June 3, 1928

I currently occupy Hannibal's spare bedroom. He is so different than other men I have known. It is refreshing to meet a cultured and considerate gentleman. I have stored my "stuff" in Hannibal's garage until we move to Chicago. Where will our relationship go from this point? I don't know, but I'm excited!

No one has made another attempt to kill me, at least as far as I know. Hannibal keeps a close watch. I carry my revolver in my purse.

Susie left for Chicago last week. Hannibal put her in contact with agents in Chicago, and she is scouting out real estate. Hannibal and his managers at the lab set Susie up in a beautiful brownstone apartment building near Lakeshore Drive. Very glamorous!

I sold both of my resident houses to nice young families. I offered them fair prices, and both families have the usual mortgages with the bank. I cleared seven thousand five hundred each on the houses. Given that I paid six thousand for each four years ago, I made a little over five and one-half percent internal rate of return on my investment. Of course, my property taxes and maintenance were much less than rent that I would have paid if I didn't own, so I came out pretty well and so did the two families.

Emily and Clara decided to join Maribel in Pittsburg. Thanks to Hannibal, both have tutors and are preparing to attend secretarial school. They share an apartment right next to Maribel.

Maribel has a good secretarial job now, and a nice apartment. She writes long letters about the wonderful young man she has been seeing. I hope it all works out. In the meantime, she is guiding Emily and Clara as they complete their education.

So, what's next? Hannibal suggested that I get my finances in order. I agree. For most of my life, I was dirt poor. Now I suppose that I qualify as being rich. It's a whole new experience.

I just scratched out my current net worth and sources of income on my notepad. Including the sale of the Victorian, the sale of my two residences and cash from my previous savings, I have just over three hundred seventy-five thousand in cash in my safe deposit box. The present market value of my preferred and common stocks and treasury bonds is about three million. Dividends and interest run about twenty thousand per year. Last year, I got about thirty-five thousand from my share of the car dealership in Terre Haute, twenty-five thousand from the trucking company in Indianapolis and thirty thousand in rents from my real estate in Chicago.

So: I have about three million, three hundred seventy-five thousand in cash, stocks and bonds and an annual income of about one hundred ten thousand. Wow! I will talk with Hannibal over dinner. He promised to grill steaks for just the two of us.

Monday morning, June 4

I am still in bed. The sun is shining through the window, and I have time to write. Mrs. Dot, Hannibal's cook, brought me coffee and toast. I wear a silk robe and lounging pajamas now. What a life!

Hannibal and I had a long talk about finances last evening. To begin, Hannibal said: "The economy has reached a dizzy place, Caroline." He paused a moment and then added: "It can't last."

I reached over and poured more coffee for both of us from a silver coffee pot. "My gut tells me the same," I replied. "However, I can't put my finger on why I feel uneasy." I looked into Hannibal's eyes. I'm sure my face had a questioning look.

Hannibal was quiet for quite a while. I waited patiently and sipped my coffee.

After a couple of minutes, Hannibal said: "Speculation has pushed up stock prices far beyond reasonable business asset values. I know the Federal Reserve is getting concerned."

Hannibal sipped his coffee and then added: "I have friends at the Chase National Bank, the Bank of New York and the Mellon National Bank in Pittsburg. My friends keep me informed on sentiment in the banking industry."

My mouth opened, nothing came out, and I closed it. Finally, I asked: "Why?"

Hannibal smiled and then replied. "You know my net worth. I have substantial accounts in all three banks."

"Oh," responded. I sure my face still had a quizzical look.

Hannibal leaned back in his chair and sipped his coffee. After a few moments, he said: "Bankers in the know are concerned that the Federal Reserve will raise interest rates, which makes the cost of borrowing money more expensive. This would reduce the amount of money borrowed to buy stocks. He paused and then added: "It would also increase the cost of business and consumer loans in general. Businesses and consumers would buy less, and the economy would slow down."

"I see," I replied slowly. "I understand that less borrowing to purchase stocks would put a damper on further increases in stock prices."

"Right," said Hannibal. "However, the situation is even more fragile. Stock prices may drop really fast."

"How so?" I asked.

"Well, many stock buyers have opened margin accounts. Buying on the margin means, for example, that they may pay ten percent down on stock purchases and finance ninety percent. They use shares they already own as collateral. However, margin accounts require a minimum balance measured by the value of the stock and cash held in the account."

"I think I see where this is going," I said. "If the market value of the cash and stocks in the account falls below the minimum, the lender may require the account holder to add cash or stocks to the account to maintain the minimum balance."

"Right," said Hannibal. "This is termed a margin call. The account holder can't add more stocks to the account because he has no cash to buy them. He must sell stocks to raise cash to put into the account."

"I see," I replied. "Are there lots of margin accounts?'

"Thousands," Hannibal responded. "If lenders start making margin calls in large volume, margin account holders would have to sell lots of stocks to raise cash. The values of stocks in the market could go down really, really fast. People could lose a large portion of the market value of their investments."

"I understand, I replied. "And I could lose money, even though I have never bought on the margin."

"Hannibal nodded and said: "Big time losses."

I mused a few moments, then asked: "All of this could happen if the Federal Reserve raises interest rates?"

"It could happen," responded Hannibal. "My banker friends are concerned." He paused and then added: "If the market falls really fast, it could cause a panic. Who knows where this would go?"

I thought a moment, then said: "So what should we do?"

"Good question," replied Hannibal. "I think we should review our stocks and make sure we keep only stocks in good, solid companies that are likely to survive a panic. Treasury bonds are also a safe bet." He paused, then added: "We should also keep enough cash and revenue producing assets to maintain our desired standard of living during a long down time in the economy."

"I see," I replied. "The stock market is pretty high right now."

"A good time to sell," Hannibal responded. "We may not hit the peak, but who knows when the slide will start?"

I thought for quite a while. Finally, I said: "I remember a panic when I was a kid. Banks failed. Should I be concerned about my local bank?" I paused and then added: "We both know my broker there is a speculator, and I use him only to make transactions that we want."

"Very good, Caroline," Hannibal said with a smile. "I suggest we move your accounts and safe deposit stuff to one or more of the big banks that I deal with. They have all been around over a hundred years, and they have survived many panics."

"Agreed," I replied. "Shall we toast to our future financial security with another cup of coffee?"

Hannibal laughed and said: "Hear, hear!" And we clinked our coffee cups.

Thursday morning, July 5

Hannibal and I watched the fireworks at the park out on Ninth Street last night. Hundreds of people, mostly families, were there. Fat Benny the mayor got up on a platform and made a speech. Other than that, it was a pleasant evening.

Jim Hansen has worked his way into the accounting department at Benny's car dealership. According to Johnny, Jim went to the university for a couple of years before he ran out of money and became a bartender at Scottie's old place. It's a shame he didn't finish his degree.

According to Jim, Benny doesn't concern himself with day-to-day operations at the dealership. The business employs about fifty people, including salesmen, mechanics, clerical staff and so on. Benny doesn't know Jim works at the dealership, which is a good thing. Given Benny's usual state at Scottie's old speakeasy, I doubt that he would recognize Jim if he saw him. We'll see what develops. Keep a low profile, Jim!

Johnny is also on the job. On the weekends, he takes a cab to various speakeasies around the Valley. He sits quietly at a table and listens. He has reported nothing new yet, except that the booze flows freely, and the Chicago based gangs are still at war. I want to find out who ordered Scottie's murder. Who is the local Capone gang boss? We still don't know.

Sunday morning, July 29

Mrs. Dot brought in my coffee and toast a few minutes ago. I'm still in bed, lounging about. It's a good time to write.

Susie called on Friday. We have good long-distance phone service to Chicago now. What a convenience! Susie found a spacious two-floor suite for Hannibal and me north of downtown Chicago, right along the lake. She sent photos.

Friday evening, August 10

We got Susie's letter and photos today. The new place is in a beautiful, new high-rise apartment building.

The penthouse has spacious living quarters that include three bedrooms, each with an adjoining bathroom. It also has a living room large enough for entertaining, a smaller intimate parlor, a kitchen and large dining room, and two rooms for offices. The view from the living room windows looks out over the lake. The next floor down has very nice living quarters for a maid, valet and cook. The basement has a parking garage. Elevators go from each floor all the way down to the main floor and also to the garage. Susie recommended that we buy both the penthouse and the servant quarters on the next floor down. How wonderful!

Sunday morning, August 19

Hannibal and I bought the Chicago suite with cash. We have joint ownership, half and half. With new furnishings, our initial outlay was one hundred seventy-five thousand each. Staff, taxes utilities and maintenance will cost about forty thousand per year. Even a few years ago, I couldn't have imagined such a place.

Hannibal has plans for our little detective enterprise. He and I will handle cases for private clients. Hannibal's lab will do our forensic work in addition to its existing contracts. Eddie has already established relationships with key police detectives in the Chicago area; there are still some honest cops.

Of course, we will keep our contacts in the Valley. We have unfinished business here, and there is a Chicago connection. I try not to worry about further attempts to kill me. Still, it causes me to jump at the slightest unexpected noise.

Based on Hannibal's market research, he thinks we can turn a profit for the agency within a year. Even if the economy declines, there will still be rich folks who need and want our services, especially in Chicago. I must ask Hannibal how he plans to collect fees.

Sunday morning, September 9

Moving day! Hannibal sold his house and shipped our stuff to Chicago. We both have rooms in the local hotel downtown. On Wednesday, we board a train for the Florida Keys. We will spend two weeks at the Casa Astoria Resort and then return to Chicago. The new place should be ready when we arrive. Adventures await!

Sunday morning, September 16

We arrived at the Casa Astoria Saturday morning. The train trip down was luxurious and peaceful. After a quiet day of rest, we began our resort activities: Saturday night at the Casa Astoria.

The evening began with a romantic touch. Ramone Flores, the Resort General Manager, met Hannibal and me as we stepped off the elevator.

"Good evening, Miss Case, and Major Jones," said Ramone. "My Maître d'hôtel has your favorite table ready for you." He looked at me with a big smile and added: "You look especially lovely tonight,

Miss Case." He continued with "Please," as he graciously motioned us toward the dining room.

"Thank you, Ramone," replied Hannibal. "It's good to see you again."

I smiled and nodded. "Ramone is such a nice man," I thought to myself. "Hannibal knows so many people."

I tucked my right arm under Hannibal's left as we walked just ahead of Ramone toward the dining room. Sconces along the walls gave off a golden glow, and lighted crystal chandeliers sparkled along the hallway ceiling.

"It took long enough to get ready, but it was worth it," I thought to myself as we walked. Indeed, I had made a special effort. My hair was cut in a bob and coiffed in the latest style. I wore a Chanel white silk backless chemise evening dress that showed my slim figure to its best advantage. The delicate beadwork of my dress was accessorized with a single rope of cultured white pearls that Hannibal had given me and long white gloves. I wore silk silvery hose and my shoes were silver silk-satin heels that glistened in the evening lamplight.

I felt elegant, and I'm sure my smile was radiant.

I looked up at Hannibal's face and saw his usual smile. He was dressed in a white jacket, white silk shirt, black pants, black tie and black cummerbund. His dark hair was touched with grey at the temples. What a handsome man!

"You are beautiful, Caroline," said Hannibal as we walked. His blue eyes twinkled in the golden glow of the lights along the hallway.

"Thank you, sir," I replied, and laughed lightly for the pure joy of the moment.

Antony Perez, the Maître d'hôtel, met us at the podium by the dining room entrance. After the usual pleasantries, he escorted us to a perfect table, just back far enough from the orchestra to hear the music and still carry on a pleasant conversation.

I looked around. The room was open to a courtyard, and our table provided a perfect view. A fountain just outside flowed and tinkled in the silvery light of lamps set all around in the tropical foliage. Two wings of the resort stretched away on each side of the fountain and spacious lawn. I could see a few guests on balconies far above. The setting was stunning.

"Quite different than the view from my old houseboat on the Wabash," I thought to myself. Memories of my humble beginnings touched on my mind for a few seconds. I quickly returned to the present.

Hannibal was requesting a bottle of champagne, which would be delivered to the table. I looked around. The consumption of alcohol was quite common throughout the dining room. I laughed inwardly at the irony.

Our waiter brought the champagne and an ice bucket. Soon we were sipping the bubbly and reviewing the menus. I didn't know where to start.

Hannibal helped out. Soon we were savoring a shrimp cocktail. This was followed by a creamy lobster bisque, a light salad, and then a Florida grouper with sautéed vegetables topped with a sprig of parsley.

As I nibbled on the last of the grouper, the waiter brought us each a little crystal glass with lime sorbet to cleanse the palate. We sipped more bubbly as we reviewed the dessert menus. I ordered a piece of carrot cake with a dip of vanilla ice cream. As I licked the last of my ice cream from my spoon, I decided that it was time for more bubbly.

As I sipped my champagne, I heard chimes of a clock in the distance. I glanced out the courtyard in the direction of the sound. I could see a large ornamental clock in the distance on a pedestal on the lawn near the fountain. "Nine o'clock," I mused.

Hannibal heard me. "Are you tired, Caroline?" He asked.

"Well, a little," I replied. "We had a long trip." I smiled and added: "But let's enjoy our champagne for a while; it's such a lovely evening."

Hannibal nodded and reached over. I extended my hand. Hannibal took it in his, and his touch was gentle and soothing.

Suddenly a terrible scream rent the evening air. I involuntarily tensed and looked toward the sound. The scream came from above, outside, nearby. Just as I looked, I saw something swish down from above. A sodden thump punctuated the end of the scream.

My hands flew to my face. A body, a man in white, lay face down on the lawn. He was just under the balconies outside the dining room. I was horrified. My hands flew up to my face. "What on earth?" I exclaimed.

21

ROOM AT THE TOP

Sunday evening, September 16, 1928

I have time for a few notes. Back to Saturday night: after the scream, the thump of the body and the ensuing commotion, events passed in a whirl.

"Oh Hannibal," I exclaimed as I stared at the white, smashed lump just twenty feet from our table.

Hannibal got up from his seat and motioned to Antony, the Maître d'hôtel. Antony saw Hannibal's gesture and hurried over. "Call the police," said Hannibal quietly, just as Antony arrived.

"Will do," replied Antony, and he hurried back to the podium. I saw him pick up the phone and dial.

I turned my attention back to Hannibal, who was speaking to me. I caught his words in mid-sentence. "…and walk over to the corner there, Caroline." He then pointed to the corner formed by the dining room wall and the edge of the courtyard. He added: "I will check out the body, you look up."

"Right," I responded. Hannibal looked at me closely, then turned and headed toward the body. I got up from my seat and headed toward the corner.

As I passed tables on my way, I noticed that other restaurant guests seemed frozen in place. A few were speaking, mostly variations on "What happened?"

I arrived at the corner and looked up. Obviously, the man in white fell from above. I counted the floors. "One, two, three, four," I thought. I saw balconies that extended out from the rooms on each floor. "The man fell from one of those balconies directly above," I concluded.

Suddenly another scream echoed through the night air. Startled, I looked for the source. I saw a figure appear on the third-floor balcony directly above the body. It was a woman, and she was looking down at the white figure on the ground. I stared. The woman was young, attractive and wore a fluffy white bathrobe. Her hands were at the sides of her face. She screamed again, a high-pitched penetrating sound.

The hair on the back of my neck prickled. I felt a presence at my side. I turned. It was Ramone. "Antony called the police; they are on the way," he said. His voice quavered a little; I could tell that he was a bundle of nerves.

I watched in silence as Ramone took a couple of deep breaths. In a calmer tone, he said: "This is bad, very bad." He stared toward the body, just a dozen feet away.

I turned from Ramone and back toward the body. Hannibal was bending over, looking closely at the man. I could see his gaze examining every detail, but he touched nothing.

Several other men approached. Hannibal straightened and spoke to them. I heard him say in a quiet, commanding voice: "Help me keep people away from the body."

Two men stepped forward.

I watched as Hannibal and the other two spaced themselves at intervals about ten feet from the body. I then heard the phrase: "Please stay back, folks, the police are on the way." Hannibal and the two men by the body repeated the phrase several times as people walked up. The phrase had the desired effect.

"Good," I thought. "Hannibal is preserving the crime scene." I looked at the clock in the courtyard. "Five minutes after nine," I muttered.

The woman on the balcony above stopped screaming. I looked up. She was gone.

As I continued to look up, I saw another figure appear on the fourth-floor balcony directly above. After a couple of seconds, the figure disappeared. I didn't get a good look.

I turned back to the dining room. Waiters and other staff were moving among the tables. In quiet voices, they were talking to patrons. I heard the voice of the nearest waiter: "Please, remain seated. The police are on the way." I saw Antony. He was directing the staff as they moved among the tables.

"Efficient," I thought. My gaze swept back and forth around the room.

After a few more minutes, I saw two men enter the dining room by the podium. One wore a suit; the other wore a dark uniform. Antony hurried over to the podium and spoke to the two men.

"Police," I concluded. I looked back at the clock. It read nine fifteen. "Very fast," I muttered. Fifteen minutes had passed since the man's body hit the ground.

After conferring with Antony, the man in the suit headed for the body. I saw his face as he passed me and approached Hannibal. "About my age," I thought.

"Major Jones," I heard the man say as he approached Hannibal. I watched as Hannibal turned. Recognition showed in his face.

Hannibal nodded and said: "Hello, Lieutenant Wright." The pair shook hands. Hannibal then said: "I'm glad you're here." Both men turned back to the body.

"That Hannibal!" I thought to myself. "He knows everyone!"

I turned and looked in the direction of the podium. The uniformed policeman had a notepad. Waiters were escorting patrons to the podium. I watched as the policeman spoke briefly to each person and wrote on his notepad. After each encounter, the patrons left the dining room.

"Taking names," I concluded.

I looked back toward the body. Hannibal was pointing to the balconies above and speaking quietly to Lieutenant Wright, who nodded periodically.

After a few minutes, Lieutenant Wright looked around the dining room, spotted Ramone and motioned him over. Wright pointed to the balconies and conferred quietly with Ramone.

Ramone nodded, turned and headed toward the podium. He motioned to several staff members on the way. They followed Ramone out the dining room entrance.

"They're probably headed to the rooms above," I surmised.

Soon the dining room was empty except for Hannibal, hotel staff, Lieutenant Wright, the uniformed policeman and me.

After a minute or so, Hannibal and Lieutenant Wright walked toward me. "Caroline," Hannibal said as they approached, "please meet my old friend Lieutenant Bill Wright." He paused and then completed the introduction: "Bill, this beautiful lady is my partner, Miss Caroline Case."

I offered my hand, and Bill took it formally. "Miss Case," he said in a friendly tone. "So nice to meet you."

Monday morning, September 17

The clock on my nightstand says five o'clock. The sky is turning pale pink out the window. Hannibal will knock on my bedroom door in just over two hours; he is very punctual. Last night, we arranged to have juice, coffee and toast via room service at seven-thirty this morning. I will write before I shower and get dressed, since I can't sleep.

Last night, we also had room service. After the waiter set up a table and dinner for us on the balcony of our two-bedroom suite, Hannibal tipped the waiter; he left, and we were alone. We both sipped our ice-tea quietly.

After a few moments, Hannibal began the conversation. "This is first case for our new agency, Caroline," he said. "Ramone has put us on a retainer."

"After your performance Saturday night, I thought he might," I replied. "I'm sure Ramone wants to solve this quickly, so he can reassure resort guests." I paused and then continued: "The tourist season will soon begin, and rumors spread fast."

Hannibal nodded and sipped his tea. He then lifted the silver covers off our salad plates and re-arranged our dishes, bread basket and drinks. "How elegant," I thought to myself. I was also hungry.

As we began to eat our salads, I said: "Tell me about Lieutenant Wright."

Hannibal nodded as he spread butter on a couple of dinner rolls. He passed one to me. After a moment, he replied: "Bill and I met in France during the war."

I'm sure there is a story behind Hannibal's brief statement, but I could tell he wasn't going to elaborate. "Still secretive," I thought to myself. I nibbled on my dinner roll. It was warm and delicious.

Hannibal gestured with his dinner roll, and said: "Bill settled in Key West and joined the police force after the war." After a couple of bites, Hannibal continued. "The force is small; he is the only detective." He took another bite and added: "Bill reports directly to Chief John Harger, who has also become a friend."

"You have many unexpected friends," I responded. "Is there anyone of importance whom you don't know?" I finished my salad and looked at the silver cover over my entrée.

Hannibal noticed and lifted the cover. "Sautéed Florida red snapper," he said. In answer to my question, he added: "A few." He grinned and his eyes twinkled. "Anyway, both Bill and John are glad we can help, and we will have full access to coroner reports, the scene where the body landed, the rooms above and any evidence."

Hannibal lifted the cover on his own red snapper. Soon both of us were savoring the entrée, which included the fish, asparagus tips and white rice.

"Witnesses?" I asked, as I polished off my snapper.

"That too," replied Hannibal. "We have a long list." He paused, took and finished another bite of fish, and then added: "Lieutenant Wright has stopped all potential witnesses, including those in key rooms above the landing spot of our victim, from leaving the island."

Hannibal laid his fork down with a satisfied look and dabbed his mouth with his white linen napkin. He then said: "One highway, the train and boats in the marina provide the only ways off the island. Bill has them all covered."

"We have just under two weeks," I responded. "Can we do it?" I looked around the table for dessert.

"I think so," said Hannibal. "There's air mail service from Key West every Wednesday with mainland connections to Chicago, and Lieutenant Wright has agreed to use the services of our lab."

Hannibal saw my search for dessert. "Over here," he said as he lifted up a dish cover. Two wedges of pie rested on two plates set on a silver tray. "Key lime pie, I think."

After a few bites, I decided that key lime pie is my new favorite. After due diligence with regard to the pie, I said: "If we get a package together by Wednesday, how long will it take for the package to get to the lab?"

"It should be there by Friday," Hannibal responded. He also began to pay appropriate attention to the pie.

"Let's see," I said, as I counted the days in my head. "Given a quick turn around at the lab, we could have a report back by next Wednesday, September 26th."

"And we are not due to leave until Sunday, September 30th, Hannibal responded. "Plenty of time."

"I like your confidence," I replied. "What a great way to spend a vacation!" I laughed, and Hannibal joined in.

I then leaned back, picked up my ice tea and sipped. "The key lime pie was wonderful," I stated. So, dinner ended.

Tuesday morning, September 18

Five AM again. I'm awake, I think. Anyway, I'm up. "Breakfast at seven-thirty, downstairs, courtyard," said Hannibal last night. Time to write before I shower and get dressed.

Yesterday was a swirl of events. After our quick breakfast, Hannibal and I met with Bill, Ramone, Antony and the uniformed policeman who took names Saturday night. The policeman's name is José de León. He seems to be a bright, ambitious young man. He also has a direct way of stating facts.

We gathered in a conference room just off Ramone's office on the second floor. We had a great view of the courtyard out the window. The fountain was visible in the morning light, and early risers strolled on walkways in the courtyard. "Beautiful," I thought to myself as I turned from the window and sat down.

Hannibal, Bill, Ramone and José all had leather notebook binders. "I must get one of those," I thought to myself.

After we were all seated, Hannibal began by asking: "Did any of the patrons in the dining room Saturday night have useful information?"

"No," replied José as he looked at his notes. "They saw the man hit the ground, and they described events that happened around the body after you took over." He looked at Hannibal.

"The dining room staff had similar stories," added Antony. "Nothing new."

Hannibal nodded and said: "I think we can let everyone in the dining room that night go on about their business." He looked at Bill.

"Yes," agreed Bill. "We have their names, and we can contact them if necessary." He turned to me and asked: "What did you see from your vantage point?"

I thought a moment and then replied: "Four floors, balconies extending from guest rooms and two people on balconies above the body." I paused as Hannibal and Bill nodded. I then continued. "A young woman in a white bathrobe came to the balcony on the third floor. She was the screamer. Another person very briefly came to the balcony on the fourth floor. I couldn't tell if it was a man or woman."

"Rooms three twenty-five and four twenty-five," said Ramone. He flipped through some notes, looked up and then added: "I personally visited room three twenty-five on the third floor at about nine-thirty." He glanced at his notes again. "The lady who screamed is Mrs. Nina Scarlatti. She is the wife of Frank Scarlatti, our victim. Mrs. Scarlatti called her husband Frankie."

"How about room four twenty-five?" Asked Hannibal.

Ramone flipped through more notes. "Joe Donnelly, one of my bellmen, went to four twenty-five and talked with a Anthony Anaselsi," he replied. "Mr. Anaselsi was cooperative, but didn't say much."

Ramone looked at Bill. "I instructed Mrs. Scarlatti to remain in her room. Joe did the same with Mr. Anaselsi."

"Yes," responded Bill. "I followed up with Mrs. Scarlatti and Mr. Anaselsi at about ten o'clock." He looked at me and then at Hannibal and then added: "I had Ramone move them to different rooms. They were allowed to take only necessary clothes and toiletries."

"It was done," said Ramone. "I watched Mrs. Scarlatti pack and escorted her to a new empty suite down the hall. Later, I did the same with Mr. Anaselsi."

"Good," said Hannibal. He turned to Bill. "Can Caroline and I visit the two rooms?"

"I thought you would ask," replied Bill with a smile." He handed Hannibal two room keys.

"What did you find on Mr. Scarlatti, the victim?" I asked.

"Not much," replied Bill. "He had a wallet with identification and two hundred dollars in cash. He also had this in his shirt pocket." Bill took surgical rubber gloves out of his jacket pocket, put them on, opened a folder and took out a torn sheet of paper.

We all looked closely. The paper was a half-sheet of standard hotel stationary, the kind kept in every room. Two numbers were scrawled on the sheet. The numbers were four twenty-five and twenty-five.

"We have a connection between Mr. Scarlatti and Mr. Anaselsi," said Hannibal.

We all remained silent for a few moments. Finally, I asked: "When will the autopsy report on Mr. Scarlatti be available?"

"The preliminary report will be ready tomorrow," replied José. I'll bring it to you by noon."

I nodded and said: "I also would like to talk with Mrs. Scarlatti in the afternoon. She might open up to another woman."

"Good," said Hannibal. The others nodded in agreement.

"I want to talk with Joe Donnelly," said Bill. "His impressions of Mr. Anaselsi might prove useful." He looked over to José. "Would you canvas the hotel service staff and talk to the maids that clean those two rooms?" I want to know as much as possible about the habits of the occupants."

"Will do," responded José. "I already know that Maria Sanchez cleaned three twenty-five and Anne Brown cleaned four twenty-five on Saturday about noon."

"Very thorough," replied Bill. He smiled at his young assistant.

Hannibal pulled out a folder and laid it in the center of the table. He opened it. We all saw strips of a transparent, film-like material. "Cellophane," said Hannibal. "It has a transparent adhesive on one side of a strip." He looked at me and grinned. "Perfect for lifting fingerprints after I have dusted them with this."

Hannibal then picked up a small box from the empty chair next to him. He took out a little jar and a small brush with soft hair fibers, like the brush a barber would use for shaving cream. I could see that the jar contained a black powder.

Where did you get that?" Bill asked. We all were intrigued.

"Well," replied Hannibal, our lab guys know a chemist named Richard Drew." He paused for a moment and then added: "Drew works for a company called Minnesota Mining and Manufacturing. I think the company plans to market something Drew calls cellophane tape in a year or so." My lab guys made the powder from lampblack and other ingredients."

"So full of surprises," I thought to myself. I then said: "A mobile fingerprinting kit." I laughed and then added: "I know what you want to do in three twenty-five and four twenty-five." Everyone joined in the laughter.

"I will do some background checks on the Scarlatti's and Mr. Anaselsi," said Bill.

Ramone said: "Antony and I will help José and Bill with staff interviews."

"We all have our assignments," said Hannibal. "Shall we meet again tomorrow?" We all agreed. Off to work!

22

CONNECTIONS

Hannibal took our package of evidence to the seaplane dock Wednesday morning. The package contained evidence from rooms three twenty-five and four twenty-five. The evidence included documented fingerprints on cellophane tape, fabric fibers, the note found on the body, selected blank sheets of stationary taken from room three twenty-five, undeveloped film with numerous photos and the preliminary coroner's report.

We should have a written reply from the lab next Wednesday morning when the seaplane arrives at the Key West dock. Amazing new technologies!

Our team met Tuesday and Wednesday afternoons to compare notes. On Tuesday, my interview with Mrs. Scarlatti and Bill's interviews with Anthony Anaselsi and Joe Donnelly were of primary interest.

I talked with Mrs. Scarlatti on Monday afternoon. Bill and I made an appointment and went to her new room at about two PM.

Mrs. Scarlatti answered the door. She was wearing a fashionable afternoon tea dress. It was light grey in color and looked to be made of linen. It had three-quarter sleeves and draped well over her tall, slim figure. She wore rope pearls and grey suede pumps. Her hair was light brown and cut short in perfect fashion. "Beautiful," I thought to myself." I made a mental note to review pictures and check out the design when I got to Chicago.

Bill smiled as he noticed my once-over of Mrs. Scarlatti. He provided the introduction and told Mrs. Scarlatti that I was working with the police on circumstances surrounding her husband's death. Mrs. Scarlatti invited me in, and Bill left for his own interviews.

Mrs. Scarlatti led the way to her sitting area near the windows. She had been moved into a beautiful one-bedroom suite. The view from the windows was lovely. I could see a set of French doors that led out on a balcony that extended the length of the suite. Except that it had a single bedroom, the suite was similar to the one occupied by Hannibal and me.

After we were seated, Mrs. Scarlatti offered me tea from a silver pot. The pot rested on a tray that also had cream and sugar condiments in matching silver containers. Fine china teacups and saucers and silver spoons rested on a separate tray.

After tea was poured and we were comfortable, I said: "I'm so sorry for your loss, Mrs. Scarlatti."

"Thank you," she replied. "Please, call me Nina."

"And I am Caroline," I responded with appropriate good manners. "If you can, please tell me what happened Saturday night." I took another sip of tea, smiled and waited.

"Well, Frankie and I arrived by train Saturday morning," said Nina. She then looked at me closely. "I think I saw you on the train."

"Yes," I replied. My business partner and I arrived on the train Saturday morning." I paused and then asked: "Are you here on holiday?"

"Well, no," responded Nina. "Frankie had business, and we came together." She paused a moment and then said: "Well, I suppose the trip was also an attempt at reconciliation."

"Oh?" I said. "You and your husband were having problems?"

Nina nodded, and said: "We weren't speaking to each other when we arrived. I went into my bedroom, undressed, and lounged in the adjacent bathtub for a couple of hours. Afterwards, I had several glasses of sherry and then took a nap. I don't know what Frankie did. I woke up at about nine PM when I heard Frankie scream."

"What happened next?" I asked.

"Well," replied Nina, "I got up, put on my robe and looked around our suite, including Frankie's bedroom. We had a two-bedroom suite. I couldn't find Frankie. I heard a commotion outside below our balcony, so I went to the rail and looked over."

Nina's voice tightened as if her throat was suddenly constricted. After a moment, she uttered: "I saw Frankie on the lawn below." Tears formed in the corners of her eyes.

"I saw you on the balcony," I said. "I was at the edge of the dining room below."

I waited for a couple of minutes. Nina's tears seemed genuine, and I gave her a little space. Finally, I asked: "Do you think Frankie committed suicide?"

"No," replied Nina. "Frankie wasn't that kind of person." Nina paused a moment, and then added: "Frankie was often belligerent with other men, a tough guy, I suppose. He sometimes even hurt me. But he was never depressed or despondent."

"He hurt you?" I asked gently.

Nina nodded and then replied: "Sometimes we had fights. He slapped me." Nina was quiet for a long minute. I think she saw a distant time and place. Finally, she said: "I deserved it, I suppose." She sniffled a little.

"No woman deserves to be slapped by a man," I stated matter-of-factly.

"You think so?" Nina replied.

"I do," I said. I paused a moment and then said gently: "I have to ask: did you ever want to kill your husband?"

"Oh, no," replied Nina. "I got angry sometimes, but I would never hurt him." She paused and then added: "He could be so nice. I loved him."

My conversation with Nina lasted a few more minutes, but I had heard enough.

Objectively, Nina had motive and possibly opportunity. However, she would have had to hit Frankie with something or given him an unexpected shove to get him to fall over the railing, which looked to be between thirty-six and forty-two inches in height. I made a mental note to measure ours at our room; the balcony railings were the same height throughout the hotel.

We needed more information. The autopsy report and Hannibal's findings in the original room would help.

Also, on Tuesday afternoon, Bill gave the team an account of his interview with Anthony Anaselsi and Joe Donnelly.

"Anaselsi was most interesting," Bill began. "He wouldn't say much, but he did provide short answers to direct questions."

The rest of us looked at Bill in expectation.

Bill continued: "According to Anaselsi, he is here on import business. He imports coffee and sugar from the big Caribbean plantations."

"Nice," responded Hannibal. "Anything else? Rum perhaps?"

"Rum in Key West? Good heavens!" Ramone said with a grin.

Bill laughed a little and said: "I checked with my friends at the docks." He paused and then added: "There were several sealed containers assigned to an A. Anaselsi on a manifest from a coastal ship that arrived from Cuba on Sunday." Bill paused again and then said: "Anaselsi has yet to pick up his containers."

"Can we get a peek inside the containers?" I asked.

"Not legally without a warrant," Bill stated. "I don't have probable cause that Anaselsi committed any crime."

Hannibal looked around the table. "Anything else?" No one spoke. "Let's meet again on Wednesday afternoon." We all nodded, and the meeting ended.

Our Wednesday meeting brought more revelations.

Hannibal began by stating: "We have evidence from both room three twenty-five and four twenty-five. I sent fingerprints, photos and a small piece of fabric to the lab." He paused a moment and then said: "The fabric was white, and I found it on the sharp latch for the French doors to the balcony off room four twenty-five."

Bill then asked: "Anything else?"

"Yes," said Hannibal. "I found a large manila envelope in Mr. Scarlatti's suitcase. It contained four thousand dollars in cash, mostly in one-hundred-dollar bills, although there were some smaller bills. The envelope had the number $6,000 written on it. Underneath was a minus sign and the number $2,000.

"Interesting," responded Ramone. "I checked with my front desk clerk, and Scarlatti paid cash for the room up front, and set up a tab for himself and Mrs. Scarlatti. The total deposit was two thousand."

"The Scarlatti vacation money," I stated. "Sounds reasonable for this resort." I looked at Ramone and smiled. Ramone smiled back. The others in the room chuckled.

Hannibal then asked: "Anything from the autopsy?"

José answered. "Smashed face, broken neck, collapsed lungs and torn pants," he stated matter-of-factly. "Our victim died from a fall. He landed face down."

I shuttered a little, but recovered quickly. "Any damage to the back of his skull?" I asked. "Anything that suggests that he was hit with something before he hit the ground?"

"Nope," responded José. "Nothing specific. However, the face was a mess, and he could have had facial injuries before the impact with the ground." José looked at me closely, with respect. I think he resolved to be a little less graphic in his explanations.

I then looked at Bill and asked: "Did Anaselsi admit that he was in the room at the time of Scarlatti's fall?"

"No," responded Bill. "In fact, he said that he had arrived at his room after nine, past the time of the fall." He looked at me closely and asked: "Could you identify the person you saw on the fourth-floor room balcony?"

"Hmm," I muttered. I looked at Bill and said: "No. It could have been anyone, man or woman. I just caught a glimpse."

"Does Anaselsi have an alibi as to his arrival at his room?" Asked Hannibal.

"Yes," replied Bill. "And that is very interesting. Joe Donnelly said he saw Anaselsi in the lobby at about nine o'clock." Bill paused a moment and then said: "If it was nine, Anaselsi would not have had enough time to ride the elevator up to the fourth floor and walk to his room before Scarlatti fell."

"Tell us about your interview with Joe Donnelly," I said.

Bill nodded and then said: "At first, Donnelly talked openly about his role in going up to room four twenty-five and checking on the occupant. He said he arrived about nine-thirty, and he knocked on the door. He said Anaselsi, whom he had met during check-in earlier in the day, answered the door. When I asked more questions about Anaselsi, he became reticent."

Ramone then said: "I saw Donnelly in the lobby at about nine-twenty or a little later. I told him what had happened and that he was to go up to room four twenty-five, which I knew was just above the body, and see if the occupants had seen anything. I also asked him to look around when the door was open to see if anything looked suspicious." Ramone paused and then added: "Donnelly rode the elevator up with me. I got off on the third floor, and Donnelly continued up."

There was silence for a moment as the team digested this account.

Bill then said: "According to Donnelly, he told Anaselsi about the death of a man due to a fall from above the courtyard near the dining room. He said that he asked Anaselsi if he had seen anything. Again, according to Donnelly, Anaselsi's answer was "No." Donnelly said he looked around the room and then left for downstairs."

"On Monday, you indicated that you followed up about ten o'clock," I stated. "Anything new to report?"

"Just that when I arrived and Anaselsi opened the door, he got agitated when I told him he would have to move to a new room," replied Bill. "At the time, I thought it was just a matter of his inconvenience."

"I followed up about ten minutes later," Ramone responded. "Anaselsi was still agitated, and he was looking around the suite for something." Ramone paused and then said: "I politely told Anaselsi that the police wanted him to move, and to take only his necessary clothes and toiletries. I waited and watched until he gathered his stuff, and I escorted him to a room at the other end of the hallway."

"Did Anaselsi say anything else?" Hannibal asked.

"Just that he couldn't find his briefcase," replied Ramone. "I assured him that the police would keep the room and its contents safe."

"Did anyone see Donnelly between nine-thirty and ten o'clock?" I asked.

For a moment, no one spoke. Finally, Antony said: "I saw Donnelly about ten fifteen. He arrived at the podium where I was standing. He was all out of breath."

Everyone was silent for a while. Hannibal broke the silence. "We have a missing briefcase, and Donnelly was not seen from nine-thirty until about ten fifteen." Hannibal looked at Antony and Ramone and then asked: "Can you keep an eye on Donnelly?" He paused and then said: "I'd like to know what he does."

Ramone and Antony both nodded. "I will also follow up with staff to see if anyone saw Donnelly or Anaselsi in the lobby around nine o'clock and between nine-thirty and ten fifteen," volunteered Antony.

"Good," responded Hannibal. "Anything else?"

"Yes," said Ramone. "A Mr. Parker Henderson checked into the hotel yesterday. He asked a lot of questions about the death of Scarlatti." Ramone then looked at Hannibal and then me. "He also asked who was investigating the death." Ramone paused again and then added: "My front desk clerk thought his questions were unusual, and he reported it to me."

"Interesting," replied Bill. "Does your register give an address for Mr. Henderson?"

"Yes," responded Ramone, as he flipped through his notes. "He's from Miami Beach. His address is listed as 93 Palm Island."

"I will ask Chief Harger to make inquiries," said Bill.

That was it. Hannibal adjourned the meeting.

Saturday morning, September 22

It's five AM, and I have time to write. Hannibal will knock on my door at seven-thirty; he always does. One revelation at the Friday team meeting was a bombshell!

Antony began with some interesting facts. After we were seated, he said: "Anaselsi and Donnelly were in the lobby at eight forty-five on the night that Scarlatti fell."

"Earlier than nine, then," I responded.

"Yes," Antony replied with a smile. He looked around the room and then continued: "I talked to Mike McGregor, our head front desk clerk. On that Saturday night, Anaselsi stopped at the front desk and asked for messages. The desk clerk found a telegram envelope in the box for room four twenty-five. He handed the envelope to Anaselsi and wrote the name, date and time in the message log. I looked at the log. The time was eight forty-five."

"What about Donnelly?" I asked.

Antony nodded and replied: "Donnelly was there, by the bell-stand. The clerk remembers that Anaselsi opened the envelope, read the telegram and then talked briefly to Donnelly. According to the clerk, the pair seemed on friendly terms."

Bill then asked: "Did the clerk remember anything else?"

"No," replied Ramone, "except that both men left the lobby."

"Time enough for either or both to get upstairs to the rooms before nine," I stated. Everyone nodded in agreement. Which room?

Silence for a few minutes, and then Ramone spoke. "As I said I would during our last meeting, I interviewed the maids for the third and fourth floors in that section of the hotel."

Ramone flipped through his notes and then said: "Maria Sanchez saw nothing unusual on the third floor, but Anne Brown said she saw Donnelly on the fourth floor near room four twenty-five. He was locking a linen closet. He then hurried down the hallway."

Everyone perked up. "Time?" I asked.

"About nine-forty-five," Ramone replied. "Anne has a watch, she has to be punctual."

"I think we need to look in that linen closet," responded Hannibal. Everyone agreed.

Bill then said: "I found out more about our inquisitive Mr. Henderson. Chief Harger got word from the Police Chief in Miami Beach. Henderson is a well-known agent and a front man for the real resident of 93 Palm Island."

Hannibal asked the obvious question: "Who?"

Bill smiled. I could tell he was savoring the moment. He then replied: "Al Capone."

23

SOLUTIONS

Thursday evening, September 27, 1928

Everything came together last night. This morning, we met in the dining room. Everyone was there. How exciting!

The courtyard clock chimed ten o'clock as Hannibal and I passed the podium near the dining room entrance. Antony, who stood by the podium, smiled and nodded as we passed.

Hannibal wore a light-grey single-breasted morning suit, a white shirt, contrasting blue silk tie and black shoes. He looked trim, fit and businesslike.

I wore a silvery-blue silk crepe de chine dress with a dropped waist and a sash that had a silver buckle in front and ties in back. The tan georgette collar and full sleeves contrasted nicely with the blue of the dress. My collar and skirt were trimmed with pleated rouchings and my sleeves had silk cuffs. The skirt line ended just below the knee, and I wore tan silk hose. My tan medium-heeled shoes matched my small handbag that contained my lipstick and revolver. I was prepared!

Bill and Ramone were already there, sitting at a table centered on the room but at the edge of the open courtyard. Hannibal and I joined them at their table.

I looked around the room and out to the courtyard. The dining tables were all covered in white linen. Coffee cups and saucers and sweet rolls in baskets rested on our table and three nearby tables. A waiter stood at a serving station with coffee and tea. The open-air side of the dining room faced west, and the sun high in the eastern sky had not yet evaporated the dew on the shaded lawn around the tinkling fountain. Fluffy white clouds moved slowly in a blue sky. Cool air wafted through the room. Other than the fountain, the room was very quiet.

Ramone motioned to the waiter, who brought over coffee, tea and condiments on a silver tray. All four of us had coffee, and we waited. Hannibal, Bill and Ramone all had leather binders with notes. I still need to get one of those!

Ramone motioned to Antony at the podium. Antony nodded, turned and motioned to a group of people who were just approaching the dining room entrance. José walked in, followed by Nina Scarlatti and Anthony Anaselsi.

I noticed that Nina wore the same outfit that she wore during our tea a few days earlier. "Poor girl can't get to her other clothes in room three twenty-five; the police still have it blocked," I thought to myself.

These three were followed by Joe Donnelly, Anne Brown, Maria Sanchez and Mike McGregor. All of the newcomers filed in and took seats at the two nearby tables. The waiter served the newcomers with coffee and tea, including the four hotel employees.

Two uniformed policemen appeared by the podium and stood discretely in the background.

After everyone was seated and served coffee, Hannibal stood up. He looked around the room with his steady, unwavering gaze. Several people squirmed as his eyes searched their faces.

"As you know, Frankie Scarlatti was killed as a result of a fall from a balcony on Saturday, September 15, at nine PM." Hannibal paused and looked at Nina Scarlatti, then Anthony Anaselsi, and finally at Joe Donnelly. He then said: "Mr. Scarlatti was murdered." The three suspects squirmed.

Hannibal looked at me. I remained seated, and I said: "At just after nine PM, I walked to the corner of the room over there." I pointed for emphasis. "I saw Mrs. Scarlatti on the balcony of the third-floor room above the body." I paused and then added: "The room turned out to be three twenty-five."

I looked directly at Nina. Tears welled in her eyes and she sniffled a little.

"I also saw a figure on the balcony directly above Mrs. Scarlatti," I added. I looked at Anaselsi and then Donnelly. Anaselsi squinted and the muscles in his jaw tightened. Donnelly looked slightly surprised.

Bill, who also remained seated, said: "The timeline around the time of the murder is crucial." He looked at Anaselsi and said: "You and Mr. Donnelly were seen in the lobby at eight forty-five." He then looked at Donnelly. "You both had time to go upstairs, to either room three twenty-five or four twenty-five, before Mr. Scarlatti fell from a balcony attached to one of those two rooms." Both Anaselsi and Donnelly squirmed again.

Ramone then said: "At ten-twenty, I met Mr. Donnelly in the lobby. He looked carefully at Donnelly and then added: "You seemed nervous." Donnelly's face had a slightly frightened look.

Ramone then continued: "We went upstairs. "I told you to go to room four twenty-five, check it out, and tell the occupant to prepare to move; the police wanted to go over the room." Donnelly nodded. Clearly, he was comfortable with Ramone's statement.

Ramone then said: "Anne Brown, the fourth-floor maid, saw you locking a linen closet door just outside room four twenty-five at nine forty-five." Ramone looked at Anne, who nodded. He then looked at Donnelly, whose mouth fell open for a couple of seconds before he realized his expression and closed it. Donnelly turned to Anne and stared. Anne stared right back.

Hannibal then motioned to José at the podium. José walked in, carrying a briefcase. Everyone seated at the tables turned their heads and stared. José set the briefcase on the table in front of Hannibal.

Hannibal looked directly at Donnelly and said: "We found this briefcase in the linen closet, hidden on a top shelf, behind some seldom-used room decorations."

Hannibal looked at Anaselsi, whose eyes widened. Hannibal then said: "I believe this briefcase belongs to you. Your fingerprints, as well as Mr. Donnelly's, were on it." Hannibal then looked at Bill.

Bill said: "The contents included twenty-five thousand in cash and a map of the Palm Island area of Miami Beach."

Anaselsi's face contorted into a snarl. He looked at Donnelly and exclaimed: "You!"

Donnelly scooted his chair back a little. His face looked like a frightened rabbit. One of the policemen at the podium moved forward a little, ready.

Both Anaselsi and Donnelly saw the movement and remained seated.

Bill then turned to Anaselsi and said: "At ten o'clock, I arrived at your room. I told you that you would have to move temporarily; we wanted to inspect your room."

Ramone picked up the narrative. "At ten-ten, I arrived at your room and escorted you to your present temporary room down the hall from four twenty-five." Ramone paused and then added: "From that time forward until now, room four twenty-five, as well as three twenty-five, have been under constant surveillance."

Hannibal then said: "Not surprisingly, you couldn't retrieve the briefcase from the fourth-floor linen closet, because the hallway was also being watched." Hannibal looked directly at Donnelly, who was becoming more frightened by the moment.

Bill then said: "Mr. Donnelly, you are certainly a thief, but are you also a murderer?" He looked first at Donnelly, then at Anaselsi and then at Nina Scarlatti.

Hannibal continued the narrative. "Which room? Did Mr. Scarlatti fall from room three twenty-five or four twenty-five?" Hannibal then looked at me.

I turned to Nina. "You had both motive and possibly opportunity to murder your husband," I said. "During our interview, you said that your husband had slapped you during fights. By your own admission, you were in your suite all afternoon until just after ten PM, when you were moved down the hall to your present room."

Nina shook her head slowly from side to side. "No," she uttered. "I loved my husband." Her face had a sad, yet frightened look. I then looked to Hannibal.

Hannibal looked at Nina and said: "We have other evidence." He paused and then added: "I found Mr. Scarlatti's fingerprints in both rooms. In room four twenty-five, his fingerprints were on a glass pane of the French doors leading to the balcony and on the balcony rail. We also found spots of blood on the balcony floor. The blood type matched the blood type of Mr. Scarlatti."

Hannibal looked at Anaselsi and then Donnelly. "We also found cloth fibers in the sharp balcony door latch that matched the fibers in a tear in Mr. Scarlatti's trousers."

Both Anaselsi and Donnelly looked back and fourth at each other. Anaselsi's jaw muscles quivered and he ground his teeth. Donnelly's mouth was open and his eyes widened even more than earlier.

Hannibal continued. "Clearly, Mr. Scarlatti was involved in a struggle on the balcony of room four twenty-five. He went over the rail and fell to the courtyard below."

Both Anaselsi and Donnelly tensed and half-raised from their chairs. The two policemen near the podium moved several steps closer.

Hannibal's eyes squinted as he stared first at Anaselsi and then Donnelly. "You both had opportunity, but what about motive?"

Bill picked up the narrative. "I found a folded half-sheet of hotel stationary in Mr. Scarlatti's pocket when I inspected the body in the courtyard. Someone had written two numbers on the half-sheet: 425 and 25." Bill paused and then added: "Later, we matched the half-sheet to its other half found next to the phone in room three twenty-five."

Bill looked at Anaselsi and then Donnelly. At first, both looked puzzled; then I could see the light come on in their eyes.

"The number four twenty-five matches your room number, Mr. Anaselsi, said Bill. "The twenty-five matches the amount of money in your briefcase." Bill paused for a moment, and then said: "Mr. Scarlatti received a phone call that gave him your room number and information that included the number twenty-five." '

Ramone then said: "We checked the message log at the front desk." He looked at Anaselsi. "The log shows that at eight forty-five PM on Saturday, September 15th, you picked up a telegram." Ramone then looked toward Mike McGregor, who was sitting with the two maids. "Mr. McGregor, our head front desk clerk, remembers that you were with Mr. Donnelly when you picked up the telegram." Mike McGregor nodded in agreement.

Bill opened his leather binder and took out a file. "We made some inquiries," he said. "Frankie Yale, in cooperation with the Chicago North Side Gang, has offered $50,000 to anyone who killed Al Capone. My sources include New York and Chicago police bulletins." Bill then added: "The information was obtained by those departments from gangland informants."

Hannibal then said: "You, Mr. Anaselsi, are a known associate of Frankie Yale."

Bill added: "We also know, from our local sources, that you have been involved in rum running in Key West since 1922. Unfortunately, we have never been able to prove it." He paused, then said: "From our sources with the New York and Miami police, you have been arrested several times in conjunction with unsolved gangland murders, both in New York and in Miami."

Hannibal then said: "I found paper fragments in a wastebasket in your room. Miss Case and I pieced it together. It was a telegram that read: To A. Anaselsi, Casa Astoria Hotel, Key West, Florida stop. 25 down, 25 upon completion stop." Hannibal paused and then said:

"The origination mark shows that the telegram was sent from New York."

Bill said: "You appear to be, Mr. Anaselsi, both a rum-runner and at least a part time hit man."

Hannibal added: "However, Al Capone has his own intelligence sources. We made some inquires with regard to Mr. Frankie Scarlatti."

Bill then said: "Frankie Scarlatti was seen leaving the 93 Palm Island residence on September 10, 1928. My source was the Miami Beach police department; they have had the Palm Island residence under surveillance for some time." He then turned to Nina and said: "We checked, and you and your husband arrived in Key West by train from Miami on September 15, correct?"

Nina nodded, and uttered: "Yes."

I then asked: "Do you remember being with your husband at the 93 Palm Island residence?"

"I think so," Nina replied. "We were invited to a party by a Mr. Henderson."

I then said: "Ramone and I also did some checking. Mr. Parker Henderson Jr. checked into this hotel on Wednesday, September 19th. He asked a lot of questions about the death of Mr. Scarlatti."

Bill then said: "We also checked on the 93 Palm Island residence. The fact that Al Capone is the real owner of the residence is well-known to Newton Lummus, Jr., the Mayor of Miami Beach, the local Miami Beach newspapers, and several citizen activist groups who have lobbied to have Capone run out of town."

I then added: "It is public record that Parker Henderson Jr. bought the 93 Palm Island residence from James Popham for $40,000 on March 28, 1928. Also, Parker Henderson bragged to many people, including Mayor Lummus, that he was friends with Al Capone." I paused and then said: "Capone moved into the 93 Palm Island residence in June of this year. My sources include several Miami Beach newspaper editorials."

Bill then said: "It is public record that Henderson sold the residence to Mae Capone, Al Capone's wife, on September 10, 1928, less than six months after his purchase from James Popham."

I turned to Nina and said: "You were invited to a party at 93 Palm Island on the 10th with your husband. Did you observe any discussions between your husband, Mr. Henderson and Mr. Capone?"

Nina was silent for a few moments, then said: "My husband, Mr. Henderson and a Mr. Costa talked in the parlor, but I couldn't hear what they were saying."

Bill looked at me and then at Nina. He then said: "Costa is a name Al Capone often uses while he is in Miami Beach."

Hannibal rose from his seat and looked closely at Anaselsi. He then said: "We have enough evidence to show that you have accepted a contract from Frankie Yale and possibly others to carry out a hit on Al Capone." He paused and then added: "Clearly, Capone found out about the contract. He first sent Mr. Scarlatti to investigate. After Scarlatti was killed, he sent Parker Henderson."

Hannibal looked at me, then Bill and then Anaselsi. "Mr. Anaselsi, you had both opportunity and motive for Mr. Scarlatti's murder."

Events then happened with blurring speed. Anaselsi jumped up, pulled a knife and tried to grab Nina. Nina screamed and tried to twist away. José and the two other policemen rushed forward as they drew their service revolvers. Hannibal stood and pulled out his forty-five. Bill pulled his service revolver. I fished my revolver from my handbag. Six guns were levelled at Anthony Anaselsi.

Anaselsi saw the guns. He took a deep breath, laid his knife on the table and slowly raised his hands. José and one of the other policemen soon had Anaselsi in handcuffs, and they led him away.

Joe Donnelly, the thief, was not forgotten. The remaining policeman put him in handcuffs, and he was also taken out.

I comforted Nina for a minute or so, she was obviously shaken. I signaled to Anne and Maria, and they came over. They left with Nina after a couple minutes. They escorted her back to her room, I suppose. I wonder what will happen to her?

In less than five minutes, the room was clear except for Antony, Ramone, Bill, Hannibal and me. The waiter also remained. He came over to our table and politely asked: "Would anyone care for more coffee?

24

TWO KINDS OF PAYMENT

Saturday night, September 29, 1928

Time to write before I go to bed. Tomorrow morning, we board the train for a three-day trip to our new home in Chicago. Adventures await!

We had a very interesting dinner earlier this evening. After we were seated at our favorite table, a well-dressed middle-aged gentleman approached us.

"Excuse me," the man said: "Are you Mr. Jones and Miss Case?"

"Yes," replied Hannibal. His face had a questioning and cautious look.

"My name is Parker Henderson. May I join you for a few moments?" He extended his hand. Hannibal stood and shook hands.

Henderson turned to me and said: "You look lovely tonight, Miss Case. Your reputation as a sophisticated lady precedes you. I had imagined your appearance, but you are even more beautiful in person."

At that moment, I decided that Mr. Henderson could stay. After all, it was a public place, and I was flattered and intrigued. "Why this?" I thought to myself.

I looked at Hannibal, who was watching me with a slight smile. I nodded.

Hannibal turned to Henderson and said: "Please join us." Hannibal then motioned to a waiter, who came over. "Please bring a chair for Mr. Henderson."

Soon it was done, and Parker Henderson sat across from us at our small round table. For half a minute, we looked at each other. Henderson smiled the whole time.

Finally, Henderson asked: "May I order champagne?"

"Please," I replied. "Where is this going?" I thought to myself.

Soon the champagne arrived, and we each sat back and sipped.

After a couple of sips, Henderson said: "I heard that you solved an interesting case."

Hannibal and I waited in silence. Finally, Henderson said: "My client is grateful."

Henderson put down his glass and added: "As I said earlier, your reputation precedes you. I know about your activities in the Wabash Valley."

I gulped involuntarily. I put my hand up to my mouth and pretended that it was the bubbly.

Hannibal frowned a little and then said: "Oh?"

"Yes," replied Henderson. "My client sometimes has a need for expert investigators. Perhaps we can call on you in the future?" He paused and then added: "Money would not be a problem."

My mind raced as I thought about the implications. "Money from Al Capone?" I took another sip of champagne. I saw that Hannibal was watching me intently. After a moment, I looked at Hannibal and shook my head from side to side, slowly.

Hannibal understood. He then looked at Henderson and said: "I doubt that we could be of future service to your client."

Henderson looked down but continued to smile.

Hannibal then said: "However, there is one favor that would be nice."

Henderson looked up and took another sip of champagne. "Name it," he replied.

"Miss Case has a bounty on her head," Hannibal responded. "Perhaps your client can make it go away."

I looked at Hannibal, first in surprise, and then with a slight smile. "My dear, you think of everything," I thought to myself.

Henderson nodded, turned to me and said: "Consider it done."

He then stood and added: "It was a pleasure to meet you both." He extended his hand to me and said: "Please enjoy the rest of the champagne."

I extended my hand. Henderson took it in his, bent over and kissed it lightly. He released my hand, smiled, stepped back, turned without another word and walked out of the dining room.

After he was gone, I looked at Hannibal and said: "Thank you."

Hannibal grinned and replied: "Well, we already got a very generous check from Ramone. We don't need more money right now."

I laughed and responded: "Let's toast to our first successful case," I said. I then held out my glass for more bubbly.

Hannibal filled my glass and then his. As we raised our glasses to toast, Hannibal said: "To the River Rat Detective Agency. May it have many more successful cases."

I laughed again as we touched glasses. I then leaned over and kissed Hannibal on the cheek.

ABOUT THE AUTHOR

Frank L. Gertcher is a retired senior scientist and a current storyteller. His publications include six books and a number of papers in scientific journals. He was born in Clinton, Vermillion County, Indiana, and grew up on a farm in Sullivan County. His mother's ancestors lived and died on the Indiana frontier. When Frank was a boy, he and his father fished and trapped on the Wabash River for a major portion of their family income. As an adult, Frank traveled to and lived in many places around the world, but he is still a Hoosier at heart. Frank and his wife Linda now live in a retirement community in Florida.

CAROLINE CASE WILL RETURN IN 2020

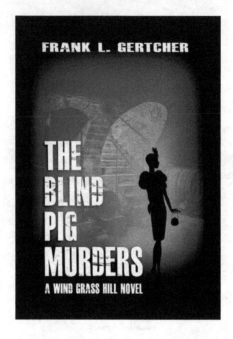

The year is 1928, and Prohibition is the law of the land. Caroline is now a wealthy, full-fledged private detective in Chicago. With her partner Hannibal Jones, she visits upscale yet scandalous salons near Lakeshore Drive and prowls dangerous and dark underworld dens in sleazy, industrial neighborhoods. Booze, murders, kidnappings and daring rescues abound. Caroline and Hannibal employ the latest tools of forensic science to solve murders and bring the culprits to justice, legal and otherwise. Although fiction, Caroline's story rings true to the fascinating history and colorful characters who lived, loved and died in the "murder capital of the world" during the heyday of Al Capone, speakeasies and Chicago-style jazz. *The Blind Pig Murders* is scheduled to be released in the fall of 2020.

October 2020 • Wind Grass Hill Books • ISBN: 978-0-9835754-6-7 • $29.99

CPSIA information can be obtained
at www.ICGtesting.com
Printed in the USA
LVHW040305020819
626231LV00005B/6/P